DESCENT

A Novel by
Donald R. Avoy

Outskirts Press
Denver, Colorado

This is a work of fiction. The events and characters described here are imaginary and are not intended to refer to specific places or living persons.

Descent
All Rights Reserved
Copyright © 2004 Donald R. Avoy

This book may not be reproduced, transmitted, or stored in whole or in part by any means, including graphic, electronic, or mechanical without the express written consent of the publisher.

Outskirts Press
http://www.outskirtspress.com

ISBN: 1-932672-02-8

DESCENT

A Novel

This is dedicated to the one I love--To Nancy

Chapter One

He began to sense his return to consciousness the same way he always had; strains of music were fluidly flowing through his brain, tugging on the hem of his awareness, demanding attention. He would passively follow the melodic line for several moments and then become actively engaged, adding the harmony or augmenting the rhythmic background.

As he became more involved in the musical game, sleep would fall away and he would either choose to pursue the melody for a while longer, or open his eyes and start another day.

He had presumed for many years that everyone started their day as he did, and had been surprised, and a bit embarrassed by the fuss his mother had made when he described his awakenings to her. It was hardly a big deal. It was just what he did.

Christopher Childs smiled before he opened his eyes, savoring the realization that his way of entering the day was very pleasant as well as unique. He rolled over and saw Shawn's lovely, green eyes studying him.

"Why were you smiling just now?" she asked.

"It's just a thing that happens to me," he said, reaching for her and pulling her toward him. "It's kind of like a cerebral CD alarm that goes off and starts playing music in my head."

"Really?" she said, snuggling up against him. "What kind of music?"

"All kinds," he said. "I never know what it's going to be."

"Is it like current stuff, or favorite oldies or what?"

"No," he said, beginning to stroke the skin on her back. "It's original."

"You mean your mind just goes ahead and plays original music

1

to wake you up?" she asked as she nuzzled her lips in the warmth of his neck.

"I don't know that it does it to wake me up," he said. "It just does it."

"Wow," she said. "That's really weird."

"I suppose so," he said pulling her body on top of his. "Look at you. You're so goddamned beautiful." He took her head gently in his hands, her long blonde hair flowing over his hands, and pulled her toward him and kissed her.

"You're not so bad yourself," she said, beginning to move her body over his in slow rhythmic undulations.

They prolonged the foreplay until his urgency overmastered him and he plunged himself deep within her. When they were both spent they remained quiet for a few minutes until Shawn looked at her watch.

"Jesus, I have to get going. I'm going to be late for the sales meeting." She worked for one of the high tech computer companies that populated the area.

"Are you coming back tonight?" he called to her from bed as she dried off from a quick shower.

"Did you forget?" she called back. "I'm going to New York for ten days. My plane leaves at four from San Francisco."

He got out of bed and joined her in the bathroom, watching while she blow-dried her hair. "Yeah. I forgot. I guess I didn't want to remember."

"Well, I'm sure you'll be fine without me. You always are. So behave yourself," she said, kissing him and looking him in the eye.

"You know me," he said, smiling.

"I do. And because I do, I'm going to call you at odd hours to check up on you. See you," she said and was gone. He walked to the door and watched her car disappear down the road. She was a fine woman, he thought. She was bright, beautiful and confident. She had a good sense of humour. His affection for her made their physical pleasure meaningful and satisfying, but there seemed to be limits to the potential of their relationship that he didn't understand, nor did he choose to pursue the thought any further.

He returned to the shower, turned on the water and adjusted the temperature. He thought again about his musical wake-up system which led him to thoughts of his mother, the source of the music

2

that was so important a part of his life. A piano prodigy herself, she had given up the certainty of a concert career to marry the handsome young physician who had swept her off her feet.

He remembered his childhood days when, sitting on her lap, he watched, fascinated, as the gentle hands that smelled so good would fly effortlessly over the shiny keys of the piano making wonderful sounds come out of the huge instrument. Those sounds, the repertoire of Chopin, Mozart, Schumann, Beethoven and the others, had become intimately familiar to him and had resonated powerfully throughout his still-developing nervous system.

He stepped into the shower and let the warm water massage the stiffness out of his neck and back.

With the constant exposure to his mother's playing and the sounds of the recordings that were always present, it was not surprising that he began to poke at the piano keys when he was still very young, demonstrating that he was not content to be only an audience. He wanted to produce the sounds he was hearing in his head. A series of small toy keyboards had given way to more expensive instruments as his pudgy hands grew.

By the age of five, he had become the most prized of his mother's pupils. In her mind, there was no question that he had the potential to fulfill her dream; that he could replace her aborted career with his own. But it was not to be.

As he had grown, his musical attention had drifted away from the more formal demands of the piano to the gentle allure of the guitar. As his mother had watched with growing disappointment, he had begun to spend less time at the keyboard and more in his room, his arms embracing the guitar, enjoying the vibrations of the instrument against his chest and the feel of the frets under his fingertips.

Whereas the music he made on the piano seemed to be the product of his mother and the departed composers, a combination to whom he always paid deference and respect, he felt much more free to impose his own spirit on the guitar and extract music that was his.

But as it finally turned out, it wasn't only the guitar that lured him away from a career as a concert pianist. When he reached his teen years, the other side of his brain, his father's side, had begun to assert itself. He still loved his music but he had become fascinated with the broader scope of the intellectual world, particularly that of natural science.

3

He had pursued astronomy with passion, staying in the cool night air for hours with his celestial maps, then burrowing himself into the warmth of his bed to read more about the subject. On the one hand he had experienced the frightening sense of being shrunk to insignificance by the vastness of the spaces he had been required to imagine. On the other, he had felt magnified by being a part of something so awe-inspiring and majestic.

As breathtaking as the firmament was with its infinite scales of space and time, even more thrilling to him was the world at the other end of the size spectrum--the microscopic and submicroscopic world of biology. His father had watched with growing pride as he had devoured books on physiology and chemistry. There had been frequent, intense conversations between the two about how the fundamental scientific facts that he was accumulating in his fertile mind related to the practice of medicine.

Then it had been his father's turn to project his ambitions onto his talented offspring. Academic medicine had seemed to be a very attainable dream and his father had drunk deeply from the cup of vicarious ambition.

But again the son's independent spirit had shattered parental dreams. After he had scored in the top three percent on the MCAT and had been accepted to five outstanding medical schools, Chris had changed the course of his life again.

He had carefully watched his father's professional life. He knew the demands of being a physician---the late nights, the interrupted sleep, the times he would suddenly have to leave in the middle of a concert or a play. It had been a source of pride to him that his father did such important work and made these sacrifices that others didn't have to. But now, mentally trying on the medical mantle, he realized that a life in medicine would require sacrifices he was unwilling to make. Foremost among those was his music.

So he had made another mid-course correction and had informed his father that he had decided to pursue a Ph.D. in molecular biology rather than going into medicine. With that degree, a career either in academics or in the biotechnology industry would provide him with more control over his life. Then he could have the best of both worlds, music and biology.

His father had been devastated and angry. It had been the first time Chris could remember his father showing so much passion.

But the storm had passed and both parents had satisfied themselves with the knowledge that their talented son was pursuing his own happiness, not theirs. Since neither had achieved his or her own dream at the expense of the other, they were able to be mutually consoling to an extent that would not been possible if one had won and the other lost.

Chris shut off the water, toweled off and dressed. Then he walked out into the driveway to retrieve the morning paper. He looked around at the neatly trimmed lawn and gardens, and inhaled the fragrant morning air. Friends of his parents, spending a few years on assignment in Europe, had asked him to live in their home during their absence. It was an ideal place to live, larger than he needed, wonderfully secluded, yet conveniently located close to the campus and with easy access to the freeway routes to San Francisco or San Jose.

He decided to have his breakfast on the patio, so he prepared his cereal and juice and carried them out with the paper, pausing to turn on some Bach on the CD player. When he finished paper and food, he went back into the house. He turned off the CD player, gently picked up his guitar and sat down on a stool. He played some chromatic scales and runs to limber his fingers.

Then he drifted into some improvisation, seamlessly evolving from baroque figures to jazz riffs. His eyes were half closed, his lips were moving gently and a humming sound was vibrating in his chest and throat. As he played, he rocked slowly to and fro. His mind and spirit were completely absorbed in the music. He had left the world of his surroundings and was in the deep, warm chamber of his soul.

After a period of time, his fingers stopped. He took a deep breath, smiled faintly, then rose and put the guitar carefully, lovingly, away. The session had ended and he was ready to begin the rest of his day.

Chapter Two

Chris threw some books and papers into the back seat of his car and backed out of the driveway. He had been driving the silver Porsche since it was given to him by his grandparents for high school graduation, twelve years ago. In some ways he found it difficult to conceive of himself ever driving another car. But their were times when his musical instruments and amplifiers had made him consider it seriously.

He took the quiet road which intersected with others of increasing size and began the familiar trip into the Stanford campus. He had traveled extensively, both with his parents and with friends, but he found himself most comfortably rooted in this valley where he had always lived.

He looked up at the crest of the Coast Range of mountains, the spine of the San Francisco Peninsula, which separated the chilly beaches and picturesque, small towns along the coast from the bay side of the peninsula with its upscale towns and residential communities. The mountains, although not very high, were extremely rugged with deep, dark ravines that defied the developers. Pockets of old growth redwoods still stand as testimonial to the difficulty loggers faced in the nineteenth century, trying to make their fortunes by removing the woody giants from their centuries of quiet repose.

He thought about the times he had spent tramping through the trails, camping in the sheltered ravines which led down to the dry creek beds that came alive during the rainy season. He remembered the moments of terror when a sudden sound in the underbrush would send chills up the spines of the group of terrified friends who would quickly deny any fright.

He remembered bicycle trips along secluded roads and days in the hot sun at the beach in Santa Cruz. The memories were part of a web of experiences that made it difficult for him to consider living elsewhere.

The road wound down the gentle slope of the piedmont which floated down to the San Francisco Bay, creating lovely valleys and ideal places to build the prized residences. As was typical for the early spring, there was an overcast which persisted until mid-morning, delaying the warming influence of the sun and moderating the temperature.

He passed by tennis clubs and shopping centers and was slowed as traffic coming off 280 from both the north and south joined the moving queue onto the campus. He parked his car in the parking lot behind the Institute for Molecular Biology and went up the stairs to the cubicle which he used as his office.

He was now in the third year of his post-doctoral fellowship. His work had gone well and he had authored a series of papers with his mentor, Dr. Jack Current, the head of the immunology section. They had collaborated in elucidating an important pathway by which signals are transmitted in effector cells in the immune system.

The work he had done had made him virtually a shoe-in for a junior faculty position. The problem he faced was that there were no such positions available at Stanford or at UC, which meant that if he wanted to begin an academic career he would have to leave the Bay Area.

The prospect of temporarily moving somewhere else had some fascination for him. He enjoyed Boston, and had developed good connections with investigators in some institutions in that area. The problem was that he would have to give up his musical connections. Specifically he would have to leave the band that he had been playing with and composing music for since his undergraduate days.

Another local possibility was to take a position with one of the biotech companies in the area. There were quite a few. Some were mature and had already successfully brought products to market through the labyrinth of the regulatory pathways.

More interesting to him were the many start-ups, small groups of bright, eager, ambitious young people who had an idea or a patent and were embarking on the difficult journey of becoming financed. Venture capital companies on nearby Sand Hill Road hired cadres of ravenous young MBAs from Stanford and Berkeley who

7

spent endless hours sifting through the data and interviewing people; doing their due diligence in deciding which of the proposals had the best chance of succeeding in the breathless, Darwinian environment, in which fitness for survival had to be demonstrated with razor sharp precision and lightning speed.

The contacts he had already made with some of the principals had convinced him that such a career was not only possible, but likely, if he so chose. At this point he was not prepared to make his choice. He preferred to wait as long as possible and continue to gather information. He could tolerate the ambiguity.

When he reached his cubicle, he found another of the post-docs, Peter Webber, sorting through some of the papers on his desk.

"Good morning, Peter," he said as he put his things down on the floor. "Doing a little cleanup or did you lose something?"

Startled and embarrassed, Webber stiffened and spat back, "I was afraid you weren't coming in since you're so late."

"Ah. The company man, as usual. What were you looking for? Maybe I can help you."

"Never mind that," said Webber. "Here, sign this form. Jack asked me to get your approval."

"Did he? Now let's see. What do we have here? He examined the form. It was a document declaring who was to be the presenter of a collaborative paper scheduled to be one of the key papers at the upcoming Federation Meetings. In the case of projects with multiple authors, the principal author was required to sign a waiver if another was designated to present.

"This lists you as the presenter," said Chris. "Is that what Jack wants?"

"Yes. That's what he told me," said Webber sullenly.

A secretary poked her head into the cubicle and said, "Chris, Dr. Current wants to see you."

Chris turned to Webber. "I'll talk to you about this after I talk to Jack."

He strolled down the corridor and knocked on the half-open door.

"Come in, Chris. Sit down," said Dr. John Current, the Full Professor of Experimental and Molecular Immunology, and Chairman of the Division. "I wanted you to be aware of something. Peter came to me and asked if he could present the paper at the Federation Meetings. I told him that since you were the principal author it was your call. That's the way I feel about it. He's uptight about his chances of landing a job and he thinks this would help. He argues that since you already have so many papers and presentations it won't affect you. I think that's self-serving bullshit, but I'll leave it up to you."

"Thanks, Jack. I appreciate your telling me how it came down. I'll take care of it."

As he stood up to leave, Current said, "Don't let this get to you. This has happened before, and it's going to happen again. These are bright, competitive guys, and they work hard. For some of them it really gets under their skin that no matter how hard they work, they can't produce the results that you can. Just remember, it's their problem and you have to do what's fair and what's best for you."

"Thanks, Jack. I appreciate that."

He walked back to his cubicle and sat down, looking over some papers, waiting for Webber to reappear. He did shortly, looking anxious and angry. "Well?" he asked abruptly.

"Well what?" asked Chris with an innocent smile.

"Don't give me that crap. What did he say? Are you going to sign it or not?"

"You know, Peter, it's very interesting. Jack's version of what happened is substantially different from yours."

"What difference does that make?" snarled Webber. "Are you going to sign it or not?"

"I haven't decided," he said. "Tell me, did it ever occur to you just to come and ask me rather than concocting this ridiculous lie?"

"Right. And I'm certain that you would have done it out of your great respect for me," snorted Webber.

"Perhaps out of respect for the fact that you had the guts to come out and ask."

"So now I suppose you want me to kiss your ass," said Webber. "Well, I won't do that. Present the fucking paper. You're the prin-cipal. You're the one who's pathetic. You could stay in academics and really make a contribution. It's so easy for you. But you're going to sell out and go for the big bucks."

"An interesting statement, particularly since I haven't decided what I'm going to do," said Chris. "But let's say that I had decided to go into industry. I would have done so believing that I would also have an important opportunity to contribute. Industry is doing first-rate science. More than that, they're the bridge between places like this and the real world where real humans live and benefit from their products."

"Real humans, profiting from IPOs and making megabucks on other people's creativity and hard work," said Webber.

"Ah, and those within the pristine palace of academics don't profit, is that it? They don't get large consulting fees and stock options, I suppose. They don't travel around the world first class, making speeches and basking in the light of their expert status. It's really amazing to me that there are still sanctimonious hypocrites like you who look down on industry until their first opportunity comes along to join up. Then the distinctions begin to blur and it's much more difficult to tell the saintly academics from the rotten money grubbers."

"I'm not surprised that you have it so well rationalized," said Webber. "Go your own way and live with it."

"Oh, I will. I certainly will. You can count on that. By the way, Peter, you can present the paper."

"Why? Just to rub my nose in the fact that I haven't had a big one of my own?"

"No. Not at all. Quite simply I want you to do it because it's more important to you than it is to me."

Webber looked away and was silent for a moment. "Well, I guess I should thank you, but right now it wouldn't be very sincere."

"Whatever," said Chris, turning back to his desk. He noticed that the light indicating that he had voice mail was lit. He listened to three messages, one of which was a call from his best friend, Rick, which he returned.

"What's up?" he asked when Rick answered.

"I wondered if you were going to bring Shawn to the gig tomorrow."

"She's in New York for a couple of weeks," said Chris.

"I thought I'd bring somebody," said Rick.

"Really? Got a date?"

"Yeah. Kind of. Yeah." said Rick.

"Do I know her?" asked Chris.

10

"I don't know," said Rick. "I don't think so. She was three years behind us in undergrad. I met her again through a complicated deal I'm working on. She works for the other company."

"Way to go. I'd like to meet her," said Chris. "God, am I looking forward to the weekend and getting away from this place. "

"What happened. Somebody piss you off?"

"It's that ass-hole Webber again. I am really fed up with uptight hypocrites like him. I think I'm going to go into industry."

"Whoa, good buddy. There're a log of sound reasons to make that decision, but that is definitely not one of them. The biotech world is certainly not a prick-free environment. I guarantee you, they're even more rapacious than the academics. There are enormous pressures to produce, fast."

"Yeah, I know," said Chris. "But somehow it seems less hypocritical. No one bullshits himself about the purity of his calling."

"I can definitely see that you're going to need some more of my wisdom before you fuck up your life forever. I'll see if I can't schedule you in for an appointment real soon."

"I can't wait," said Chris. "By the way, what time do we start?"

"I think we're on at ten," said Rick. "Oh, I remember what I wanted to tell you. I ran into Cal Martin. He said he's going to come by with some friends."

"That sociopath?" said Chris. "I thought he'd be in jail by now. Where'd you see him?"

"In a bar," said Rick. "He was with a real knock-out. He spoke fondly of you."

"I'm sure. Look, I've got to go. See you tomorrow. I'm going to be in The City. I'll meet you there."

Rick and Chris had been thrown together as roommates on their first day at Stanford and had quickly become inseparable friends. Rick had also grown up in the Bay Area and they had many things in common, including their common goal of going to medical school.

Rick's progress toward medical school had run into the formidable, and for him, impenetrable, obstacle of organic chemistry. The realization that he was not going to be able to fulfill his childhood dream had been painful. For a short while, it had strained their relationship because Chris had been able to breeze through organic as he did through all his courses.

But they had talked it out. Chris had felt very protective of Rick and had been determined not to let the issue become a reason for any distance between them. When the immediate pain had passed, and Rick had replanned his studies and his life, their friendship was stronger than ever, and remained a constant in both lives.

Rick had veered away from the natural sciences, majored in political science and flirted with the prospect of law. Eventually, he ended up getting an MBA just when the field was beginning to take off. He had joined a large corporation with headquarters in San Francisco and had made enough early progress to feel secure about his future.

But the strongest bond between them was music. Rick also played keyboard instruments and the guitar. In the first few weeks of school, they were able to find three other freshmen who played bass, drums and another guitar, and formed a band "The Perimeter" which had played together for almost all of the ensuing years. A couple of the members had dropped out temporarily when they went away to graduate school, but they eventually ended up back in the Bay Area so the band was still together, playing a large repertoire of familiar tunes augmented by new compositions, most composed by Chris.

There was a warm, collegial understanding among the members of the band. Chris was unquestionably the best musician and composer, and also the leader, but that fact never became a negative presence. They all played together because it was a joy to do so. More than that, it was the fulfillment of dreams they had all shared when they were growing up and fantasizing about becoming successful performers.

They were all good enough musicians to have been able to eke out careers in the field, but for various reasons had all decided not to pursue the possibility, unwilling to spend their lives fighting that difficult, uphill battle so fraught with uncertainty and frustration. So, "The Perimeter" became the temple where they assembled to pay homage to their individual and collective muses.

Chris had been approached frequently in the early days and had received offers to join other groups for tours or recording sessions. Some first rate people had appreciated the magnitude of his gifts.

He had tried it a couple of times during undergraduate summers, but it hadn't worked for him. The awareness that to be successful in this highly competitive world he would have to play "their" music in "their" manner made it unpalatable to him.

He had understood that ultimately he might become successful enough to be able to have it his way, but for a time of undefinable length he would not be free, and he would have to give up his science, his band and his friends. It had not been a difficult decision for him. He had no regrets.

Chapter Three

The Cardiff was one of many small hotels in the South of Market district of San Francisco. It had been built in the early part of the century and had, so far, survived grandiose plans to turn the ground it occupied into someone's concept of "a vision of the future."

The current owners maintained the original redwood bar and backbar with the beautiful beveled mirrors and proudly displayed the ornate wood fixtures that gave it a stamp of Edwardian authenticity to those who cared about such things. The original elegant dining room had not survived, but pizza and a few other trendy, non-challenging dishes were served in the bar area at prices which provoked no arguments.

A wide variety of alcoholic and non-alcoholic beverages were available but beer and wine were preferred by the predominantly young crowd. Week nights tended to be a bit slow, but the live music on the weekends guaranteed that the rent would be paid with a bit left over.

The first groups started playing at eight or eight-thirty while people were still interested in their food, so these less well established musicians had to compete with the menu and appetites for attention. Many of the serious listeners began to show up at nine thirty or later, having already eaten, eager to hear their favorite groups, local ensembles which had gathered a faithful following and had a tape or two or even a "recently-released CD" which they made available for a reasonable price after their set.

Since The Cardiff had been built with a magnificent ball room in its hey day, it was now one of the favorite spots for the bands and their followers because it could squeeze over one hundred fifty people in just for the music. The old bandstand, which had been the platform for the bands that drove the dancers wild during the twenties and thirties, now served as a stage.

The appearance by one of the bands was usually announced by flyers and mailers to loyal followers. The announcement that "The Perimeter" was appearing was enough to ensure a sell-out crowd and a solid night at both the bar and the kitchen. The local newspapers agreed that they were among the best of the groups that now circulated in the area.

Chris arrived alone and a bit early. He was finishing off his pizza and beer when Rick came in the door. "Hey. You don't get a free ride," he shouted from the door. "Help us with this crap."

Chris went out side, where Jimmy Garza, the drummer, was unloading the van that they all had chipped in on years ago. "Hey, Jimmy," said Chris, giving him an embrace. "Good to see you. Was traffic bad? You're a little late."

"Nah. We had to pick up a passenger. Jan," he shouted. "you might as well get out now. I'll have to drive all over the frigging area to find a parking place."

The passenger side door opened and a pretty young woman climbed down out of the van. "Hi Chris," she said extending her hand. "I told Rick and Jimmy that I was sure you wouldn't remember me. I'm Jan Appleby. I was a couple of years behind you at Stanford."

"Hi, Jan," said Chris, looking at her intently. "You do look familiar, but I'm damned if I can remember where we met."

"It was at the Spruce Goose in Menlo Park. You were all playing there. Some of my friends and I were like groupies. God, that's so embarrassing to recall."

"Why so?" said Chris, laughing. "You were obviously very discerning in your musical taste."

"Hey, will you get off your ass and move some of this shit," shouted Rick. "You can do the charming memories routine later."

After they had unloaded and put their equipment out of the way, they all sat at a table waiting for their turn on stage.

"Jimmy, don't bullshit me," said Chris. "Did you remember Jan?"

"Of course I did," he said smiling at her. "Of course she's continued to send me fan mail all these years."

"Oh right," said Chris.

A handsome man with dark hair and complexion, who looked like an older, larger version of Jimmy, walked up to the table. "Hey are you guys here to eat, drink and bullshit or are you going to play some music?"

"Carlos!" they said in unison and stood for friendly embraces.

"How's my favorite little brother?" he asked Jimmy.

"I'm your only little brother, shit head, and I'm just fine."

"How's the doctor business?" asked Chris.

"I think I got in on a rapid growth curve in the ER," said Carlos. "Sometimes I think I'm going to run into myself coming around a corner. But I love it. So how could life be any better than that?"

"You here for the booze or the music?" asked Rick giving him a hug.

"Booze I can get anyplace," said Carlos. "I gotta find out if you guys still have your magic."

"Just you wait," said Jimmy. "We'll show you some magic."

A trio of singers was just finishing a lively set and responded to the applause by playing an encore number. They then left the stage and "The Perimeter" set up their equipment.

The owner, who was also the master of ceremonies then announced, "Let's give a warm welcome to one of our favorite groups, "The Perimeter," and the audience responded enthusiastically.

They opened with some of the pieces that were expected by their followers, mostly jazz renditions of familiar older tunes, some with vocals, some without. When they were warmed up, they began to play their new material which was also well received.

They ended their first set with a new piece, a solo by Chris.

"This is an adaptation of a poem by one of my favorite poets, William Butler Yeats," he said.

It opened with a guitar solo in a minor key. The audience was silent as Chris took them on a voyage of inventiveness. His fingers flowed with an insistent inevitability producing a compelling melody in which each phrase anticipated and gave way to the next. The ballad that he sang was tender and honest, with power that came from a graceful melding of sorrow and wisdom. When he finished,

16

there was a prolonged hush as he sat still, his eyes still closed, breathing quietly. When he raised his head slowly and smiled, there was an enthusiastic ovation.

The lights came on and the MC announced a ten minute intermission.

"You really got it that time," said Rick. "Never been better."

"Thanks," said Chris. "It felt good. I felt like I really got around it."

"That's gonna be a bitch to follow, man." said Jimmy. "I'm glad we've got an intermission to figure it out."

"Yeah, I think we ought to put on cowboy outfits and do all our shit-kicking stuff," said Dale, the keyboard man. "Ain't no point in going anywhere near that."

"How about a little John Philip Souza?" said Jimmy. "We can sell war bonds and make a little extra scratch."

"Jesus, Chris, they said you were good, but I had forgotten how amazing you really are. That was sensational," said a young man of their age who had walked up to the bandstand. He was stocky and self-assured.

"Well, I'll be damned, Cal Martin," said Chris, holding out his hand. "It's been a while, hasn't it?"

"All the way back to the spring of our sophomore year," said Martin. "Right before I took my leave of academic pursuits."

"Not that you ever pursued anything that looked or smelled academic," said Rick, also shaking hands.

"Just didn't fit my needs, or my gifts," said Martin. "I was glad to leave that to the likes of you. Here, I'd like you to meet Erin Leahy, a good friend of mine. You already met Rick and this is Chris, who I've told you so much about."

She stepped forward and held out her hand. "I'm very pleased to meet you, Chris. Your music is extraordinary." She had dark, auburn hair and deep, blue eyes that looked at him with gentle confidence. Her smile was warm and sincere. He realized he was staring at her and attempted to regain his his balance, feeling self-conscious, which was unusual for him. "Uhm, thanks. I appreciate that, Erin, did I get your name right?"

"Yes," she laughed. "Just a bit of Irish. Sincerely, I'm really astonished at your music. I'm studying English and poetry is my field. Yeats is probably my favorite poet but it would never have occurred to me that someone could use his words and create a piece of music that was worthy of the poetry. But you've done it. I'm very impressed."

Chris was also impressed. She was obviously intelligent, but completely natural and at ease. Her appreciation of his work was also at a much more thoughtful level than he usually experienced. He relaxed, feeling less awkward but still very much aware of how attractive she was to him.

"Thanks again," he said. "I guess I've read about everything Yeats wrote and most of them wouldn't work, but there are a few I can connect with musically. I really get a kick when it works out well."

"Come on, Erin," said Martin. "We better be heading out. We've got another stop to make. Good to connect with you again, Chris. Let's keep in touch."

"Sure," said Chris. "Let's do that."

"Good-bye, Chris," said Erin. "I'd like to hear more of your work, not only the Yeats pieces."

"Any time," said Chris, taking the hand she offered and looking again into the welcoming warmth of her magnetic eyes.

"Whew," said Jimmy after they had left. "You could almost hear the chemistry that was going on between you two. Que pasa?"

"I don't know," said Chris. "But that was clearly a moment. Well, she's probably deeply attached to Martin and I'm happy with Shawn. I certainly don't need any complications. She was a stunner, though, wasn't she?"

They continued with the second set which was also enthusiastically received, but Chris was distracted by the persistent memory of the compelling blue eyes and the warm intelligence of the beautiful girl he had just met.

When he reached home that night he took out his guitar and played all the Yeats poems that he had set to music. The melodies stayed with him until he fell into a deep, pleasant sleep.

Chapter Four

When Cal Martin brought her home the night before, Erin had gracefully, she hoped, repulsed his effort to come into her apartment. She wanted to be alone with her thoughts. She had turned on some quiet music and poured herself a glass of wine and sat down to review the events of the evening. More disturbing than the events themselves were her responses to them.

The music played by "The Perimeter" was very skilled and attractive. But the Yeats poem set to music by Chris had been astonishing in its sensitivity to the poem and the inventiveness of the marriage of lyric and music. But that wasn't the central core of her disquiet. She had responded to him in a very profound way, one which was exciting, but also a bit frightening. She did not sleep well that night.

She awoke the following morning and went for her usual run, trying to focus on the natural beauty of the park and woods where she ran, but feeling viscerally uneasy. When she got back to her apartment, she was doing some winding down exercises when her next door neighbor called to her. "Hey, Erin, come on over for some juice and coffee. I never get a chance to talk to you."

"Hi, Ellie," she responded. "Sure. I'll be right over."

Ellie Gordon was a divorcee who was several years older than Erin. She worked as an administrative assistant at the University. She had never been to college herself, but her native intelligence and determined diligence made her very effective in her work. Her apartment was always in perfect order with all the knick knacks she had accumulated in their proper places. She had survived a difficult divorce and seemed to be in solid control of her life.

"So come on in, Erin," she said with her exuberant smile.

"There's some decaf and orange juice. How have you been. How are the studies going."

"Everything's going well. I think I have a good topic for my thesis and my advisor agrees."

"Well, that's good. How about your social life. Are you serious about that guy that you're seeing? What's his name?"

"Cal," said Erin. "No. Nothing serious there. I think he'd like it to head in that direction, but it won't. He's nice but there aren't any real sparks for me."

"Well, you hold out until you get sparks, you hear? I latched onto the first guy that wanted me, even though I knew he wasn't the dream I'd been chasing. I ended up paying for that in the long run. Better to keep looking. Have you ever experienced the sparks?"

"Strange you should ask," said Erin with a smile. "Can I talk to you about something?"

"Of course, honey. We all need some one to bounce off of every once in a while."

"I'm feeling uneasy. I met a guy last night and I think we really connected in a very unique, powerful way. At least it was that way for me. I don't know how he feels."

"Wonderful," said Ellie. "Where did you meet him?"

"He's a musician. We heard him playing with his band in The City."

"Oh, Honey. You be careful of musicians. They can be nothing but trouble."

"This is a bit different," said Erin. "He's a PhD in molecular biology at Stanford. He just does the music on the side."

"Well, that is different. So what's the problem."

"It's me," said Erin. She paused for a long moment, and sighed. "There's a part of me that I don't know very well. I think I told you I was adopted."

"Yes, you did."

"My adoptive parents are wonderful to me. They always have been. But I can't find myself in either of them. There are times when I'd like to be able to look at my real mother and find those parts and be able to talk to her about them."

"What kind of parts are they?" asked Ellie.

"There's a kind of impulsiveness that sometimes drives me to do things that can be dangerous. Things that absolutely shocked my adoptive parents because neither of them were like that. Nothing real bad has ever happened but the potential is there. I had some friends in high school and undergraduate school who were really marginal to most people, but to me, they were really nice, misunderstood people who became friends. I just followed this impulse and it worked out."

"And now?" asked Ellie.

"I feel a very strong impulse to pursue this guy. I don't think I've ever had such a strong attraction. It's more than just physical, although that's certainly present. It's really wierd, and disquieting."

"Well, let me tell you what I think," said Ellie. "I think you should pursue it if it's that strong. Maybe you'll learn something about him that will make it necessary to back off. You can do that, but I think you should go for it. We all have places inside of us that cause us to make impulsive decisions. Some may turn out bad, or not so good. But some of them really turn out to be winners. Go for it."

That same morning, after a leisurely period of quiet music and pleasant reflections, Chris drove through the backroads of the valley toward Atherton, a small, exclusive residential community north of the Stanford campus where he had grown up and where his parents still lived. Sunday brunch was a pleasant tradition, one of the connections with his childhood. The morning overcast had burned off and a warm, spring sun bathed the gently curving hillsides. Blue and yellow wildflowers floated in a sea of green grasses.

He drove through the familiar, wooded, winding streets and pulled into the curved driveway and over to the side of the garage.

"Hello," he called, entering the rear hallway through the back door. "Anyone home? I'm a robber and I've come to relieve you of all your earthly possessions."

"Come in, honey," called his mother's voice. "I'm just finishing up a few things."

He entered the kitchen and embraced her warmly. "You're looking particularly beautiful on this wonderful spring day," he said.

She was a thin, elegant woman, with dark hair that was softly, gracefully, turning gray. She always appeared to be perfectly outfitted for the moment, with no detail overlooked.

After their embrace, she kissed his cheek. "Where's Shawn? I thought she would be coming," she said with a cordiality that belied her concern that Shawn was not quite right for her only son.

"I forgot to tell you," he said. "She's in New York for a couple of weeks. So you have me all to yourselves."

"Lucky us," she said, laughing. "How was the music last night?"

"Well received. Genuinely appreciated," he said, idly picking at a fruit salad. He paused for a moment as he recalled the meeting with Erin. "Genuinely appreciated," he repeated.

"You hesitated," she said. "Did something cross your mind?"

"Oh, nothing," he said offhandedly, amazed that she was still so finely in tune with him that she was able to perceive the subtlest of signals.

"Where's Dad?" he asked. "I saw his car in the garage so I know he's back from the hospital."

"Where do you think?" she replied. "He's in front of the TV watching another boring baseball game."

"Ah, that's right. The Giants are in Atlanta. I'll go check on him, just to make sure he's OK."

"Don't even bother with those lame excuses, I'll call you when everything's ready and I'll expect you two to respond quickly."

"Hi, Dad," he said walking into the TV room. "What's the score?"

"Oh, good morning Chris." His father rose and gave him a hug. "Sit down. They just blew a double play and now the bases are loaded. They should have been out of the inning. They're still leading three to one, bottom of the seventh."

Dr. Childs still had a full head of brown hair that was the envy of his colleagues and contemporaries. His skin was remarkably free of wrinkles for a man nearing sixty. His weight was the same as it had been in medical school which he attributed to his continuing commitment to swimming, tennis and golf. He was almost exactly the same height as Chris, just a shade under six two. and from the back they looked like brothers, so similar were their builds. They also shared the twinkle in their gray eyes and the quick, broad smile that was so warming and comforting to the doctor's patients and which had gotten Chris out of many childhood scrapes.

They chatted about the progress of the game until they heard the call to the dining room.

"Now, am I going to have to share you two with that infernal ball game?" she asked.

"No," said Chris. "It's essentially over. They blew it. They had it and they blew it."

"Praise the lord," she said as they took their customary seats.

"So, Dad," said Chris. "How are things going? Last time we talked you were pretty frustrated."

"I can't remember exactly what the issue was then," said his father. "But frustration is where I live right now. You know, it was a big disappointment to me when you decided not to go into medicine, but I'm glad now that you didn't. In fact, if I had it to do over again, I'd advise you not to."

"Really?" said Chris and his mother simultaneously.

"Really," said his father. "The frustrations of practicing in HMOs or managed care or whatever they call it, are unimaginable, particularly for those like you two who really haven't really felt the impact. Just a couple of years ago it would have been impossible for me to believe that they could seize the profession I love so much and the practice I have enjoyed for so many years and make them almost unpalatable.

"Look, I know how lucky I've been. I came into practice at the best of times. The physicians controlled everything, particularly the surgeons. No one ever questioned what you did and insurance companies paid your fees without question or delay. The hospitals catered to our wishes. We worked very hard, but we were well compensated and had the rare sense of being in control of our profession, our practices and our patients' welfare."

"But, Dad," said Chris. "That system was a financial disaster. Medical costs were rising at about twice the inflation rate for other sectors. We were looking at predictions that medical costs would reach fifteen percent of GNP."

"I know, I know," his father agreed. "It couldn't last and shouldn't have. But it wasn't only the physician's fees that were going through the roof, which I also think was unconscionable for some of the surgeons and sub-specialists. It was all the other businesses that became a part of the feeding frenzy, the medical suppliers and home treatment companies. Everyone was scrambling around to pick up some of the golden eggs the system was laying."

"You have to admit that managed care has squeezed a lot of waste out of the system," said his mother.

"I do admit it," said his father. "And for that, I salute them."

"What then?" she asked.

"Most people aren't going to realize what's been lost until it's long gone. Pursuing the bottom line, not only for cost savings but also for huge profits, these HMOs have squeezed the humanity out of medicine. I know that there always were callous technicians in white coats who didn't bother to give any of themselves to their patients, but most of the guys I practiced with were diligent and caring. They spent the time that was necessary to let their patients know that they cared and were concerned. They knew them as human beings, not only as the next appointment on an impossibly crowded schedule. You just wait. As soon as the markets become stable, prices will begin to rise. Then we'll see how satisfied everybody is with this new system. Well, enough of this. How are things at the lab?"

"They're going well. We have the feature presentation at meetings that are coming up."

"Are you going to present?" asked his father.

"Nah. Another guy in the lab's going to do it. I'm the principal author but he's going to present. He wanted to do it. It's no big deal."

His father raised his eyebrows. "No big deal? I'd think that presenting would be important to someone who's just building his career."

"I've made the contacts that I need to, if I decide to stay in academics."

"If?" his father asked, irritation evident in his voice. "And just what else would you do?"

"Well, I'm thinking about the biotech industry. There are some very interesting career opportunities."

"Chris, that's not worthy of you," said his father. "You have a gift for science. You can make some real contributions. Don't even consider going into industry."

"It's not quite as simple as that, Dad," said Chris. "Industry is doing some very good, innovative science. Don't sell them short. Then there are other considerations."

"Like what?"

"Like my music."

His father looked briefly at his mother and then was sullenly silent.

"Speaking of which," said his mother, "you were certainly enigmatic when I asked you about last night."

"You're just trying to make something out of nothing," Chris said with a laugh. "Everything went very well. I played that new Yeats number and it went well."

She looked at him and smiled. "All right. Well, why don't we finish up here and play some together."

They played for a half hour and then Chris took his leave and drove back to Portola Valley. He did some reading and then picked up his guitar. He was absorbed in his music when he became aware that the phone was ringing. Because he had not heard the first few rings, the answering machine cut in before he was able to pick up the receiver.

When he first heard the female voice he expected that it would be Shawn calling from New York, but it was not.

"Chris? Hi. This is Erin Leahy. Remember me? We met last night at the Cardiff. I was with Cal Martin. I'm the Irish Yeats freak. You said to call anytime I wanted to discuss your other work. So here I am taking you up on your offer. Give me a call." She gave him her phone number.

He could have picked up the receiver and interrupted the answering machine at any time, but he did not. He was already engaging in some serious self-examination.

He and Shawn had a warm, comfortable, honest relationship. Although he had never committed himself to its permanence and all that was encompassed by that word, he was committed to the present tense and what that included; good companionship and fulfilling, delightful sex. He wasn't certain what else. Not that it was bad, even if there wasn't much else. He just hadn't spent any time examining the relationship because there hadn't been any reason to do so. But now?

The phone message was about much more than music. There had been a biochemical exchange at the Cardiff; an occurrence, a subtle transaction. A connection had been made that transcended the polite words that had been exchanged.

He had felt it but dismissed it, partly because of Shawn and

25

partly because she was with Martin. Now she was calling and there had been very little delay. He remembered her warm smile and absorbing, deep eyes.

"Shit!" he said out loud. He knew that if he picked up the phone and called the number, he would be embarking on an adventure and he did not consider himself to be a trifling adventurist. It might be exciting, but would also be destructive. Just to call was an act of disloyalty to Shawn and he would have to accept the consequences if he called.

He stomped around the room muttering epithets and obscenities, berating himself for the act of treason he knew he was about to commit.

"Maybe I'm making too much of this," he lied to himself. "Maybe this is only about Yeats. What the hell. Why shouldn't I respond? It would be ridiculously stiff not to. For chrissake, it's only a phone call."

Fortified by his rationalization, he submerged his honest concerns and dialed the number. After a couple of rings, he heard her voice.

"Hi. This is Chris. Just returning your call. I had stepped out for a minute. I'm glad you called." He felt the words tumbling awkwardly out of his mouth.

"Really?" She sounded surprised. "I didn't want to intrude, but you did say 'anytime', so I just decided to go for it."

"How'd you get my number?" he asked, still feeling tense and self-conscious.

"Ah," she laughed. "That's my secret. Listen, the reason I called is that I was just blown away--I still am--by that song you did last night. Do you really have more Yeats ballads?"

"Sure. And I feel pretty good about some of them," he said.

"I know this is intrusive and forward, but could I come down and have you play them for me?"

He knew he was at the Rubicon, and he felt himself wading in.

"Well, I guess so," he stammered. "I don't want to create any complications. I mean, you were with Cal and I...well."

"That's not a problem," she chirped brightly. "No commitment. We just go out. Oh, I'm sorry. You're probably seeing someone and this would be awkward for you. I tend to just blunder ahead without thinking it through. I'm sorry."

He was now up to his waist and heading for deeper water.

"No," he said. "That is...there is someone that I'm seeing. Actually she's away now. I don't see any reason why we shouldn't get together. I mean, even if she were here....it's not as though....we're just talking about music. So, sure. Let's do it."

"Are you certain?" she asked after a brief pause. "You still sound hesitant. Listen, if this is going to cause problems, let's not do it. I'm serious. I don't want this to be uncomfortable."

"No. Don't worry," he said, completely taking the plunge. "I insist. What did you have in mind?" He closed his eyes and shook his head silently, feeling the cold of the immersion surrounding him.

"Well, since you're going to provide the music, I thought maybe I'd come down and bring some food for a kind of a picnic."

"Okay," he said. "That'd be good. When?"

"What about late this afternoon? I have a paper to finish. You live near Palo Alto, don't you? I could be there around five."

"Perfect," he said. "That'd give me a chance to get some stuff done." He gave her directions and then placed the receiver back in the cradle and stood there with his hand still touching the phone, as though he were unable to break the connection, paralyzed by the step he'd just taken.

The phone rang at that moment, startling him. He jumped and the phone fell to the floor, where he could hear the female voice, "Chris? Are you there? Chris?"

He grabbed the receiver and stammered out a greeting. "Shawn, is that you? I dropped the goddamned phone."

"Are you drunk?" she asked. "You never drop anything."

"No. No." he laughed nervously. "I guess it's a sign of my advancing age. How are you doing?"

"I'm exhausted," she said. "God, I hate trade shows. In the booth all day and then I'm supposed to be able to drink with these idiots the rest of the night. This pace is going to kill me. How'd your gig go last night?"

"It was good," he said, relieved that the conversation was evolving so normally. "No major screw-ups. The crowd was lively and responsive."

"Well, you take care. I'm going to bed. I begged off the dinner and drinking. I've go to get some sleep or I'll collapse. I'll call you tomorrow."

"Good. You take care of yourself. No one else will."

After he hung up he walked out onto the patio and stood thinking for a long time.

Shortly after five, the front door chimes sounded. He opened the door and Erin was standing there. In the artificial light of the hotel, she had been very attractive. Now, standing in the filtered, afternoon sun in the entryway she was breathtakingly beautiful. Her auburn hair picked up the reds of the soft light and formed a diffuse halo. Her skin was clear and lightly tanned. Her intense blue eyes were large, framed by dark brows and lashes. Her lips parted parted with a broad, beaming smile that gave way to a laugh.

"My father says I'm about as subtle as a semi. He thinks I should be a teamster rather than an intellectual. Thanks for letting me come over. I should have devised a more clever approach, but I just had to hear more of that music."

He laughed and held out his hand to take the basket she was carrying. "Come on in," he said, studying her face and enjoying her disarming candor.

"What a great place," she said, looking around the large living room, with its elegant, comfortable furniture and tasteful art.

"It's not mine," he said. "Friends of my parents. I'm house sitting for a couple of years. It's perfect for me, if a bit large. Secluded and private and very close to the campus. Let me show you the outside."

He led her out through the large French doors onto the brick patio, covered by an arbor. Brick paths led out to a trim lawn framed by large, graceful cedars. Roses, rhododendrons and zinnias were flowering and a gentle floral scent permeated the warm air.

"Just look at these flowers," she said examining and smelling her way around the yard. "Look at these beautiful poppies. I've always been drawn to them. Do you know how lucky you are to have a garden like this? I'm so envious. Flowers are my first love."

"I guess I don't pay them as much attention as I should," he admitted. He was drinking in her sincere enjoyment, almost childlike in its spontaneity.

"So, do you want to hear some music?"

"Oh, yes," she said. "Could we do it out here?"

"Sure," he said. "Why not. Wait here."

He went into the house and returned with his guitar and a stool. "Have a seat," he said, indicating one of the padded chairs. He sat on the stool and played some introductory runs, then he played a graceful introduction. He began to sing and was transported by his own music into the realm of sound and rhythm where he was aware of nothing else. His voice and the guitar blended as he traveled the familiar journey of the melody he had created to provide a setting for the words of the great poet. The phrases and dynamics worked perfectly with the meter and rhythm of the poem.

He was removed from his surroundings, existing only in the floating ethereal sounds of his music and the poetry. When the song ended, he stopped, opening his eyes only after the last vibrations of the guitar ceased.

He looked down at Erin. She was sitting quietly, her eyelids down. When she looked up he could see that her eyes were moist. She smiled and rubbed her eyes.

"I feel foolish," she said, looking down again. "I don't think I've ever had anything move me like that." She shook her head, as though to clear it, and took another deep breath. "I'd like to walk around a bit and gather myself."

They walked silently for several long moments. The only sounds were from the birds. Then she stopped, turned to him and asked. "How can you do that? That was the most beautiful melody I've ever heard. Where does that come from? How does it happen?"

"I'm glad you liked it," he said smiling back at her, pleased that he had touched her so profoundly. "I don't often receive that kind of a response."

"You should," she insisted. "Your music is pure genius. Tell me how it happens."

"To a certain extent, it just happens," he said. "My mind creates melodies spontaneously." He told her about his awakening music. "But when I'm after something specific, like when I want to capture an image or do a setting for a poem like this one, I just concentrate on the words, the images and the meter for a few times through and the melody and rhythm kind of assemble themselves. Then I smooth it out and polish it up."

"What an incredible gift," she said. "Do you have any idea how uniquely talented you are?"

"I think I have some perspective about that," he said, smiling. "I don't want to sound conceited, but people I love and respect have been telling me that for as long as I can remember." he told her about his musical background and his mother's guidance.

"How can you not just plunge yourself into music full time?" she asked.

"I thought seriously about that," he said. It was expected that I would, but as I got closer to the reality, I realized that you can't just surround yourself with music. You have to be willing to enmesh yourself with all the people and processes that turn music into profit and transform musicians into stars. I don't want any part of that. My music is too important to me to let that happen. Besides, I have this other side to my brain that's also important to me. So I'm trying to work out the best possible compromise."

The light was fading now, and the temperature was beginning to fall noticeably. He watched for an instant, experiencing the admiration she obviously felt for him as it was reflected in her beautiful face and eyes. As enjoyable as it was, he felt uneasy and decided to change the subject.

"It's getting a bit cool," he said. "Why don't we go in. I can play another of the Yeats pieces if you'd like."

"I don't know if I'm ready for another dose of that intensity," she said. "Sure. Let's do that. Please play anything you'd like."

He played another number that he had composed. When he finished, she said, "That's it. I can't hear anymore for a while. Let me fix us something to eat."

He opened a bottle of chardonnay and she set out the sandwiches and salad that she had brought.

"Tell me a little about you," he said. "How did you get to where you are?"

"Just a girl from a small town north of Los Angeles, Simi Valley. Have you heard of it?"

He nodded affirmatively.

"An ordinary childhood. Loved and adored by my parents. An only child. Actually I was adopted, so they really doted on me."

"So the Irish part isn't really you?" he asked.

"Oh, it 'tis," she said in an Irish brogue. "My adoptive parents knew something of my mother. She was an Irish lass that had gotten into some trouble and had no way of raising a young one. I've seen pictures of her and the map of Ireland is clearly on her face."

"Did she tell them anything about your father?" he asked.

"I don't think she knew much. Anyway, I grew up loving Irish music and Irish tales. I did well in school and went to U.C. Santa Barbara for undergraduate. Berkeley has a very strong English department and I wanted to come to Northern California anyway, so here I am."

He watched her carefully, enjoying the candor with which she made personal parts of her history open and available. He wondered if she were always so forthcoming. "What do you plan to do?" he asked.

"It always gets to that question, doesn't it?" she asked, smiling. "The old identity crisis. 'Who am I really?' I'm not sure. I had some excellent teachers in high school, undergrad and now in Berkeley. They're the models that made we want to pursue English, and, I guess, teaching. If I had to make the choice right now, I might opt for academics rather than classroom teaching, but I really don't know. I haven't done any teaching."

Again, her bewitching openness and lack of pretense or guile captivated him. He found himself wishing he could get her to keep talking so he could just watch and enjoy. But he felt compelled to respond in kind and so he related the circumstances that created his current dilemma.

"On the one hand, I'd love to stay on here and continue my work, but that's not possible," he said "If I want to stay in academics I'll have to leave, at least for a while, and I don't want to do that right now."

"No," she said. "That just won't do. You must stay here. I haven't heard all your music. Oh, look at the time. I really should go. Can you grant me one last wish?"

"If I can," he said.

"Do you have any tapes of your music?"

"It just happens that I have several gross cartons of tapes by our band, and only slightly fewer of my own solos. We're having a special, so I could let a few dozen go at a special introductory price. How about zero? How about I pay you something? I can't afford much."

She laughed. " I really would treasure anything you'd be willing to part with."

As he walked her to her car, he was rehearsing his lines, already committed to doing whatever was necessary to see her again, soon.

"I know this may not be any of my business, but, do you have any commitment to Cal? I've known him for a number of years, and I have to admit, we were not always good friends."

"Oh, really?" she said. "He implied that you were. No, no commitment. We've dated for a while, but it won't become more serious than that. Why do you ask?"

"I was wondering if I could see you again," he finally blurted, dissatisfied with the clumsy formality of the declaration.

"I thought you were seeing someone," she said, stopping and looking at him squarely.

"Well," he stammered, "That is...that was true, but something has changed that. I'd really like to see you again. What do you say?"

"I'd love to," she said. "I just don't want to cause any problems."

"Life is full of problems. This is one I'll manage. When can we get together?"

"Why Mr. Childs," she said laughing. "You sound positively eager."

"All right, so I'm not subtle either. Look," he said, still feeling the flush in his face, "you started this with your Irish impetuosity. When do I get to see you again?"

"Call me tomorrow," she said. "I'll see what I can arrange. Chris, I really want to thank you. This has meant a lot to me."

"Talk's cheap," he said holding onto the hand she had offered. "I want more. I'll call you tomorrow. By the way, how did you get my phone number?"

"Jan Appleby is from Simi Valley," she said. "I knew her younger sister in high school."

He watched her back out of the driveway and head back to Berkeley. There was no question now. He was smitten and was enjoying it thoroughly. He was completely obsessed with his memory of her. He recreated the different views he had seen: her face, her hair, her smile, her voice, and her eyes. God, those eyes-- so full of the unmistakable strength that comes from the center of people who like themselves and feel no need to dissemble or impress.

And yet, there was a vulnerability, the kind that is usually associated with children; an innocence that opens doors wide, but also exposes them to unknown dangers from which they need protection. He felt himself particularly responsive to that innocence and wanted to follow her exploratory adventures and be there to protect.

He sat down with his guitar and let the music flow. It did, from his fingers, from his brain, from the deep centers of his spirit, from his soul. From the well of his uniqueness, the music tumbled out in joyous conceits, exultative motifs and exhilarating figures. He was in touch with a multidimensional labyrinth of joy and love that was creating a paean to her coming into his life. He was wrapping himself in a voluptuous fabric of extravagant happiness. He was experiencing the joy of her memory and of anticipation — the anticipation of seeing her again and beginning the next episode of their lives.

Chapter Five

Chris left the laboratory at noon and hurriedly drove to the on-ramp of Interstate 280, part of the Interstate 80 system which rings the San Francisco Bay Area. 280 begins in the south of San Jose and winds north along the peninsula toward San Francisco. On the lower peninsula, it passes through Portola Valley and other rural valleys. It crosses through the Stanford Campus, and over the linear accelerator. As it proceeds northward through the middle of the peninsula, it gains enough altitude to permit intermittent views of the bay.

This was all familiar scenery to him, and on many of the days he had driven this route he had enjoyed the rich panorama of the unspoiled hills. Today, he was distracted, barely aware of the beauty, driving the familiar terrain on automatic pilot.

Traffic was light in the early afternoon and Chris was soaring along in high spirits. He had called Erin when he got into work that morning and had insisted on seeing her in the afternoon. He would not delay any longer. When she agreed, he took the rest of the day off and was now on the way to Berkeley.

He drove past the Crystal Springs reservoir, sparkling sapphire blue under the clear mid-day sun, surrounded by the splendid foil of the rugged, heavily forested green hills.

He sped north to the southern edge of San Francisco, and then followed the freeway as it headed east to its rendezvous with the Bay Bridge. Crossing through this portion of the route, the vista of the San Francisco skyline stood out boldly, surrounded by the water of the bay, often gray-green when the sky is overcast, but deep blue today.

He sped east across the bridge and then headed north, taking the second Berkeley exit and beginning to follow the detailed directions she had provided.

While she had sounded pleased to hear from him so soon, and was willing, even eager to see him, there was a faintly detectable fiber of resistance that hadn't been present before. He puzzled over what it might signify, but his native self-confidence convinced him that it wouldn't be a serious impediment.

He pulled up in front of the small duplex and checked the address one final time. He retrieved his guitar from the back seat and walked up to the door, aware that his heart was beating faster than normal. The door opened and she was there in front of him, smiling her warm welcome.

"Hi," he said, self-consciousness competing with the thrill he felt seeing her again. "Thanks for letting me invite myself up."

"I certainly owed you that much," she said. "Come on in. It's not much, but it's home for now."

"Do you have roommates?" he asked.

"No. I lived in a sorority house for three years. I wanted my privacy back. Oh, you brought your guitar. More Yeats?"

"No. Not today," he said. "I have something that I want you to hear. It's kind of a work in progress. Brand new, but essentially complete. Do you want to hear it?"

"Of course I do," she said, and for the moment, the shadow of hesitation that he had detected was gone, consumed by the brightness of her enthusiasm.

He took the guitar from its case and tuned it quickly, sitting on a kitchen stool. He became quiet, waiting for his mind to become completely focused. Then the music began, the recently composed music of her, of his joy at finding her. It told how eager he was to welcome her to his life and to begin their adventure together; to begin spending their time together, sharing the moments that would forge their separate lives into one. It was an invitation to intimacy and commitment. The music he was playing was saying these things to her, but he had no idea whether she heard the meaning or only the melody.

Then it was over and he stopped, his eyes still closed while he took several deep breaths. When he opened his eyes, she was sitting quietly, her eyes down. He waited silently, watching her.

"How can I possibly respond to that?" she asked quietly. "That was the most beautiful love song I've ever heard and you did it without words."

"Then you understood?" he asked.

"Of course I understood," she said softly as she looked up at him. "It spoke to someplace deep inside me. It was so profound, so powerful, yet gentle and caressing. I just can't believe you can do that."

"I can't do it for anyone else," he said.

"Oh, Chris, I'm frightened," she said, rising and coming toward him. "Please hold me."

He put down the guitar, rose and enfolded her gently in his arms, burying his face in the scented softness of her hair. He could feel her heart pounding against his chest, and the deep irregularity of her breathing.

"Why are you frightened?" he asked. "I don't understand."

"You don't understand? I don't understand," she said looking up at him and pulling away slightly. "Look, I was very attracted to you when we first heard your group singing. I was really blown away by your music. I thought it would be fun to pursue you a bit and find out what was behind all your talent. I was ready for a bit of an adventure, but I'm not sure I'm ready for this."

"For what?" he asked, still puzzled.

"For you. For us. For this. This is serious. I've never felt this way about anyone. I never knew I could. I think I'm deeply in love with you and we just met. That frightens me."

"I thought I felt you pulling back a bit when we talked on the phone," he said.

"You detected that? God help me," she said.

"Erin, what are you afraid of?" he asked, looking at her steadily, intently. "You heard my love in my song. You know what I'm offering you. That you even understood my song means that you're in tune with the deepest, most important parts of me. I'm as overwhelmed as you are. You've hit me like a bolt of lightning. But I know that I adore you. I want to be with you and to love you and protect you and care for you forever. You must know that."

"Oh, I do, I do," she said. "But I just can't believe this could really happen so quickly." She looked at him with a combination of concern and tenderness. Then she gently took his face in her hands and brushed his lips with hers.

"Please be patient with me," she pleaded, kissing him again, tenderly, but with greater firmness. "I need time to assimilate this. It's too enormous."

"Of course," he said. "We have a lifetime."

Then her arms were around his neck and she kissed him longingly, deeply, fervently. The feelings of hesitation and self-consciousness they had both felt melted in the growing heat of their passion. Their exploratory caresses were gentle, inquisitive, adoring and then, finally, insistent.

She took his hand and led him to her bedroom. They began to slowly remove each other's clothes, kissing and caressing the newly exposed flesh. They were both giddy from the overwhelming thrills that they were simultaneously evoking and experiencing. The singular experiences of the smooth softness of skin against skin, the scents of hair, face, body and perspiration blended into a symphony of sensuality.

She opened herself to him and he was enveloped a in deep, warm, welcoming embrace that drew him into the most sacred chambers of her body and soul. They soared upward through a thrilling crescendo of the most exquisite pleasure in which the meaning of 'give' and 'take' lost all relevance. They reached the pinnacle of their passion simultaneously, in a moment of the most intense ecstasy and then floated down in each other's arms, overwhelmed by what they had experienced and what it predicted for their lives together.

Chapter Six

Now the music flowed from his soul in torrents. Whereas it had previously tumbled easily, like a summer stream, meandering jauntily but insistently along its course, now it burst forth like a fountain, under the pressure of his passion, with the urgency and volume of early spring run-off.

Previously, there had been no program. The spontaneous melodies with which his mind and spirit nudged him had been inventive, usually playful. Now there was a central core, a focus, an imperative. The music now was an anthem to love, his love, his Erin, his happiness.

Every moment they spent together was additional stimulus for more melody. When they were apart, his thoughts were dominated by his memories of her and anticipation of their next meeting.

Shawn returned, called and came over. He greeted her with a self-conscious embrace and a perfunctory kiss, separated himself and said, "We need to talk."

She looked at him quizzically but without alarm.

"I've met someone," he said, feeling awkward and guilty. "I think this is the important one. Not that you haven't been important, but... well...this seems to be different."

"Oh, Chris," she said easily. "You look so miserable. So forlorn. This is really difficult for you, isn't it. You're so sweet."

"You're not mad?" he asked, with visible surprise, and a touch of disappointment.

"No," she said with a smile. "I'm not. As a matter of fact, I'm a bit relieved."

"What do you mean?" he asked.

"I always get job offers at these trade shows. Some of them are just sexual come-ons, but some are legit. None of them has seemed to be just right. Last week a guy offered me a great job in Boston. The salary's good and the job has the right scope for me. I've always wanted to spend some time in Boston."

"And the guy?" he asked.

"Interesting," she said. "Very Interesting. Who knows? But I think it'll be fun."

"When are you leaving?"

"I've given my two weeks notice, and I have some leave coming, so I'm going to leave next Monday. I'm going to drive back so I can take a load of my stuff."

He shook his head and then looked at her and smiled. "It's amazing how quickly things can change. I'm really happy for you. I really felt awful."

"I know you did," she said. "And that means a lot to me. I have to admit, I did feel a twinge of something like jealousy when you beat me to the punch. But that didn't last long. I have a lot of affection for you, Chris. We had fun, but it was never going to be more than fun for us. I'm glad you found someone who can really light you up. Come here. Give me a hug."

They embraced warmly and then she was gone

Erin was at home, working on a paper that was due the following day. She usually did her assignments well in advance of the deadline, but recently she had become distracted. She was having difficulty concentrating on her studies. Her mind would constantly, insistently, drift to her mental picture of Chris's face, his music, his scent, his voice. She would find herself remembering fragments of their conversations, or creating situations in which conversation would take place. Then she would find herself in the midst of such a reverie and guiltily return to her work.

She had slipped into another mental distraction when she was startled by her doorbell. She opened the door and found Cal Martin standing there.

"Hi," he said, smiling warmly. "I was in the neighborhood and thought I'd come by and take you to dinner."

She flushed, not prepared to deal with this inevitability.

She was awkward and hesitant as she responded. "That's nice, but I'm afraid I can't. I'm in the middle of a paper that's due tomorrow. I'm way behind."

"That's not like you," he said. "How'd that happen?"

She hesitated a moment then took a deep breath. "Come in for a minute. I have something to tell you." She turned as he followed her in. She motioned to a chair and he sat down.

"I've begun to see someone seriously," she said measuredly. "I'm not going to be seeing anyone else. I'm sorry. You and I had some very nice times together. I hope you understand."

A look of disappointment spread across his face. He sat silently for a moment, then shrugged. "Well, I guess these things happen. I was hoping it might happen to us. It must have been sudden."

"Very sudden," she agreed, watching him carefully, relieved that he seemed to be taking it calmly.

"Is it someone I know?" he asked.

"Yes."

"Will you tell me who?" he asked. "I'd rather hear it from you now than from someone else, or just run into you."

"Of course," she said. "It's Chris."

Whatever relief she had felt was immediately erased by the dramatic change in his features. The quiet, soft understanding expression had instantly been transformed into something cold, hard and, perhaps, sinister. As the change took place, she could see his body becoming tense.

He stood up suddenly with a grim smile on his face. With a voice that strained from control, he said, "Chris Childs, is it? The wonderchild. Wouldn't you know. And I introduced you. So you win this one, eh Christopher? Please give him my regards, and accept my apology if I don't gush over your good fortune. Good bye."

She stood and followed him to the door. "Cal, wait," she said, grabbing for his arm. "What's going on? Don't go like this."

He shrugged her hand away and turned to face her. "Good bye, Erin," barely controlling the fury she saw so clearly in his eyes and face. He slammed the door and she stood there, shaken and confused.

The morning fog had been evaporated by the insistent rays of the warm spring sun. The sky was a hazy blue with no clouds in sight. On the bay, there was enough surface wind to create the white caps that crowned the waves and created a speckled appearance. The larger whites were the sails of the small boats which carried weekend sailors on their Sunday adventures.

Traffic, lighter than workdays, moved well in both directions on the Bay Bridge. Chris and Erin were traveling from the East Bay toward San Francisco, on their route to Tiburon.

"I had my talk with Shawn, the 'other woman'", said Chris, looking in the rear view mirror, preparing to change lanes to exit.

"How did it go," she asked.

"Amazingly well," he said. "She had been on the east coast and found not only another job but another potential relationship. She's moving to Boston."

"Just like that?" she asked

"Just like that."

"Well, that worked out well. How do you feel about being so easily replaced?" she teased, poking him in the side.

"You know, I have to admit that it bothered me a bit," he said. "I was all prepared for this big, dramatic scene in which she'd be emotionally destroyed and tearful, and I'd have to be consoling but firm. It never happened. I guess it was a bit of an affront to my ego. But I'm really pleased for her. She's a fine person."

He drove down the exit ramp and onto the streets that head for the Golden Gate Bridge.

"Well, I'm glad it went so smoothly for you despite your bruised ego," she said. "It certainly wasn't like that for me."

"Really?" he asked. "What happened?"

She described the scene at her apartment. "I was astonished, completely taken by surprise. I had known that he wanted more out of the relationship than I did. I wouldn't have been surprised if he'd been angry with me, but he was very understanding about my role. It was you, your name, that brought out this incredible anger. I thought you two were friends."

"Not quite friends," he admitted," shifting gears as they drove up the hill on Franklin street. "It started out friendly enough when we were in the freshman dorm. Then it became competitive. For him, I mean. He made a big thing about being 'pre-med'. We had a lot of the same classes."

"And you made better grades than he did?" she anticipated.

"Yeah, but it wasn't a big deal. I mean, his grades were good."

"So what happened?   I know there's more to this."

He geared down as they descended toward the bay. "In our sophomore year, he began to get behind. He was doing a lot of drugs, mostly marijuana and cocaine. Some LSD and shrooms. Anyway, we were both taking organic chemistry and he was missing lab. You just can't do that. The experiments are long and involved. Not that they're difficult. It's like cooking. You just have to follow the recipe. But if you start missing you get into a hole that's tough to get out of."

He swung the car down Lombard Street and then onto the approach to the bridge.

"He knew he was in bad shape. He came to me and asked if I'd help him out. He wanted to falsify his lab workbook by using mine. Just changing some of the data. I told him I couldn't do that, and he really got pissed off. All the old competitive shit erupted again and he really lost it. I think he would have strangled me if there hadn't been some other guys around. Man, was he furious."

He slowed down and maneuvered the car through the lanes of the toll plaza.

"Anyway," he resumed as he settled the car into the traffic flow crossing the bridge, "He got somebody else to help him. He paid them, I think. But they got caught and both were expelled. Honor code violations. He was gone. Just like that. I'm sure he believes I turned him in.

"I hadn't seen him since, until I saw him with you at the Cardiff. We'd hear from time to time that he was involved in some kind of deal. I mean, he's a smart guy. Highly motivated. There was never any doubt that he could be successful, he just had this penchant for living on the edge. Apparently now he's got it all together. He's successful isn't he?"

"He's making a lot of money, if that's what you mean," she said. "But I have the feeling that he believes he's not in the place he deserves to be and resents it. I had that feeling before any of this came up, but now it makes more sense. He certainly hasn't gotten over the episode with you, despite being so cordial and charming at the Cardiff. I was amazed at the fury on his face."

"It's so strange to have him pop back into my life. Particularly under these circumstances. Is he still doing drugs?"

"Nothing serious that I'm aware of," she said. "We've smoked pot a couple of times."

"Well, I'm sorry that you had to take the brunt of his old anger toward me."

"It certainly wasn't your fault in either situation," she said. "It'll be O.K. As I said, he's disappointed, but I don't really think he's angry at me."

"Well, that's the way I'd rather have it," he said.

"Don't worry," she said, putting her arm around his shoulder. "It's really not that important. Now, you and me, that's important."

They continued north, past Sausalito and up to the exit for Tiburon. The road wound past the Belvedere lagoon on the way. In Tiburon, they found a parking place in one of the public lots and wandered around, browsing in some of the shops, spending some time in a book store.

They went to a cafe on the wharf and sat out on the deck, enjoying the warm sun, some beer and hamburgers. Boats pulled up to the dock and hungry groups of people would disembark and join the throng on the deck.

"This is such a colorful place," said Erin. "My parents brought me here during one of our trips to the Bay Area. They loved it, too."

"Amazing," said Chris. "My parents introduced me to this place. They still come here when they can. Where else did they take you, I mean, within California."

"Most of my travel with them has been within California. They took me to Yosemite a few times. We always stayed at the Awanee. They weren't too big on roughing it."

"Just like my folks," said Chris. "Although I did some backpack trips to Yosemite with my buddies."

"Was Rick one of them?"

"I didn't meet Rick until Stanford. I don't think I ever went there with him. Although we did go skiing a few times together. Do you ski?"

"I've gone a few times, but I've never progressed far enough to really enjoy it," she said. "Actually, that's one example of my barging ahead without really thinking it through. I just presumed I could ski and so I took a lift that had only bad alternatives for me. I was just a mess. The ski patrol had to take me down. I was so embarrassed."

"You just need someone to teach you and protect you from those destructive impulses. That's something that I'll accept as a challenge. My folks have a place at Tahoe. It's great to go there either winter or summer. I can't wait to show it to you."

"I have this feeling that I'd like to go back over my whole life with you," said Erin. "I mean, I'd like to show you everything I've been and everything I've done, so you'd know me completely."

"I'd be up for that," said Chris. "I'd love to see the whole story. No, more that I'd like to experience the whole story. We'll just have to do it all in narrative. You tell me yours and I'll tell you mine."

For Chris and Erin, conversation flowed effortlessly. They exchanged stories about family, about vacations, about friends and school experiences. They talked about things they would do together, places they would go, experiences they would share. Each drank in the visage, the voice, the style and the mannerisms of the other, delighting in each new nuance revealed and discovered.

He reached out and took her hand. "I can't believe this is happening. I feel like I'm in some kind of suspended space, that this isn't real. It couldn't be real. I'm just crazy about you. I can't get enough. It just keeps getting better and better."

"That's exactly how I feel," she said, putting her other hand on top of his. "I'm just so full of love for you I want to shout or sing, but that would ruin everything because I'm such a lousy singer."

"O.K. Hold the singing," he said. "If you feel the need to express all that pent up affection and passion..."

"I didn't say anything about passion," she said with a laugh.

"Yes you did. You just didn't say it out loud. Now, don't interrupt. As I was saying, if you need some sort of a physical release, I have an idea."

"And what would that be?" she asked coyly. "I can't imagine what you have in mind."

"Well," he said slyly. "There's this little motel nearby that might be willing to provide a refuge for us if we give them some money."

"I'm not even going to ask how you know about this motel," she said. "All right, you smooth talking devil. What are we waiting for? This is so sinful and decadent. I love it."

They drove to a motel and he went in and registered. "I'm so cool he didn't even ask me where my luggage was. So I just told him it was in the trunk."

"You volunteered that even though he didn't ask you? You are cool."

As soon as they entered the room, they were in each other's arms. Their kisses were deep and hungry, their embrace pressured by their intense excitement. They quickly took off each other's clothes and he carried her to the bed. There was no foreplay. They were both electrified by the heat of their passion and overwhelming desire. They plunged themselves together and quickly experienced a powerful, mutual orgasm.

They lay quietly for a few moments, entwined in each other's arms.

"Wow!" he said. "That was incredible. I felt like the two of us had become the same person. There were no boundaries."

"I think we have some very rare magic," she said, clinging to him and nuzzling his chest. "That explosion happened deep inside me, in a place I never even knew existed."

"I love you so much," he said, kissing her hair. "I just can't get enough of you, but I'm going to spend my life trying. Well, will you look at that. Shall we go searching for that place again?"

"You've got to be kidding," she said. "Already?"

"I told you I couldn't get enough."

They spent the rest of the afternoon and early evening in each other's arms.

Chapter Seven

Chris and Rick were sitting at one of the outdoor tables at Zotts Beer Garden. The sun was warm and the tables were filled with young people enjoying the sun and the camaraderie. Laughter errupted intermittently from one or another of the groups, and the intercom occasionally interrupted the music to announce that someone's order was ready.

Rick filled their glasses from the pitcher he had carried out from the bar. "O.K. so what's your big news?"

"Did I say there was big news?" asked Chris.

"Cut the crap. What's behind this excitement that you can barely contain?"

"I'm that transparent?" Chris asked.

"Like glass," said Rick.

"All right, you asshole. I'm in love."

"With Shawn?" asked Rick. "She's great looking, and I know you two have a lot of fun, but I never thought you planned to go all the way."

"No. Not Shawn. She's moving to Boston, coincidentally."

"Well who, then," insisted Rick. "Come on. Out with it."

"It's Erin," said Chris with a big smile.

"Erin?" Rick repeated, not immediately able to place the name. "You mean Erin, the gorgeous one who was with Cal Martin?"

"None other," said Chris, refilling their mugs. "Aren't you going to drink to my everlasting happiness?"

"You son-of-a-bitch. How in the world did you pull that off? Man that was fast."

Chris explained about the Yeats music and their subsequent meetings. "I still can't believe it happened to me like this. I mean she flattened me. It's as though she turned on a light and all the flat, stale, bromides about romance suddenly became profound, three-dimensional truths. I am completely in love with that woman."

"And how does she feel?" asked Rick.

"The same. That's what's amazing. You can't feel this way about someone unless they feel the same about you. It seems obvious, but I never understood that until now."

"You son-of-a-bitch, as I find that I've already said before. You really have been smitten, or smote, or whatever. Look at you. You're like a radiant, fucking bride. You ought to be ashamed, or at least a little embarrassed."

"Not me," said Chris. "I couldn't be more delighted. Shame and embarrassment is for cynics like you."

"So tell me, Mr. Romantic, what are you going to do now? Get married, or something stupid like that?"

"Not immediately," said Chris. "Eventually we will. But we'll probably move in together when her semester's over. Then she'll be done with her course work and starting to work on her thesis so she won't have to live in Berkeley. Man, I don't think I could stand living in that town. But for her I'd try."

"So where do you think you'll live?" asked Rick.

"Probably in the city," said Chris. "I can commute."

"Man, look at you," said Rick, laughing. "The commuter. If this is what love does to a man, I don't want any part of it. But I'm really delighted for you two. She really does come across as a very straightforward, bright, and beautiful woman."

"She's all that and more. I just can't describe the way we fit together. I never would have believed it."

"Have you told your folks?" asked Rick.

"Yeah, I told them. I'm taking her over to their place for dinner tomorrow night to meet them."

"I bet they'll be pleased," said Rick. "Everybody'll be pleased. Everybody but Martin. Jesus. What about him? He'd be pissed at losing her to anyone, but to you? Jesus. You better hire a bodyguard."

"You applying?"

"Shit no. I don't want any part of that. Jesus, as I find I've said before, is he going to be pissed."

Erin had driven to Chris's and they were now in his car, heading for Atherton. The light of the late afternoon sun was casting shadows on the road as they sped along.

"I don't know why I'm so nervous," she said. "I've met parents before and it never fazed me."

"It's entirely proper that you should be nervous, my dear," looking at her from under arched eyebrows. "In the first place, these are among the meanest human beings on the face of the earth, or at least in the conference. Secondly, I don't think there's a chance in hell they'll like you or accept you. So, after they throw us out we'll just head for the golden arches and get something to eat."

"I really appreciate your bolstering my confidence like that," she said.

They drove in the driveway, parked, and he helped her out of the car. "Do I look all right?" she asked. "Is my lipstick on straight? Is..."

"You look terrible and the lipstick is all over your face. Now relax."

They entered the back hall and he stopped her. "Listen," he said, holding a finger to his mouth. "It's Mom. She's playing Chopin."

They stood quietly and listened to the rest of the movement. "Oh my God," Erin said. "It's like being at a private performance."

"Come on in," he said. "Mom? We're here. Erin says she doesn't like the way you play."

They entered the living room as Mrs. Childs was getting up from the bench of one of the twin pianos. "Christopher, your manners are atrocious. You're a constant disappointment to me. Erin, I can't tell you how pleased I am to meet you." She went to the young woman and embraced her warmly. Chris has just raved and he was absolutely right."

"Thank, you, Mrs. Childs. I'm very pleased to meet you. I feel awkward in asking, but would you play some more? The two of you?"

"Where's Dad?" asked Chris.

"He just called," said Mrs. Childs. "He's been delayed, so

maybe this would be a good time to play. We can save all our questions and answers until after he gets here. Come on, Chris. Make your mother happy. Let's play together."

They played flawlessly while Erin sat enraptured. When they were finished, she applauded excitedly. "That was incredible. You're both so wonderful. I'm just overwhelmed."

"Thank you, Erin," said his mother, "You must forgive me my self-indulgence. I try to get to play with him whenever I can. It's a special thrill for me. And you're playing very well, Chris. Have you been practicing or is just your happiness that I'm hearing?"

"It certainly isn't practice," he said. "I'm just showing off for my girlfriend. Come on, let's take a tour of the house."

"You two do the tour while I finish up a few things in the kitchen," said his mother.

He walked her around the house, showing her pictures and momentos of his childhood, including awards he had won for his music. There were pictures of his parents, his mother alone in her days on tour, his parents together at the time of their wedding, and a series of the three of them at different ages.

"See," he said. "I wasn't always ugly."

He was showing her his room when they heard his father's car drive up and they returned to the living room.

Dr. Childs was taking off his coat, when they entered. "John," said his wife, "Here's Erin. We're just getting acquainted."

He turned to meet her, with a warm smile on his face. He took her hand in both of his and held them firmly. "We're so pleased to welcome you to our home. It's the kind of moment one dreams about when one reaches our age. I think it has something to do with renewal." He put his arm around her shoulder and guided her to a seat on the sofa, where he sat beside her.

"Dad," said Chris. "I'm here, too."

"Oh, hello, Chris. Would you please get me a scotch? What would you like, Erin? We have a nice chardonnay chilled."

"That would be perfect, thank you."

"A glass for me too, please, Chris," said his mother.

"We try to make him feel useful," said his father. "Now, Chris says you're originally from the south land. What brought you up here? I, we, will ask you a lot of banal questions, partially because we're interested in the answer and partly because we just want to see how well you tolerate this kind of boring interrogation."

"I don't mind at all," said Erin. "It's something we have to go through to get to know each other. My parents used to try to show me the places they thought were the most beautiful and most unique, so they brought me to San Francisco. I fell in love with this whole area. So when I had a chance to come here for graduate school, I leaped at it. Plus, the English department in Berkeley is very good."

"See what I told you two," said Chris carrying a tray with the drinks, "She talks real good. Like one of them real intellek-chewuls."

"And what does your father do?" asked Dr. Childs.

"He's an attorney with the public defender's office," said Erin. "He grew up in Simi Valley, as did my mom. They love visiting other places, but for them, that's home."

"I believe Chris told us that you're an only child," said Mrs. Childs.

"Yes. Adopted by two wonderful people who were told they couldn't have children. So I've been the recipient of all their love and attention."

"Well, we know something about how only children can be spoiled," said Dr. Childs.

After their drinks they went into the dining room and enjoyed the meal that Mrs. Childs had prepared. The conversation was continuous and lively. Revelations by Erin or Chris about experiences they had already shared or planned to share stimulated memories and stories from one or both of his parents, several that Chris had never heard before.

"Wait a minute," he protested. "How come you never told me about that? How come I'm getting all this information now, all of a sudden?"

His parents paused, looked at each other and smiled. "Let me try to explain," said his mother. "Seeing you two together, seeing the way you interact and how much you obviously care for one other, has, I think, stirred a lot of our old, precious memories. That's the way we felt about each other in those thrilling days when we first met."

"That's right," said his father. "It was love at first sight for us, too. Every moment we spent together was another affirmation that

50

we had each found the perfect mate and that the most important thing in our lives would be to spend them together. You haven't said those words, but, having lived through it, we can see it in your faces. It's thrilling to recall the feelings we had. I'm afraid we've just let our emotions run away with us, boring you with all this history."

"Nothing could be further from the truth," said Chris. "Until I met Erin, I couldn't have understood what you two had gone through. Now, I do. We both do. We understand perfectly."

"I'm still overwhelmed by it," said Erin. "I guess I never believed that it really existed, or that, if it did, it would happen to me. My parents have a very solid, loving relationship, but nothing like this ever happened to them. I think that's more what I expected for me."

"Well, let's drink to true, romantic love," said his father, raising his glass. "And to those fortunate few who are lucky enough to find it."

As the evening was ending, and Chris and Erin were preparing to leave, his mother said, "Chris, you two should take advantage of the San Francisco apartment. We use it so rarely. It's a shame that it just sits there. It might be convenient for you two while Erin's still living in Berkeley and you're still living down here."

Chris was surprised and delighted. "Great idea. I'm sure we can find some use for it. Thanks."

Driving home, he said to Erin. "I think they were as taken by you as I am. I've never seen them just completely welcome some one like that before. I mean, they're friendly and all, but it was like they had known you for a long time. And Mom offering the San Francisco place. That would never have happened with anyone else. I think you have a second family."

"That's the way I felt," she said. "It was just wonderful."

Erin was working on a paper that was due the following week. She was refilling her coffee when she heard the doorbell. It was Ellie. "I just wanted to check up on you. I wanted to find out more about that musician you seemed to be so stuck on. Is that still going?"

"Oh, Ellie, come on in. Let me tell you. I am completely in

love. Sit down. Let me get you some coffee."

She did and the two sat on the sofa. "I've had affectionate relationships before that were very enjoyable. But as I think back on them, I realize that I invested only a part of myself. It was as though I were standing back and watching the whole thing evolve. But this. This is complete and total immersion. I just want to give every part of myself to him and hold nothing back. And I know he feels the same way."

"Wow," said Ellie. "I've never had that experience. You mean that there aren't any parts of you that you feel that you have to protect?"

"Exactly. I feel that he understands everything about me, and loves the whole package without reservation. It is such a wonderful feeling of safety and warm comfort that goes far beyond the passion, I feel that he is the one person that was meant for me, and me for him. I am more joyfully happy than I ever realized could be possible."

"Well, it certainly shows. You just look radient. I am so happy for you, but you know, I feel a little jealous. Your talking about an experience that I never had, and probably never will. I really can't complain. My life is good. I'm in control. But suddenly I'm feeling lonely."

"I'm sorry," said Erin.

"Don't be. This is a very unusual gift that you've been given and you must treasure it and enjoy it for all your life."

"Thank you. I realize that I had never really understood the concept of intimacy before. I mean profound, spiritual intimacy and its transforming power. It makes everything seem more meaningful because you can share it with another person who feels the same way about you."

"It couldn't have happened to a more deserving person, Erin. I think I'll go out and start looking for myself. You're an inspiration."

*   *   *

Chris and Erin drove north from San Francisco, heading up 101 to Cloverdale. There, they turned northwest on route 128. The drive took them through some of the land that had recently been converted into enormously popular, successful vineyards and wineries.

Despite the arrival of these newcomers, the area retained a rural, pastoral character.

Closer to the coast, the road began to follow the course of the Navarro River through some magnificent stands of redwoods, the survivors of the last century when timber from this region was being floated down the river, onto barges and down the coast to San Francisco, where it became the Victorian homes of that era.

They reached the coast at the little fishing town of Albion and turned north to Mendocino. When they arrived they checked into the bed and breakfast where they had made reservations. Then they went for a walk.

"I love this town," said Chris as they walked along the wooden sidewalks. "It's like a living museum. I feel like I'm stepping back in time when I come here." They wandered through museums, bookstores and art galleries with other tourists from the Bay Area.

They had dinner at the Mendocino Hotel, a survivor from the last century that had been refurbished and was now enjoying the prosperity that accompanied the rebirth of the town in the fifties and sixties.

After dinner, they strolled along the headlands, listening to the sounds of the ocean below. The cloud cover obscured the stars.

"Sorry," said Chris. "No astronomy lessons tonight."

The breeze was cool and they walked with arms around each other for warmth and the thrill of the contact. They went to bed early and snuggled into the warmth of the down comforter that adorned the brass bed in their room.

The following morning, after breakfasting on fruit, scones and hot coffee, they drove south and found a small, secluded beach. It was still overcast and chilly as they walked along the damp sand. They found a large outcropping of rocks at the edge of the ocean and carefully climbed to find perches from which they could watch the ocean.

"I can watch the waves for hours," said Erin. "My folks used to take me to the ocean when I was just a toddler. They'd just perch me someplace and I'd sit there until they came and retrieved me. I could never get over the fact that every wave is different. As I got a little older, I became fascinated by the notion that they had been doing the same thing since the beginning of time on this planet.

Each wave is different, but the ocean is somehow the same."

"I love it, too," said Chris. "I can spend hours just watching. But there is change. Look at those rocks out further. You can see how the pounding of the waves has shaped them into arches. Change is constantly taking place, it's just that it's taking place at a such a slow pace that we can't perceive it. The amount of change in one of our lifetimes is probably difficult to measure."

"I guess you're right," said Erin. "It looks immovable and permanent, but that's only an illusion. We have to change our perspective about how we measure time. I like that better."

"Look at these little green plants," said Chris, pointing to clumps of plants growing on the rocks. "They really amazing to me. Think about how much adversity they have to endure to continue to survive and reproduce. There's virtually no soil, and yet they're able to get their tiny roots anchored firmly enough to withstand not only the pounding of the waves but the constant wind.. You'd think it'd rip them right off the rock. But yet they're able to get enough nutrition to survive.

"It blows me away that the power of the drive to exist and survive is that strong," said Chris. "They just have to fulfill their destiny." He turned to her and took her hand. "You're my destiny. I'm yours. That's why our attraction for each other has such force. Our love is another expression of this incredible panorama of life. It's overwhelming."

"I hadn't thought about that," said Erin. "Nicely put. I think that's worthy of some poetry. I'll have to do some work on that."

"Do you write poetry?" he asked, surprised.

"A little," she said. "Nothing I'm going to let you see."

"And why not?" he asked. "I showed you mine. Now you have to show me yours."

"Do not," she said, sticking her tongue out at him.

"Do too," he said making a face at her. "Why won't you?"

"Because, for me, writing is a very private, personal act. It's a way in which I clarify my own thoughts and challenge the precision of my thinking. But it's not something I do to show to other people."

"But it should be shared," he insisted.

"Why?" she asked. "For you it's different. You were raised to accept music as something you share with other people. That's

54

what your mother taught you. But that doesn't mean that all people should share their music."

"But music is meant to be shared," he said. "What good is it if no one hears it?"

"If it gives pleasure to the person who performs or writes it, that certainly is justification enough," she said. "I'm not saying that all art should be private, but I do insist that if that's what the artist wants it to be, that's what it should be."

"Hmm," said Chris. "I guess you're right. I just have trouble getting used to thinking about it that way. I also have difficulty believing that you're not going to share your poetry with me."

"Believe it because it's true," she said firmly. "Now, sometime in the future, I may write something that I do want to share with you and I will. What I've written so far is personal."

"And I don't get to see it?" he asked.

"You don't get to see it," she said.

"I'm also surprised that you're so stubborn," he said laughing.

"I think what really surprises you is that you're not getting your own way," she rejoined.

"Are you implying that I'm spoiled?" he asked in mock surprise.

"Rotten," she said. "And I'm going to be very careful to make certain that I don't encourage any of your bad habits."

"Oh, Lord," he said. "I see trouble on the horizon."

"More than you can handle, Dr. Childs?" she asked, climbing down from the rock.

"Not on your life, Irish," he said, scrambling after her. "I'm in this one for the long haul. You ain't gettin' rid of me just because you have some peculiar personal quirks."

"'Quirks' is it?" she said. "And what do you intend to do about these quirks?"

"Well, one of the things that I've always found very helpful in getting rid of quirks is some good old wrestling."

"You wouldn't dare," she said backing away from him.

"And it may include some water therapy," he said, moving toward her.

"Chris, don't you even think it," she said and took off running.

He ran after her, she squealing, he roaring like a monster. He caught her and they tumbled into the sand and thrashed about for several minutes until he rolled on top of her and pinned her arms beside her.

"Now, me pretty," he said. snarling. "I have you where I want you."

"Now, you big oaf, I have you exactly where I want you."

They laughed and he let go of her hands. She reached up and grabbed his neck, pulled him down to her and kissed him.

"God, I love you," he said.

"We're such a splendid match," she said. "I never enjoyed being with someone as much as I do with you. And, if forced to admit it, I love you too. Kiss me again."

As they walked back to the car she pointed to a hawk that was soaring at the edge of the forest. "Look how beautiful that bird is. He barely moves his wings. He's so graceful, but he's alone. How terrible to be alone. I don't want to ever be alone again."

"You won't be if I have anything to say about it."

That afternoon they were taking a walk along a pathway that followed the edge of a cliff overlooking the rocks and beaches below. At intervals wooden benches had been placed to permit people to rest and enjoy the view. There was a wooden railing that accompanied the pathway and separated the walkers from the edge of the cliff.

"I bet you didn't know that I was something of a gymnast," said Erin as they were leaning on the rail, watched some sea lions sunning themselves on the rocks below.

"No, I didn't. What were your events?" asked Chris.

"I wasn't very good on the rings, but I enjoyed them. I was best on the vault and the balance beam."

"Really," he said with admiration. "I would have liked to do the rings. I always thought it was a bit like flying."

"It is," she said. "And that's why it loved it. I just loved soaring, more than I did the discipline. Although, the discipline of the balance beam was a challenge that I enjoyed."

"I thought the beam was a bit boring, " he said.

"Oh, you did, did you," she said. With that she mounted herself onto the top railing of the fence and began walking as if in a gymnastic routine. She did a cartwheel that took her to the end of the fence segment and then turned to come back.

"Jesus, Erin," he said, somewhat alarmed. "Get down from

there. What do you think you're doing?" She did another cart-wheel, coming back the opposite direction. But as she landed, her weight was too much for the railing to support, and it gave way bending but not completely breaking. She began to lose her balance, and stumbled backward. Christ grabbed her jacked and pulled her towards him."

"You idiot," he said holding her closely to him. "You could have been killed."

"Well, it was a bit clumsy, I admit, but it was not boring," she said with a laugh.

"Why did you do that?" he asked. "That was really dangerous."

"Just call it spontaneity or impulsivity," she said. "It's just part of my Irish charm." She saw that he was not taking the episode lightly. "I'm sorry. I guess that was a bit foolish. It just seemed like a fun thing to do."

"But you could have been hurt," he said still holding her.

"Yeah. I guess so. I guess I didn't think about that. It's a part of me that I don't understand. I'm sorry it bothered you."

Now over his alarm, he kissed her forehead. "I told you I wanted to be able to protect you," he said. "I just didn't realize that it was going to be protecting you from yourself."

"Do you still want the job?" she asked.

"More than ever," he said, holding her close. "Now I realize how much you need protecting."

They drove back down to San Francisco via the slower coast route, stopping several times to look at the ocean.

They were working one evening in the apartment. Chris was sitting at a desk, going over a manuscript. Erin was reading a large leather bound book while sitting on the sofa. She came to the end of a chapter and reflected for a few moments on the contents and implications of what she had been reading. Then her eyes wandered to Chris. She watched him quietly for a few moments. He felt her eyes on him and smiled before he turned to her.

"I can just feel those wonderful vibes," he said, leaving his desk and coming over to sit on the sofa with her. He gently stroked her cheek and then kissed her. "So this is what love is like. I think I enjoy it. What were you thinking about?"

"I just feel so full of love for you. It's amazing to me how powerful this feeling is."

"What do you mean?"

"I think I told you that I've always felt that there are parts of me that I don't completely understand. Parts that I'm certain I could understand better if I had known my parents. Since I don't, there are just these mysterious parts that have always been a puzzle, and sometimes bothersome. Now, with you, I have the sense that you'll be able to help me open up and understand them better."

"Ah," he said dramatically, "Love reveals all mysteries."

"Don't laugh, you rat," she said as she poked him in the side. "I'm serious. I really feel that together we can find parts of ourselves that might otherwise remain out of reach. Don't you get that feeling."

"I do know what you mean, although for me it's different. How can I put this. I feel that you are the only person I've ever known who completely sees and accepts me. My parents, of course, accept me completely, but they see me through their parental prisms, and that's different."

"I'm surprised," she said pulling back from him a bit. "I can't think of anyone I've ever known that would be more universally acceptable than you. You have so much to offer."

"That's the point. Sometimes I think maybe it's too much. This is difficult for me to put into words. Most people I meet respect and admire the things that I can do. I know that." He paused for a moment. "But they tend to be either a bit awed by the whole package, which creates distance, or they become competitive and resentful, like Cal. This may sound silly to you, but I've always felt a bit lonely and estranged."

"I can see how people would have those reactions," she said, brushing the hair back from his forehead. "That's sad for you. And, think of all they miss."

"But I won't have to worry about that any more. You seem to have no reservations. I know you see me clearly and respond with no self-consciousness. What do the psychologists call it: 'unconditional positive regard.'"

"You've got that right. Kind of like a puppy."

"No, seriously. You must feel like I do when we're together, that you're in a completely safe space. I can feel completely unguarded and spontaneous. That is so important to me."

"But aren't your friends in the band like that for you?"

"To a certain extent. About music, yes. And Rick probably comes as close as anyone else in my life. But there were problems that we had to get over, and I still feel that he has a sense of frustration because he couldn't go to medical school, while I could have and chose not to. It's just not the same as with you. But you are right about the importance of those guys. That source of peace and comfort is one of the main reasons that I've been so reluctant to leave this area. Even though I still feel that way, I now feel that with you I could to anywhere in the world and be supremely happy.

"I know I'd go any place you wanted to go without hesitation," she said. "But do you really want to leave this area?"

"No. This is, and, I think, will always be number one. But if I came to the decision that academics were really the right pathway for me, I feel that I could make that decision easily if you were with me."

"I believe my place will always be with you," she said coquettishly. "What would you think if that place were the bed?"

Chapter Eight

Erin's life was now compartmentalized. She was still pushing ahead with her studies, but that compartment now lacked energy. The compartment with Chris, her love, her joy and her future, had pre-empted the energy and vitality she usually focused on her studies.

Looking at the schedule she now faced to successfully complete the semester and this phase of her Ph.D. program, she felt some pangs of concern. Not only had energy been stolen from the academic compartment, time had also been embezzled. Her audit revealed how large the debt had grown.

The only account from which she could temporarily borrow time was that allotted to sleep; sweet, delicious, dream-filled, renewing sleep, which she treasured. It was a cruel sacrifice, but there didn't seem to be any alternative.

She shortened her sleep by two hours: one at night and one in the morning, but found that schedule unworkable. She was not able to study effectively late at night so that time was wasted. Worse, although she did work well when she arose an hour earlier, she found that she was no longer as efficient in the late afternoon, and was falling asleep in some of her classes.

After discussing it several times, she and Chris came to the conclusion that for the rest of the semester they would have to limit their time together. Phone calls were to be kept to fifteen minutes, only one per night. They would only see each other one evening on the weekend with no overnights. The first weekend they tried to adhere to the new plan, they realized that this last codicil was untenable. It had been she, in tears, who had clung to him and refused to let him leave.

But the program was working. She was gradually pulling herself back toward being on schedule. She still fell into reveries about him, but with Chris's understanding and support, she felt more confident about getting through the ordeal.

One evening, a few weeks later, she was working on a paper when the doorbell rang. When she opened the door, Cal was standing there, with a bouquet of flowers.

"Hi, Erin," he said in a warm and friendly manner. "I wanted to talk to you for a few minutes. It won't take long."

She was surprised, and relieved, at how amiable he seemed, but felt guarded because of the violence of his previous departure. "Cal. How nice to see you. Come in."

He still hesitated at the door. "Look, I'm presuming Chris's not here. I checked and didn't see his car, but I don't want to intrude."

"No, he isn't here. Please come in. Are these roses for me? They're gorgeous. You know how much I love roses. Thank you so much. Would you like a glass of wine?"

"I know you're studying. I really don't want to take up a lot of time."

"Nonsense," she said, going to the refrigerator to take out a bottle of wine. "I'm at a good place for a break." She poured two glasses and brought them back to the living room where he was sitting.

"I really appreciate your being willing to talk to me," he said sincerely. "I'd understand if you didn't want to after the way I behaved last time. I don't know what got into me. I was very disappointed, but there was no excuse for my anger. I sincerely apologize."

"I'm glad, Cal," she said. "I really did enjoy our times together and I didn't want to lose your friendship."

"After I calmed down I had a chance to think about things and I can see what a natural couple you and Chris make. Maybe that was part of my anger, that I could see that he was better for you than I am. He's really one of the most talented people I've ever known. You two deserve each other. Here's to you two," he said, raising his glass."

"Thank you," said Erin. "That's very sweet." Her defenses

were now completely relaxed.

"I have a favor to ask of you," he said. "It may sound strange, but it would mean a lot to me. It would kind of seal the friendship thing for me."

"Of course," she said, feeling very relieved about his change in attitude and eager to put all negative feelings behind them.

"Would you...well, would you smoke a peace pipe with me?" he asked.

"What do you mean, marijuana?" she asked, remembering the occasions when they had done so.

"Something like that," he said. It just makes you real happy, and I wanted to share it with you. It doesn't last long."

She didn't want to get high. She had studies to complete, but she didn't want to offend Cal, since he had been so eager to apologize and reach out to her. She also felt sympathy for the pain of rejection she had inflicted so she suppressed her cautious instincts.

"Are you sure it doesn't last long?" she asked for reassurance.

"Sure," he said.

"O.K."

He opened his coat and took out a cigarette from an inner pocket. It was a commercial cigarette that had been reloaded. He lit it and handed it to her. "Take a good hit," he said. "You'll really enjoy it."

She inhaled the smoke, tasting the strange flavor, unlike the sweet taste of pot. She expected that there would be a period of waiting before she felt any effects, but within a few seconds, lights went off in her brain and she was lifted into a realm of euphoria and happiness that was unlike anything she had ever experienced. She began to feel nauseated, but she suppressed it and floated on upward into a realm of physical and mental bliss that was overwhelming. She felt that she was losing contact and control but didn't care. She relaxed and let herself dissolve in the most profound, pure enjoyment she had ever experienced.

It was a combination of spiritual, physical and sexual joy that was unimaginable. Every part of her seemed to be participating, swimming through a liquid medium of pure pleasure.

She floated at the apex for a period of time which she could not determine or appreciate. Then she gradually felt the effects beginning to diminish. She reestablished vague contact with reality which then gradually became more precise. When she felt able she opened her eyes and realized that Cal was standing near, watching her. He was smiling, but he didn't look happy, which puzzled her.

When she felt able, she said, "That was incredible. What was it?"

"China," he said, maintaining the puzzling smile.

She was confused by the reply. It made no sense. He saw her look of confusion.

"China white," he said which confused her even more.

"China white's a very powerful, pure form of heroin."

He saw the terror that spread over her face. "Don't worry, Erin. You don't become addicted with one hit, usually. You have to use regularly to get hooked. I just wanted you to have what I think is a very special experience. I'm leaving now. You know how to reach me." he said as he left.

Her confusion had changed to alarm. Heroin. The word reverberated in her brain. The drug that was associated with the darkest evil, the most heinous crimes and infinite despair. She had allowed the most vile chemical she knew anything about to penetrate the purity of her body, her mind, and maybe her soul.

"Why? Why did he do that?" she asked in despair. She saw the bouquet of roses lying on the counter and threw them in the sink. He had seemed so friendly. How could he have shown such terrible judgment? How could he have ever believed that she could want to experience — She couldn't even think the word without recalling all the gothic images of terror and ultimate evil.

She ran into her bedroom and took off her clothes. She went to the shower and turned the water on full blast and got in. She began to soap her body over and over again. She was sobbing as the warm water continued to pour down on her, offering no comfort, no relief. There was no solace. Her ablutions were pitifully superficial, far removed from the deep, dark stain that now disfigured the purity of her soul.

Now there was a third compartment in her life. She was still struggling to make up her deficient assignments, struggling to crowd enough hours of study into days with insufficient sleep. Her daily conversations with Chris were even more important to her now, but were deeply disturbing because they took place under the shadow of her duplicity.

She now had a secret--a profound, disturbing secret that she could not share with him. Just days before, the notion that there would be a part of her life that she would deliberately hide from him would have been inconceivable. The compelling desire to open herself to him completely and feel so safe in doing so was one of the most satisfying aspects of their relationship.

But that had changed. Now she was guarded. Spontaneity was suppressed. She wondered if he noticed. Certainly he must, but he had said nothing, perhaps presuming that any change could be ascribed to the pressures of her studies.

The third compartment was dark. She had to keep it so. It was the dense, palpable darkness of shame and terror. In the first days after smoking heroin, she had begun to feel that maybe the experience would be no more than what she had already experienced---a single exposure to the drug, after which she would resume her normal life.

Maybe, no certainly, she would discuss it with Chris after some time had passed. It would be important to clear the slate and close the gulf that the incident had created between them.

But it wasn't over.

Now there were dreams. Ambiguous in form, but very disturbing were the recurrent, hazy, visions that were interwoven with intense pleasure and terror. The content was not ambiguous. She realized almost immediately that these were shades of the heroin experience. Somehow the dark thing had attached itself to the part of her brain that produced dreams. It could insinuate itself into her sleep and subtly insist on her acknowledgment of its presence.

She didn't know if this was a transient phenomenon that would self-extinguish with the passage of time. She chose to believe so and awaited reassuring evidence that this would be the case. Perhaps just looking for such evidence was enough attention to keep it alive. But she couldn't stop the concern. The third compartment was a fact.

The dreams continued, but the content subtly changed. The terror was no longer present, only the vague images that connected her with the pleasure; the rush, the high. She would awake feeling unrested, still in mental contact with the images and a persistent visceral feeling of disquiet.

As the days went by she found herself experiencing a deep craving to repeat the experience. She tried to suppress the growing compulsion and tried to make herself concentrate on her studies.

One evening, after talking to Chris, she sat staring at her books. She was in no frame of mind to continue her work. Her concentration was poor and she had no energy. She didn't feel sleepy, so she tried to do some recreational reading, but she couldn't concentrate. The craving for heroin was asserting itself. She struggled, trying to suppress it, but couldn't and decided to call Cal and ask for more. "You know how to reach me," had been his last words to her.

At the time, she could not have conceived of ever doing so, but now, here she was, calling to ask for heroin. She felt giddy as the phone rang.

When he picked up the receiver, she said, "Cal, this is Erin. I was wondering..."

"Sure, Erin. No problem," he interrupted. "Is now a good time?"

"Yes," she said, and put down the phone. She felt vague nausea, similar to that which she had experienced after smoking. She felt a chill. She was involved in a desperate argument with herself. "This is crazy. Don't do this. Put this out of your life," said one voice.

"It's no big deal. Cal said you don't get hooked that easily. I need a way to relax a bit. I've been working too hard," said the other.

The door bell rang, and he was standing on the porch smiling. "Hi," he said.

She asked him in. "Listen, I was really angry with you. You should have told me what you were giving me. That was an awful thing to do."

"If I had told you, you wouldn't have done it and you would have thought I was evil for even suggesting it. Now at least you've had the experience and you know how incredible it is. You can make your own decision. Lots of people just use occasionally. It's no big deal. They don't plunge themselves into hell. That's all propaganda. Pure bullshit. Did you want some more?"

65

"Well, I'm getting a little stressed out and I thought maybe a little bit might help me relax," she said.

"No problem," he said. "Here are a few cigarettes for you."

"How much do I owe you?" she asked. "I know this stuff is expensive."

"Don't be silly," he said. "I told you. This is a way of sealing our friendship. Just let me know if you need any more."

During the next couple of weeks, she smoked the cigarettes, usually at night. She began to notice some changes. She never had the same, intense high that she had experienced the first time. The experience was pleasant, and she felt a relaxing, pleasant, floating sort of numbness but it lacked sharply focused thrill of the initial ride.

Second, she wasn't feeling well. She was having some aches and pains in her muscles, some sweating, chills, and nausea. She mentioned to Chris that she thought she was coming down with the flu. Then she noticed that when she smoked the heroin, the symptoms went away.

She called Cal again and asked if he could come by. He was happy to oblige.

"The reason you're not getting as high, is that you're developing a bit of tolerance to the drug, which simply means that you have to smoke more."

"I did," she said. "But it's just not like that first time."

"It never is as good as the first time," he said, with his knowing smile. "But, you may have to think about injecting it to get the same effect."

"I could never do that," she said, shivering in abhorrence of the thought."

"That's what everybody says. That's what diabetics say, and think, when they first learn that they're going to have to take insulin. Here, let me show you how easy it is. I'll do it to myself. I'll just inject a small amount to show you."

He took a small kit out of his jacket and carefully opened it. It had a small syringe with an attached needle, a band with a piece of Velcro attached, a small packet of powder, a spoon, some cotton and a vial of water. He took a small amount of powder, placed it in the spoon and poured in a small amount of water. He heated the underside of the spoon with his cigarette lighter until the powder dissolved in the water. Then he expertly drew the syringe plunger back, filling the barrel through the cotton which filtered the material that flowed into the needle. He unbuttoned his shirt cuff and rolled up the sleeve. He applied the band to his arm, fixing the Velcro and watched while his veins became more visible.

She noticed the small line of dots that followed the course of the vein, and realized that she had never seen him wear short sleeved shirts. He cleansed the area over the vein with a small disposable pad of alcohol and then quickly slipped the needle into the vein. He drew back the barrel and a stream of dark red blood spurted into the syringe. He released the Velcro tourniquet and pushed the barrel of the syringe down, injecting the fluid into his vein. He withdrew the needle quickly and rubbed the site with a small amount of saliva on his thumb.

"There," he said. "Wasn't that simple? It's more efficient than smoking. With smoking you get real quick jolt, but you lose a lot. You only get about thirty per cent of the stuff to your brain."

"I could never do that," she said.

"O.K. Maybe it's not for you. But I'll leave this rig here for you in case you want to practice. There's more stuff and more cigarettes."

"Thank you, I think," she said as he left.

Chapter Nine

Looking back, she had difficulty understanding how it had happened. First the combination of the intense thrill of the first high and the offsetting terror and disgust that accompanied her realization of what had happened. Then, the craving and the reluctant, continued use despite the disgust and loathing that she felt for herself. The fiber of her determination not to use again had somehow been shredded and become inconsequential, being replaced by a helpless acquiescence that was accompanied by shame and increasing desperation.

Erin now knew that she had become addicted to heroin. She knew that unless she provided the chemical to her brain, she would become severely ill in several hours. She had tested the reality, resolving to refuse to give in, but became so miserable, that she was unable to tolerate the nausea, cramping, vomiting, diarrhea, muscle and joint pains which became so intense that they were unendurable.

She was unable to sleep and knew that she would not be able to successfully take her exams. She contacted her professors and told them she had a family emergency and obtained permission to take an "incomplete" in her courses.

She did not share this with Chris. She used the excuse of her studies to limit their time together, which made her feel more isolated and increasingly desperate. Maintaining the web of deceit was becoming more difficult. Phone calls from friends and family were going unanswered and unreturned.

She convinced herself that when she was free of the pressure of her school obligations, she would be able to concentrate and rid herself of the effects of heroin, without ever having to tell Chris until it was all over. She had gradually overcome her fear and was now gaining confidence in her ability to inject the drug into her veins and she had learned that the dose seemed to last longer when it was injected.

Knowing when her finals were scheduled to be finished, Chris made plans to take her out to dinner to celebrate the end of the term. He wanted to go to one of his favorite San Francisco restaurants and then spend the night in the apartment.

Her problem would be to time the dose so she would not be too high during the meal, and would not be getting sick from withdrawal. Hopefully, she would then be able to fix again later on, without his knowledge. It would be difficult, and she was becoming desperate.

She injected a dose in the late afternoon, and waited out the period of the intense high in her apartment. Then she took a cab to the BART station and took a train to San Francisco. The train sped along the surface streets and then went underground for the trip under the bay. Under the influence of the heroin, she connected the train ride to her dark fears and found herself obsessed with the feeling that her whole life had suddenly been caught in a vortex and that she was plunging down into a dark, subterranean tunnel, unable to control her destiny. She attempted to control the fear that rose within her by convincing herself that it was just temporary, and that she would soon emerge and again enjoy her life.

Chris was waiting outside the Italian restaurant on Guerrero St. He embraced her and kissed her when she got out of the cab. She felt limp from the wonderful feeling of being safe again in his arms.

"God, I've missed you so much. I can't tell you. I don't want us to ever be separated again. It's terrible," he said. He paid the cab driver and they entered the restaurant. "You must be exhausted. Do you still have the flu? You look tired."

"It's no big deal," she said. "I'll be fine now that we're together again. Although we may have to be apart for a bit. I told my parents that I'd come down and spend some time with them." She had concocted a plan to get away and kick the habit without either her parents or Chris being the wiser. "It won't be long, but it's something I need to do."

"Maybe I could come with you," he said eagerly. "I'd love to meet them."

"Maybe after a few days, I need to be with them alone first."

"I understand, " he said. "But keep it in mind."

They went through the meal engaged in a conversation that was very different from those they had previously enjoyed. There was no spontaneity. He questioned her about her studies and exams and she deflected the questions with vague, partial answers. Her efforts to respond in a way that would satisfy him without giving herself away were exhausting and nerve-wracking.

"You don't seem yourself," he said after another attempt to start the flow of thoughts and words had again resulted in awkward, puzzling silence.

"I'm sorry," she said. "I guess the strain of the exams has taken more out of me than I realized." The stress of the situation had triggered some chills and sweating, which she recognized as early withdrawal symptoms. "Would you mind if we went home early?"

"Of course not," he said. "I'm just happy to be with you. It doesn't matter to me where we are."

They left the restaurant and drove a few blocks in Chris's car to the apartment in Noe Valley. The house was a three story Victorian which contained two separate apartments, each with a separate entrance. Trees lined the parking on both sides of the street and flowers were planted in the shallow front yards.

They entered the apartment, which was a split level duplex, the mirror image of the one adjacent. "Let me take you on a quick tour," said Chris. The large front room had bay windows opening on the street. The high ceilings had crown moldings. A fireplace had been converted to gas. It was separated by a pocket door from a room that had been converted from a bed room to a study. The furniture was Edwardian, in perfect condition.

A long hall led to a large dining room with built-in cupboards closed by leaded glass doors. "All this is original," said Chris. "The china and crystal were my grandmother's."

The dining room connected to a large kitchen in which the equipment had been modernized but the decor remained true to the period of origin. A small screened-in porch was connected to the kitchen.

They went up the stairs to the second level which had a master bed room and two smaller others.

70

"This is all so lovely," said Erin. "I wish I was in better condition to enjoy it. I think that flu must be coming back."

"You don't look well, darling," said Chris. "Look you're perspiring," he said as he brushed some beads of perspiration from her forehead. "You need to go to bed."

"I hate to on our first night back together," she said. "I'm so disappointed. I'm sorry."

"Nonsense," he said, kissing her forehead. "You need some rest. Then you'll regain your strength. We have plenty of time."

They put their clothes in the master bedroom. She undressed in the bathroom down the hall, and they both climbed in bed. "Good night, Erin," he said. "I love you."

"I love you too," she said, grateful that he did not expect to make love.

Her withdrawal symptoms were becoming stronger. She was having severe cramps and had to get up to vomit. He was still awake when she came back to bed. "Is there anything I can do?" he asked.

"No. I took some Pepto-Bismol. That's been working for me."

She was simultaneously sweating and chilled and experiencing severe aching in her back and her legs. She was determined to hold out until he was asleep. When she heard his heavy, slow, regular breathing, she slipped out of bed very carefully. She went to the bathroom and experienced more cramps and explosive diarrhea. She poured cold water over her face and attempted to calm down. Her eyes and nose were watering and her hands were shaking.

She took out the small kit she had in her overnight bag. She took out the heroin and decided to make up a heavy dose so that she wouldn't have to go through withdrawal again until she was able to get away from Chris. She tried to calculate what she thought would be sufficient. She went through her routine and injected the material. Very quickly her symptoms began to abate. She felt much better, and very high. Then she became more and more sleepy and decided to lie down on the floor until her head cleared.

Chris awoke some time later and realized she wasn't in bed. He went to the bathroom and found her lying unconscious on the floor. He was immediately alarmed, thinking she might have fallen and hit her head. Panic spread through his body as he attempted to calm himself enough to cope with the situation.

He called her name again and again, gently shaking her lifeless, unresponsive form. When he opened her eyelids, he noticed that her pupils were constricted to the size of pin points. It was then that he noticed the syringe on the counter and found the site of injection on her left arm. In a daze he left her and called 911.

After he made the call he returned to the bathroom and sat on the floor, cradling her in his arms. His mind was racing, confused and disbelieving. Filling his chest was the heavy ache of fear, accompanied by feelings concern and profound dread. At the periphery of his awareness he began to hear the crescendo of the siren that was growing louder as it came nearer. In his panic it seemed the very antithesis of the comforting sounds that usually decorated his life. It foretold the sinister dimensions of the future they would face together.

Chapter Ten

Dr. Carlos Garza walked into the small office and flipped on the light switch. He fell, more than sat down, into the chair at the desk. He took off his glasses, holding them in his left hand while he slowly rubbed his eyes with his right. He rotated his neck three hundred sixty degrees and then repeated it again, feeling some of the tension being released from the taught muscles in his neck and shoulders.

He took a deep breath, let it out slowly, replaced his glasses and sorted through the mail that had been placed in the center of the desk calendar. It was mostly junk — announcements of continuing medical education opportunities on cruise ships in the Mediterranean or Caribbean--"Two weeks of breathtaking beauty, wonderful cuisine and a completely accredited course in dermatology for the primary care physician in the HMO era. Thirty-five hundred dollars per person in standard cabin. Forty-five hundred deluxe Air fare not included."

"Jesus, who goes to these things," he muttered as he tossed several brochures into the waste basket.

He quickly sorted through the journals that arrived by the pound, week in and week out. Many were throwaways such as "MD Economics," and "Leisure for the Physician," which he discarded without looking at them. Then he sorted through the journals of substance. He breezed through the table of contents, read the abstract, then turned to an article he found interesting.

He hadn't always enjoyed reading. It had come slowly to him. His younger brother, Jimmy, had been much quicker to pick up the skill, and he had transformed that ability into his Stanford education. His older brother was also a quick study, but that ability had played no part in the tragedy of his truncated life.

There hadn't been much time for reading when he was growing up in the artichoke fields near Watsonville. The soil was incredibly fertile, the irrigation abundant, and the sun poured the transforming energy of its rays onto the green shoots with a regularity that made bankers rub their hands with anticipation. But these fields didn't grow the grains that flooded the fields of the central valley, where magnificent machines did much of the work. These crops required the careful hands of skilled workers. These hands were the last ingredient in the equation that transformed the fertile land into wealth.

Such hands belonged to the people in Carlos' family. His parents, his brothers and sisters, his cousins, aunts and uncles all had these hands. They all worked together. They shared their days, bent over in the constant sun, working silently together. They shared the noon meal which Mama had prepared, seeking the shade provided by one of the trucks. They would find a cool area and cherish the moments, gulping the food and washing it down with the lemon-flavored water, giggling when one of the siblings or cousins spilled and had to bear the shame of parental rebuke.

The summer days were long, but what else did they know? Everyone they knew did the same thing, day in, day out. On week ends they all attended the same church services and family meals and celebratory gatherings. In the cloak of familiarity there was protection from the pain of being different, and the tension of the anger it produced.

They would hear the men and the older boys grumbling their words of frustration in the evenings, after they opened their beer, but the angry words had no meaning for them when they were young. They were only interested in enjoying the delicious hours of coolness in the darkening evening, playing tag and kick the can.

They all went to the same schools, the ones intended particularly for the children of the workers. The faces and the accents were all familiar. Even the teachers were well known, through the experiences of older siblings or cousins.

It wasn't difficult to pinpoint the moment when reality began to expose itself: the fact that there were different, parallel worlds inhabited by different people. The most important event of his young life simultaneously demonstrated that ugly truth and gave him the strength and direction that would make it endurable. It was an experience of such violent transformation that he could still recall the contradictory feelings that had overwhelmed him.

He was riding in the back of the pick-up. His father and older brother were in the cab. They were slowly making their way along a fog enshrouded road near the coast when a car materialized out of the obscuring mist and ran into them. The conditions had slowed everyone's speed, reducing the force of the impact. When his mind cleared he remembered the flash of the oncoming headlights and the realization of being hurled out of the bed of the truck. The sense of momentary flight ended with the stunning impact and confusion.

Then there were more lights, sirens and numerous, unfamiliar people dressed in uniforms making clipped, unintelligible remarks. Then there was the sensation of being carried into a place where there were strange, pungent smells that were at once repellent and reassuring.

Then there was the loving face of his mother bending over him. He could still remember the familiar, reassuring scent and the coolness of her lips as she kissed his forehead.

The gringo family which had been in the other vehicle had been carried in separate ambulances to the same emergency room. They were being evaluated by the hospital staff while his family waited their turn. His mind had cleared by then and he remembered that he had been moved by the gentleness and compassion with which the staff treated the other family, reassuring them and anticipating their needs.

The other indelible part of the memory was the skill displayed by the staff. He had never been in a hospital and was mesmerized by the shining, magical equipment, completely unfamiliar to him, and manipulated with such grace and confidence by the staff.

When the doctor came in, there was obvious deference to him as the staff transferred the arcane information to the authoritative man who listened and nodded thoughtfully. He then approached the members of the gringo family individually. He appeared so wise and caring that Carlos was thrilled, expecting that he would soon have the same opportunity to come under the spell of this wonderful, powerful man.

But then the staff had turned their attention to him and his family. It was different. The concern, the compassion, the warmth and patience had been replaced by a stern, abrupt manner and a cool distance. He had never observed such a dramatic difference and it puzzled him.

It was repeated when the doctor came in to do his evaluation and examination. The same words were used, the same questions asked. The same examination was performed, but the friendly, reassuring smile was gone. There was no warmth.

He had been eager to have this interaction, anticipating the pleasant, easy exchange he had witnessed, but the doctor's reserved manner silently told him that this was not to be and he fell silent, feeling awkward and self-conscious and not knowing why.

He was distracted on the trip home after their release with assurances that they had sustained no serious injury. His parents presumed that his silence was due to the shock of the experience. They were more correct than they could have known.

His thoughts at that moment had been focused as they had ever been in his life. He had found the key to his universe. When he grew up he would work in a hospital and become a master of those wonderful pieces of equipment that could make people well. He would wear the green suit with the tag on it that bore his name. He didn't presume to aim to be a doctor, but one of those who assisted. The thought of it thrilled and warmed him almost enough to overcome the chill of the emergency room experience which he didn't understand.

On one hand, his determination to achieve medical training and become one of the healers now became a powerful engine driving his intellect relentlessly forward. Reading now had a lofty purpose. Mastery of mathematics and science was a stepping stone on the pathway to the sanctuary of the healing arts.

On the other, he was growing old enough to sit at the fringe of conversations with older boys. He heard the anger and defiance and the message began to resonate within him. He began to realize that they were speaking of powerful forces, realities which would explain the experience of his seminal pain. The shrill, angry cries of macho defiance had the deeper foundations of injustice and inequity, and it was this understanding that was moving him inexorably toward a difficult dilemma.

The most common way of acting out the Chicano rage was to stick your ass in the face of the Anglo establishment and all the institutions it used to perpetuate its arrogant posture of superiority.

The schools were such a tool. Once you recognized this, it was your duty to refuse to prostrate yourself to the learning process which was just another way of taking away your pride and your manhood and exchanging them for obsequious submission.

He felt this obligation as deeply as anyone. How, then, was he to gain the education he so deeply coveted without selling out his people.

Older cousins took him aside when word circulated that he was an outstanding student. Angry words and not so veiled threats convinced him that to betray his people for his own selfish goals was unworthy. He should be planning when to leave school, not how to succeed in it.

Abruptly his grades plummeted and his attitude deteriorated. Teachers who had been delighted with his progress watched in frustration as he turned away from excellence and coldly rebuffed their attempts to intervene.

His mother watched the transformation with pain. Knowing that her husband held the same negative opinion about education made it impossible for her to act directly. Desperate, she had a tearful conversation with her older brother, Luis, which proved to be pivotal.

Luis, whom Carlos adored, came to the house one afternoon. "Come with me," he said.

They drove in silence to the ocean. The sun was turning the clouds to red and orange when they arrived. They took off their shoes and threw them into the back of the truck. A cool onshore breeze was blowing as they walked from the parking lot to the edge of the ocean and sat down. The breeze was removing the heat from the sand faster than the fading sun could replace it and the sand felt cool on their feet.

Strands of kelp lay scattered at the edge of the water. Sandpipers scurried along the edge of the waves and gulls soared in and out over the rolling waves. Walkers, solitary and coupled, strolled along the edge of the water, some attached by leashes to eager, frolicking dogs.

"Look at the sea, Carlos," said his uncle. "Look how powerful it is. If you come back in two weeks or two centuries it will still be here, still powerful. But you and me? We'll be long gone. We are weak. Our lives are short." He walked to the edge of the water and picked up a small bit of wood that had washed ashore. Still fingering it, he sat down again.

"Do you respect me, Carlos?" he asked.

"Of course I do," the boy had replied.

"Do you admire me?"

"Absolutely."

"Why?" Luis asked, rubbing his fingers over the surface of the wood.

"Because you are my uncle," the boy said with proudly. "You are strong but you are also very kind. You are a fine man."

"It's good that you see me in this way," he said. "That makes me very happy. What you don't see is how limited I am. I have little education. I know little of the world. The big forces of the world can knock me around the way the sea knocks around this piece of wood. I am virtually powerless.

"There are so many things that I see around me that are completely beyond my understanding. What do I know? I know the soil. I know the plants. I love nature. But I cannot take my love of nature and use it to help others."

"But you're such a fine example to us because of your strength," argued Carlos.

"I have endurance, it is true. That is one source of pride to me. I don't have many. I would rather have lived my life as you can live yours. Learning all the wonderful things that scientists know and helping sick people---that's a dream worth having and a life worth living."

"But you have to let the Anglos make you a lap dog to do these things," said Carlos. "You lose your pride."

"Pride? Pride in what?" asked Luis. "Pride in fulfilling their expectations of you as an angry, ignorant person, suited only for doing menial labor to support his family? You gain nothing for yourself or your family by selling yourself short and throwing away opportunities that others would die for.

"The way of courage is to meet them on their own terms: to seek knowledge; to learn how to learn and never lose your own dignity and self respect. They cannot make you a 'lap dog', as you call it, if you will not be one. You can be an example for those who come after you if you have the courage to be different.

"Go for it, Carlito. Don't just become another pissed off Chi-

78

cano, drinking beer and complaining about the Anglos. That won't change anything. You have a fine mind. Use it to help us. Be an example of how far we can go and what we can achieve. Don't throw your life away with this macho shit. It is unworthy of you.

"Look at that sunset. It's magnificent," he said with a sweep of his arm. The soft colors were changing from moment now as the red ball of the sun was slipping below the horizon. "Make sure that when you're looking at your last sunset that you look back over a worthy life. Don't settle for anything less than being a doctor and show everyone what wonderful, kind doctors our people can be."

Without realizing it, Uncle Luis had turned the key---the notion that he, Carlos, could be a physician and be as compassionate and warm to everyone as the emergency room doctor was to the Anglos. Now it all made sense. There was no longer a dilemma. He knew his destiny.

"Whenever it gets tough for you," Luis had said. "Whenever someone's giving you too much crap and it's getting to you, you come to me. We'll sort it out together."

Many times through the years, he had called Tio Luis. In high school there had been frequent, angry calls and intense conversations by the sea. When he was an undergraduate in Santa Cruz, the calls were less frequent and less emotional but still regular.

In medical school at U.C. Davis, there had been frequent calls but mostly for sharing good news. And now, at least once a week, Carlos called to check in and see whether the chemotherapy was controlling the bone pain from Luis' prostate cancer which had been discovered last year. He called both as a loving nephew and a concerned, compassionate physician.

He was jarred by the vibrations of the pager he wore on his belt. He checked the message and dialed the familiar number that rang in the nurses station in the emergency room.

"Your flock needs you," said the nurse's voice. "They've got a good one."

"I'll be right down," he said. He put a paper clip in the journal to mark his place and headed into battle.

Chapter Eleven

"What's up?" Carlos asked the resident on duty who turned to greet him.

"I'm not sure," said John Harding, a tanned young man with chiseled, handsome features. He put down the chart in which he had been writing. Harding spoke to the intern. "Jim, why don't you present our patient.

"Shoot," said Carlos.

"Jorge Sanchez is a thirty-six year old Hispanic male, unemployed laborer and known heroin addict. He presented here two days ago complaining of difficulty with his vision and some trouble speaking. He was examined but no abnormalities were noted. Specifically, he had a normal neurological exam. Since he had alcohol on his breath, it was presumed that he was intoxicated, although his breathalyzer showed only 0.015%. He was given a shot of thiamin and sent home.

"Since then, he has had progressive difficulty with vision, droopy eyelids, more difficulty with speech and in the last few hours, difficulty swallowing. He also notes some difficulty getting his breath when he walks up the stairs. He became frightened and returned here.

"When I examined him, he was anxious and appeared to be in mild respiratory distress. His pulse was one hundred ten, respirations thirty, blood pressure one twenty over eighty and temp one oh two point five. His face was flushed."

"Was he febrile when he was here two days ago?" asked Carlos.

"One oh one," said the intern.

"Did they get a white count?" asked Carlos.

"No lab work was done."

"O.K. Go on."

"Other than rapid breathing, his respiratory system was negative. Lungs were clear. Positive finding were limited to the neurological system. He had bilateral ptosis, which was symmetrical. He had paralysis of lateral gaze bilaterally. His speech was slightly but definitely slurred. He had no cerebellar signs. His reflexes were active and symmetrical. There was no clonus. His neck was supple."

"Is that it?"

"Pretty much," said the intern.

"So, how do you put it together?" asked Carlos.

"I'm concerned about meningitis," said the intern.

"Good. With fever and rapidly changing neurological signs you should be. You didn't mention any evidence of an ear or throat infection."

"I should have mentioned that they were clear," said the intern.

"Good," said Carlos. "Did you do a spinal tap?"

"Yes. The opening pressure was normal and the fluid was clear. Microscopically there were only a few red cells, no white cells. We sent it for culture."

"O.K." said Carlos. "So we have a man with a febrile illness and neurological involvement which may or may not be meningitis. Let's go see him."

They walked to the gurney indicated by the intern and pulled back the drape that surrounded it. The patient looked ill and scared. There was an IV running into his left arm.

"Mr. Sanchez, I'm Dr. Garza. I'm pleased to meet you. My colleagues have been telling me about you and your illness. We need some more information to help us decide what we must do to make you well. I know that you're having trouble breathing and talking so we'll keep this brief. We know you've just had a spinal tap so we won't ask you to sit up since that would cause you to have a headache. Jim," he said to the intern. "Turn up the oxygen and let's see if that doesn't slow down his breathing a bit. He's having to do a lot of work at this pace. You did get blood gases, didn't you?"

"The results should be back in a few minutes," said the intern. to the patient.

"Have you had a headache? Just nod yes or no."

The patient nodded no.

"Any cough?"

The same reply.

"Do you have any pain?" asked Carlos.

"My shoulders," came the quiet, labored reply.

They carefully removed the hospital gown. There were warm, tender lumps on both shoulders.

"Have you been fixing there?" asked Carlos. The man nodded affirmatively. Carlos looked at the resident and intern. "Did we get cultures from these abscesses?" he asked.

"We missed them," said Harding. "Sorry about that."

"Let's open them now. Be sure and get some fluid for culture and gram stain. Be sure they culture them anaerobically also."

"The intern prepared the skin, put in a small amount of local anesthetic and then incised the skin over the abscesses allowing dark, infected fluid to drain forth. Swabs were saturated with the material and placed in culture media. Other swabs were smeared on glass slides to be stained and analyzed under a microscope.

"Did you start antibiotics?" asked Carlos.

"Not yet," said Harding. "We weren't sure what we were treating."

"O.K.," said Carlos. "We can wait a few more minutes until we see the slides. Have him transferred to ICU with respiratory precautions. Check on the blood gases and meet me in the Infectious Disease Lab."

He walked into the Infectious Disease Lab and greeted the chief tech. "Hi Eddie."

"Hi, Dr. Garza. What you got?"

"We need to have these specimens cultured," said Carlos.

"Are these from the guy in the ER.? We got some spinal fluid a little bit ago.

"Same guy," said Carlos. "Be sure to culture them all anaerobically also. Will you gram stain these slides for us, please?"

"Gotcha," he said. He took the slides, and went through the process of staining them. When they were ready he handed them back.

"Thanks," said Carlos. "Can I use your teaching scope?"

"You bet," said Eddie.

Carlos went into a small room that had microscopes on the

benches. He sat down at a large microscope that had several oculars attached so that more than one person could view the specimen at the same time.

He switched on the light in the microscope and moved the stage. "Look at those little mothers," he said to himself. The intern and resident entered the room.

"Here, Jim, have a look. Tell us what you see," said Carlos.

The intern looked. "Gram positive organisms. Is it staph?"

We'll let our senior resident make the call," said Carlos.

Harding looked through the microscope. After a couple of adjustments he smiled. "I'll be damned. I've heard about these cases. Finally I've got one. That's Clostridium. We've got a case of wound botulism."

"What's that?" asked the intern. "I thought there were only two types of botulism. The kind you get from canning and the kind that infants get."

"Tell them, Jim," said Carlos. "It's fascinating."

"Naw," said Harding. "You tell him. You're the expert."

"O.K." said Carlos. "Start him on twenty million units of Penicillin a day and decide whether he needs to be on a respirator. I'll come over and talk to him in a bit.

"In Mexico," he went on, "they make this junk that's called Black Tar Heroin. Some of the stuff they use in processing the poppies makes it dark and gummy. Unfortunately, there are also soil contaminants because they also manage to include our organism, Clostridium Botulinum in their final product."

"But why aren't they killed when they boil the heroin before they inject it?" asked the intern.

"Excellent question," said Carlos. "Clostridia are spore formers. Look at those little nodes on the ends of the rods. Non spore-forming organisms would be killed. Because these guys form spores they can endure. When the addicts inject the heroin, they also inject the spores. When they're injected into the skin, the spores can germinate and the organisms come to life. When enough of them have begun to grow they start putting out the botulinus toxin, which, as you know, is one of the most powerful neural toxins known."

"But I thought Clostridium can only grow in the absence of oxygen," said the intern.

"When they're injected into an area of infection or an abscess, the oxygen tension is low enough to permit the organisms to grow," said Carlos. "As they produce more and more toxin the patient begins to have the symptoms that Mr. Sanchez now has. Do you remember how Botulinus toxin works?"

"It's at the junction between the nerve and the muscle," said the intern. "At the motor end plate. I think it blocks the release of a neurotransmitter."

"Exactly," said Carlos. "The toxin is actually a protease, an enzyme that destroys the nerve terminals."

"So how do we treat him?" asked Jim.

"First we have to stop the infection," said Carlos. "We'll take him to the OR and remove all the infected tissue. Really clean up those wounds. The Penicillin will kill any we leave behind. I'll call the Centers for Disease Control in Atlanta. They'll send us some antitoxin."

"Will that stop the paralysis?" asked Jim.

"No," said Carlos. "It will neutralize any toxin that's still in his plasma. But his nerves will have to heal before the paralysis will completely go away. Meanwhile, we'll probably have to put him on a respirator to assist his breathing. I don't think he's moving enough air to get sufficient oxygen to his tissues. Come on, let's see how he's doing."

They went to the ICU and found Harding, standing by the bedside, making notes in the chart. "He's all out of balance. His oxygen level is only borderline with oxygen running full bore and he's blowing off all his CO2."

"What do you want to do?" asked Carlos.

"I think we ought to do a tracheotomy and put him on the ventilator. He's already exhausted trying to breathe."

"I agree," said Carlos. "Get the permits signed. Do you want me to talk to him?"

"He understands English perfectly well. I already told him what we were going to do."

"O.K.," said Carlos. "I'll just pay my respects, then I'll call CDC and have them fly out some anti-toxin."

"How much will they send?"

"Two vials," said Carlos. "Give him one IV and one IM. Test him for sensitivity to horse serum first. Can I talk to you a minute?"

"Sure," said Harding. He put down the chart and they walked into the clean room behind the nurses' station.

"Who saw him two days ago and sent him home without working him up?" asked Carlos.

"Look," said Harding. "I'd rather not say."

"I can, and will get it out of the ER records. I just wanted to save the walk down to medical records."

"O.K. It was Carlson." said Harding.

"Thanks," said Carlos. He walked to the bedside and took Sanchez's hand in his. "We know what's making you sick and we can make you better. I'm confident that everything will turn out fine this time. But I want you to know, that if you continue to use heroin you're going continue to make yourself sick, and maybe next time you won't be so lucky. Think it over. You really ought to knock this shit off before it kills you."

The man nodded a frightened, wide-eyed agreement. "Thank you, doctor."

Carlos went to his office. He left a page message for Carlson instructing him to come to the office. He called medical records and had them fax a copy of the ER record to him. Then he called CDC. They agreed to send the antitoxin. He was reviewing the ER record when Carlson knocked and came in.

"Hi, Carlos," he said, affably. "What's up?"

"I have a case here that I need to discuss with you. Sit down," said Carlos. "Do you remember a thirty-six year old man by the name of Jorge Sanchez? You saw him in the ER two nights ago."

"Can't say that I do. Refresh me, please."

"He came in complaining of slurred speech," said Carlos.

"Oh, you mean that junkie," said Carlson. "Yeah. I remember him. He was just drunk. I gave him some vitamins and sent him home."

"Did you examine him?"

"I went over him," said Carlson. There wasn't much of anything unusual."

"How about his vital signs?" asked Carlos.

"Nothing remarkable, as I remember," said Carlson. He was looking more concerned and shifting uncomfortably in the seat. "What's this all about?"

"Look at the record sheet. What was his temperature?"

"101.5 Well, I guess it was up a bit. I figured he was just starting to withdraw."

"But you didn't even get any lab work," said Carlos.

"Aw come on," said Carlson, nervously. "He was just a junkie who was also drunk."

"That's the second time you've used the word 'junkie'", said Carlos. "Do you mean to imply that his being 'a junkie' absolves you of your responsibility for the level of care you provide?

"No," said Carlson. "I didn't mean that. It's just that these people..."

"Before you go any further," said Carlos. "I'm going to tell you something. I had an older brother who was a heroin addict. He died of sepsis because he refused to come to the hospital where he had repeatedly been humiliated and insulted by physicians like you who seem to believe that your version of the Hippocratic Oath excludes drug addicts."

"Look, Carlos," said Carlson, now alarmed. "I'm sorry. I didn't know. I didn't mean to imply..."

"You listen to me," said Carlos sternly. "The man you sent out of this hospital after ignoring the fact that he was febrile, after doing a half-assed exam, after having failed to discharge your responsibility as a physician, that same man is now in the ICU on a respirator with wound botulism which might have been detected when you saw him if you had done your job.

"I have written these facts down on this incident report which you are required to acknowledge by your signature. If you have any comments or any extenuating circumstances to cite, you can either do so orally or write them on the back of this report."

Badly shaken, Carlson signed the report without comment.

"You have the knowledge and the skill to be a good physician," said Carlos. "But you're arrogant. You lack humility and compassion. I know you've been accepted for a residency in plastic surgery. I'm going to keep this report here in my desk. But you listen to me. If I hear of any more incidents in which your attitude prevents you from discharging your responsibility to your patients, this will be presented to the chairman of the department of surgery. Do I make myself clear?"

"Yes," said Carlson quietly.

"That's all. You can go."

Carlos had calmed down and was walking through the lobby outside the emergency room when he recognized a man sitting in one of the chairs with his head down.

"Chris. Chris Childs," said Carlos. "Is that you?"

Chris looked up. His eyes were swollen and red and his face was a mask of torment. "Carlos," he croaked, "I forgot you worked here."

"What's going on?" asked Carlos. "Somebody in your family here?"

"Not exactly," said Chris, fighting to compose himself.

"Come with me," said Carlos. He put his arm around Chris's shoulder and led him to the doctor's lounge which was empty.

"Tell me about it. Can I help? Who is it?" asked Carlos.

Chris was breathing deeply, trying to get the words out. "Someone I care about a great deal. They brought her in her about an hour ago. I can't find out what's happening and I'm going nuts with worry."

"What's her name?" asked Carlos.

"Erin. Erin Leahy."

"O.K. Here, pour yourself some coffee. I'll check it out and be right back."

Carlos went to the admitting clerk and asked for the record. He scanned it quickly. "Heroin overdose" was the admitting diagnosis. "Where is she?" he asked.

"Number three," said the clerk.

He went to the third station and looked at the unconscious girl. The chart indicated that her vital signs were now stable. She had received two doses of Narcan, an opiate antagonist.

Carlos sighed and shook his head sadly. He looked at the reddened fresh tracks on her arms. He put down the chart and walked back to the doctor's lounge. Chris was standing by the coffee machine when he walked in. He looked up anxiously.

"She's doing fine," said Carlos. "Everything's under control. She's going to be all right."

Chris grabbed him in a tearful embrace, sobbing his relief.

'Come on," said Carlos. "Sit down. I didn't know you were involved with anyone. Is this new?"

"Yeah," said Chris, drying his eyes. "Very new."

"She means a lot to you doesn't she?"

"She's my life, Carlos. I adore her."

"She's very beautiful," said Carlos, then he asked softly, "Did you know that she was an addict?"

Unable to speak, Chris just shook his head.

"You just found out tonight?" asked Carlos.

Chris nodded affirmatively.

"God, that's tough," said Carlos. "I'm really sorry for both of you. Tell you what, I'll take her off the teaching service. I'll put her on my private service. I do have a few privileges around here."

"I'd really appreciate that," said Chris. "It would mean a lot to me."

"To me, too," said Carlos. The two embraced. "You better go home and get some rest. There's nothing you can do here tonight. But you shouldn't drive all the way to Palo Alto."

"We were staying up here. I'll just get a cab," said Chris.

"Do you want to see her. She's still unconscious," said Carlos.

"Yeah, I'd like to," said Chris. "Just for a minute."

They walked into the treatment area and Carlos pulled back the drapes. Chris stood there looking at her. She was lying on the gurney, looking so peaceful, so beautiful.

With tears running down his cheeks he bolted from the room and out of the hospital into the chilly night air. His mind was trying to sort out directions in a future that had seemed so bright, so certain. But now, what loomed ahead was the ominous terror of undefined tragedy.

Chapter Twelve

Chris didn't awake to music the next day. After a fitful sleep he arose with a vague feeling of nausea. He had no appetite. He went over the events of the previous night with a sense of disbelief. How long had this been going on? How could he have not known?

He showered and drove back to the hospital. He inquired at the desk and was given Erin's room number. He went by the floral stand and bought a bouquet of flowers and took the elevator to the floor where her room was located. With a mixture of deep concern and dread he walked into her room. Erin was lying in bed with her face turned to the wall away from him.

"Good morning, Darling," he said. "I brought you some flowers."

She was silent.

"Has Carlos been in to see you?" he asked, walking around the bed.

She looked strangely pale. The vivacious colors had gone out of her skin. Her eyes looked dull. Tears streamed down her face, which was twisted in agony.

"I'm so ashamed," she whispered, barely audibly. "I just want to die."

He sat on the edge of the bed and put his arms around her. "Don't ever say that. Don't ever even think it. We have our whole lives together to look forward to."

"Oh, Chris," she sobbed. "That's over. Look at me. I disgust myself. I know I must disgust you. I'd rather have died than to ever have you see me this way. I'm so sorry."

He continued to hold her close, kissing her hair and her forehead. "Erin, my darling, you owe me no apologies. I don't know how this happened, but I know that I love you and I know we can fight this together. I don't know much about addiction but I know that love and support is important and you have that. My life is so much richer with you in it. I'll never let you go. Never. This is a problem that we'll face together."

"You mean you'll stay with me?" she asked.

"Of course I will. What did you think?" he said softly. "There's nothing in the world that could tear me away from you."

"Oh Chris, the thing that terrified me the most was that I was sure I'd lose you. I couldn't face that."

"Maybe I wasn't clear when I told you before all this happened. I'm in love with you. Nothing can change that. I'm completely committed to you---to us."

"Hold me," she urged. "Please hold me. It's been so terrible having this awful secret and not being able to tell you. It's been tearing me apart. I desperately needed your help, and your strength, but I was so ashamed. I was convinced you'd leave me if you found out."

"O.K. So now you know that you don't have to worry about that. You must never keep anything from me and I promise I'll do likewise."

"All right," she said. "There's another part to this that we need to discuss. It also terrifies me, but for a different reason."

"Is this a good time?" he asked. "Are you sure you want to do it now? Can't it wait."

"No," she said. "I don't want to live with this secret for another minute. Before I tell you, I want your promise not to do anything rash. If you do, it could take you away from me now at a time when I need you most. You must promise me. You must."

"All right," he said soberly. "I promise, but I don't understand."

He sat on the bed. She clasped his hands with all her strength. Looking steadily into his eyes, she told him the story of Cal's coming to her apartment and all that had followed. She saw his eyes widen and felt his anger surging as she related the events.

"That dirty son-of-a-bitch. That evil mother-fucker," Chris shouted. His face was distorted with hatred and fury. He tried to pull his hands away from hers but she held on.

"Chris, stop," she insisted. "You promised. I won't let you do anything to him. If you do, it'll destroy us both. You'll go to

90

prison and your life will be destroyed. Our only hope is to put it behind us."

He closed his eyes. His jaws were clenched in fury as the enormity of the evil tore at him. "To get at me, he did this to you, even though I know he cares for you. What kind of a monster is he?"

A puzzled look crossed her face. "Do you really think so? I hadn't put it together that way. I thought he was just using poor judgment, but you're right. I can see that now. He was waiting for an opportunity to hurt us. I was so immersed in my own shame that I missed it. You're right. He is a monster."

"That filthy son-of-a-bitch," Chris repeated through clenched teeth. "I want to kill him, to destroy him. I know. You're right. I won't do anything, but it will take everything I have not to."

There was a knock on the door and Carlos walked in.

"Good morning," he said. "I must say, you both look considerably better than you did last night." They looked at each other, and squeezed hands in a mutual signal of confidence. Chris took a deep breath and tried to calm himself.

"I feel much better, thanks to you and to Chris," said Erin, holding Chris' hand and looking up at him lovingly.

"We really appreciate what you've done," said Chris.

"It's what I do," said Carlos. "When I can do it and it benefits people I care about, it's a double pleasure. Chris, will you step out for a moment, please? I want to do a brief examination. Then we can talk about what we'll be doing next."

When he was called back in, Chris went to the bedside and took Erin's hand again. "She's very precious to me, Carlos. What's the next step? We're going to lick this thing together."

"That's what she told me," said Carlos. "Having that kind of support is enormously important. I was going to keep her in for another day to make certain that there aren't any infections or other problems lurking, that could surprise us later, but all the lab work is normal. So, you can get her out of here this morning. I'll continue to give you the methadone that I started last night. It'll prevent you from having any withdrawal symptoms and will be the way in which we will provide the chemical transition to get you off heroin. After you leave here, I'll want you to check in to the methadone clinic. They'll continue the process as an outpatient."

"Will she have to stay on methadone for a long time?" asked Chris.

"There are two methadone programs permitted by state law," said Carlos. "One is the long term program called maintenance. California law doesn't permit people to get on that program until they have been addicted for two years. The other is for short term treatment. It's called the detox program. They start you on a medium range dose and taper it over three weeks."

"Does that work?" asked Erin. "Can you be cured in three weeks?"

"We'll see," said Carlos. "I think we have a pretty good chance since you haven't been addicted very long."

"And it's all outpatient?" asked Chris.

"All outpatient," said Carlos. "You just show up every morning and get your dose. Pretty simple, huh? I'll give you a prescription for two days worth of methadone in case you have any problem hooking up with the program. You've already had your dose for today."

"That was those pills that they gave me?" said Erin.

"Right," said Carlos. "In the clinic you'll be getting it in liquid form, but it's the same stuff.'

"Great," said Chris. "If it works."

"If anything comes up, if you have any questions, my pager number's on this card. Don't hesitate to call. I'd rather deal with it sooner than later."

Chris embraced him. "It really means a lot to me to have her in your hands."

"Well, I'll return the compliment," said Carlos with a laugh. "I'm glad she's going to be in your arms."

"Thank you, Carlos," said Erin, as he bent over and kissed her forehead.

They filled the prescription at the hospital pharmacy and then headed south for Portola Valley to get some of his things. They had decided to move into the San Francisco apartment while she was attending the clinic.

The morning had been overcast, but now, toward mid-day, a bright spring sun was breaking through. They could see the ocean beyond the landfalls, still gray-green under the cloud cover that still hovered over the sea.

"I can't tell you how relieved I feel," said Chris, reaching over and taking her hand. I was afraid I was going to lose you. I was terrified."

"I'm sorry I put you through that," she said, kissing his hand. "I guess it had to come out one way or another. You can't imagine how comforting it is to feel reunited with you. I felt that there was a growing chasm between us and I didn't know how to bridge it because I was terrified that I'd drive you away."

"What a terrible dilemma. You were really caught, in more ways than one," said Chris. "Just remember, Erin. This is our problem. It wouldn't have happened to you if it hadn't been for me. I feel that responsibility very deeply."

"I know you do," she said. "I don't completely agree with you about that. I could have said no, but I didn't and I continued to use the stuff. It's my responsibility. But the important thing is that we're going to go through this together. I really feel so much stronger now with you beside me."

"How do you feel physically?" he asked.

"Just a bit queasy. Not bad at all," she said.

When they reached his place in Portola Valley, she took a nap while he did some work and made some phone calls. When he was finished he took out a mandolin and began quietly playing it. The music gushed out, calming and soothing him, putting him in touch the serenity that had been eclipsed by the events of the past few hours, which seemed like days.

He played for a long time, losing track of time. When he looked up, Erin was sitting quietly, watching and listening. "How many instruments can you play?" she asked.

"String instruments are all pretty much the same," he said. "If you can play one you can play them all, or sort of."

"That was really lovely. What was it?" she asked.

"Nothing. I was just noodling around a bit," he said

"You're so amazing. Go on and play some more."

"O.K." he said. "I'll play a bit more and then I want to take a walk if you're up to it."

"I'm feeling fine now. The nap was really good for me."

Thirty minutes later they drove to the head of one of the many trails in the area. It started off in fields of deep grasses interrupted by patches of wildflowers. The pathway then descended through clumps of white oaks, live oaks and laurel. Quail skittered along the road and darted into the bushes along the side of the road. Erin and Chris walked hand-in-hand, not talking much, pausing occasionally to kiss. They crossed a small creek on a wooden bridge and sat at a nearby table from which they could see the creek and hear the gurgling of the water.

"Look," said Chris, pointing to three deer that scampered up a hill and out of sight. "They're so quick and graceful."

"This was really a good idea," she said. "There really is something cleansing about getting out into a beautiful place like this. The ugliness and the problems seem to belong to another world."

"The thing that blows me away about this region is that there are so many places in which you can enjoy virtually unspoiled wilderness," said Chris. "Everybody thinks of California as all freeways and shopping malls. God knows we have plenty of both, but there are so many opportunities to see nature as it was when the only people living here were the Indians. I've always loved coming to one of the parks and just losing myself."

"You're never lost," she said. "You always have your muse with you."

"I guess you're right. But I've got some great places to take you. When you get off the methadone we should go camping. There are some magnificent places close by. There are enough to last us a lifetime."

"How could I wish for more," she said, putting her arms around his waist and her head on his chest. When they walked back to the car, the light was fading and the pleasant warmth of the late afternoon had given way to a bracing coolness.

They spent a quiet evening, and then went to bed. Their lovemaking was tender and gentle, even solicitous as though they were simultaneously sharing the scent of a delicate flower. Beneath the lightness of the caresses and touches, however, were powerful feelings of relief, protection, joy and commitment.

Chapter Thirteen

Early the next morning, they gathered his guitar, computer, some clothes and other personal items and loaded them into the trunk of his car to move them into the San Francisco apartment. They made their way north, joining the morning commuter traffic.

He drove up to the entrance of the clinic and let her out of the car. "I'll be glad to wait here if you want me to."

"I'll be fine," she said. "I'll call you when I'm ready."

He drove away and she went into the clinic and presented herself to the receptionist, who found her name on a list and gave her several forms to fill out. When she was finished, there were more questions to be answered, identification to be presented and financial details to be arranged.

When that part of the processing was completed, she was ushered into the medical area where she was interviewed by a taciturn physician. He asked her a series of questions about her general health, making notes as she answered. Then, "How long have you been using heroin?"

The question was simple and direct, but its effect on her was profound. It established her as something she could never have believed possible--an IV drug abuser, a heroin addict. The question and her answer gave her situation official status. She was now a number in a bureaucratic box. Her identity became a matter for statisticians and epidemiologists who looked for the answers to "the addiction problem" in graphs, medians, quartiles and standard deviations. She was now a part of the demographics of the most sordid problem in the world.

"Two months," she answered softly, her voice heavy with shame.

"How much are you using each day?" he asked.

She was uncertain and hesitant.

"We'll just say a quarter gram a day. What other drugs are you using?"

"Other drugs?" she asked, confused by the question.

"Cocaine, speed, crank, hallucinogens," he enumerated. "What other drugs are you doing?"

"Nothing. Nothing else," she said. The denial was momentarily comforting until she thought to herself, "Oh I don't use any of those drugs. Just heroin. Only heroin. Heroin is my only problem." She felt a wave of nausea.

The physician performed a cursory physical exam, concentrating on the marks in the skin of her left arm.

"You'll be in the Heroin Detox Program," he said without looking up from the form he was completing. "It's a state licensed program. You don't qualify for maintenance. You'll receive daily doses for twenty-one days. The amounts will gradually decrease so that at the end of three weeks you'll be down to zero. It's important that you not use any heroin or other drugs. Any questions?"

She was too bewildered to think of any; even the simple, obvious, "Does this work?"

She took the papers he gave her and followed his directions to the dispensary. On the way she passed a public phone and called Chris to tell him she was almost finished. She fell in line behind a dozen or so other people. She felt her knees buckle as she assimilated the reality that she was in line with heroin addicts---other heroin addicts like her.

Her nausea was stronger as she surveyed the other people in line. Some were disheveled, but most were well groomed. From the appearance of the people in line, the age, gender and behavior, it might have been a line at Safeway. They looked like normal people: people like her: heroin addicts.

When she reached the front of the line, the dispensary nurse took one of the forms, and examined the identification card she had been given.

"Name?" the nurse asked.

"Leahy. Erin Leahy," she said.

"O.K. give me your ID card, honey."

The nurse read the physician's order sheet and then dispensed a red fluid into a plastic cup. "O.K., Erin. This is your dose. Drink it, then drink the water, then show me your mouth so that I can see that you've swallowed it all. That's it. Open wide. O.K. Next."

The sweet, fruit-flavored fluid puckered her mouth, and she had a moment of difficulty swallowing it. She went through the exit door and burst into the sunlight which was now quite bright. She had to wait a minute while her eyes adapted to the light, then heard the honk and walked to Chris's car and got in. She sat down heavily, took a deep breath and closed her eyes.

"You O.K.?" he asked, taking her hand.

"I think so," she said. "Let's go."

He started the engine. "Pretty rough?" he asked.

"Not really," she said. "The process is benign, if a bit impersonal. It's just tough getting used to myself as a heroin addict and having other people take it so matter-of-factly."

"I don't want you to get used to that image. This'll all be over in three weeks."

They drove to Berkeley to collect some of her things to move to the apartment. She checked some messages on her answering machine. There was a call from her mother which brought tears to her eyes, realizing how far her parents now were from realizing this truth about her.

She gathered up some clothes, some books and other personal items. As she was going through the drawers, she came to the locked box she had carefully hidden among her underthings. She paused, started to reach for it, changed her mind, drew her hand back and closed the drawer.

During the next several days, Erin began to feel more normal than she had in many weeks. She was not experiencing any withdrawal symptoms and the craving for heroin had completely disappeared. She began to read productively and to think about preparing for her make-up exams.

Chris watched her carefully and was delighted to see her confidence grow. The color had completely returned to her skin. Her mood became light, even playful as the guarded hesitation receded.

Toward the end of the second week, Erin noticed that she was beginning to have difficulty sleeping and when she did sleep she was having disturbing dreams. She tried to dismiss the changes, hoping they would prove to be transient, but they persisted and became stronger.

"I'm scared, Chris," she said the next morning after experiencing a dream that was unmistakably about using heroin. "I'm afraid it's coming back."

"I'll call Carlos," he said.

He left a message on Carlos' pager and the call was promptly returned. "What's up?" asked Carlos. "How's she doing?"

"She was doing fine," said Chris. "But now that the dose is lower she's starting to get into some trouble."

"What kind of trouble?"

"She can't sleep," said Chris. "Weird dreams. A little nausea. Now she's getting scared."

"Damn it," said Carlos. "It sounds like she's coming down on the dose too quickly."

"Can't they slow it down?' asked Chris.

"No," said Carlos. "That's the crazy, irrational thing about these programs. They have to be finished in twenty-one days. That's the law in this state. The docs have no leeway. They can't use their own medical judgment. So the doses for these poor people are controlled by politicians and bureaucrats in Sacramento. It's idiotic. It's infuriating. It's just too fast."

"What can we do?" asked Chris.

"Tell her to ask them for some clonidine?" said Carlos.

"What's that?" asked Chris.

"It's a drug that blocks some of the symptoms. It's not an opiate. It works on the autonomic nervous system."

"Is it habit forming?" asked Chris.

"No. It's very safe. If they won't give it to her, call me back and I'll give her a prescription. Chris, this isn't going to be easy. I was hoping that she'd have an easier road because she's only been using for a couple of months. That's apparently not going to happen. She and you're going to have to gut this out. It might be worthwhile to get her into Narcotics Anonymous. They can provide a lot of support, even if you don't fully accept their approach."

"I'll talk it over with her," said Chris. "How do you spell clonidine?"

Carlos spelled it for him. Then he said, "Hang onto her. We've got to get her through this together."

"You bet I will," said Chris. "Thanks Carlos."

When he hung up, they discussed the situation. 'Carlos says that it could be rough but this other medicine can make it easier. I'll do anything I can to try and help you. He even mentioned considering Narcotics Anonymous. He says they can be very helpful."

"Someone I knew had a bad experience with AA. It may not be rational, but I'd rather do this with you. If you'll help me I think I can do it."

He went to her and embraced her. "I believe we can do it. I wish I could take some of the agony and that you didn't have to experience it all."

"I know that feeling helpless is going to cause you plenty of agony. So don't be greedy," she said, poking him. "You've got your agony and I've got mine. Together we're a great mess. Don't you have to go to work today?"

"I told them I was going to be working at home for the next few days," he said. "They can reach me if they need me. How are you feeling now?"

"I'm getting some mild cramps and nausea," she said. "Nothing I can't deal with."

"O.K." he said. "Let's go for a walk."

"Good idea," she said. "I'd like that."

The air was crisp but the sun was warm on their faces. They walked down to 24th street and strolled through the area looking in the small shops. They stopped at a market and bought some sandwiches and sodas to take out. They walked to Dolores street and turned left, walking toward Market street. At eighteenth street they sat on the lawn in the park and ate the sandwiches.

Then they walked down Dolores to the Mission. There were only a few visitors present. They walked through the old church marveling at the workmanship done by the Indians. They went out into a small, spare courtyard and sat in the sun. Adjacent was the graveyard, where many San Francisco pioneers had been buried.

"Look," she said. "Here are some Irish people."

"Do you find places like this morbid?" he asked, a bit concerned.

"Oh no," she said. "I love cemeteries. I love reading the headstones, figuring out how old they were when they died, how long they lived, and what life must have been like for them. I find it fascinating.

"One of my dreams is to go to Ireland and find where my mother was from. I'd love to go to the church where the family went and do the same thing that we're doing here. I have such a great imagination. I can just transform myself into one of my ancestors. I think that's why I love literature so much. It takes me so many places."

"That's great," said Chris. "I've always loved cemeteries too, but I was afraid that I was a bit perverted. At least now I know we have the same perversion. How about this. When we go to Ireland, we'll go find your family and then we'll go to Yeats' tower. What's it called? Toor Ballylee. We can stand at the battlements and I can sing you my songs. How's that for romantic?"

"Perfect," she exclaimed. "I can pretend to be Lady Gregory. See how well it fits. You the troubadour and me, the romantic heroine. This is going to be monumentally, extravagantly delicious to live out."

She went to him and kissed him. "I do believe in the magic of the future we're going to share. We will do it, together, won't we?"

"Don't you ever doubt it--not even for a second," he said, looking at her steadily. "We will do this."

Erin received the clonidine from the clinic and it began to alleviate some of her symptoms. She was less anxious and she was able to sleep better for several days. But as the methadone dose was lowered, the symptoms began to return. She reported this to the clinic and the clonidine dose was raised to the maximum. Again there was a period of relief, but again it was transient. The symptoms came back even stronger.

The methadone was lowered even further and then it was stopped. She had received the allowable three weeks of treatment. The rest would depend on her strength and the effects of the clonidine.

She was miserable. She was shivering, chilled and tremulous,

100

but at the same time, sweating profusely. She spent much of the time doubled up with strong stomach cramps. Every bone in her body seemed to be the source of relentless pain. Her eyes and nose were watering profusely and she was having frequent vomiting and diarrhea.

"I'm scared," she said to Chris, who was holding her in his arms. "I'm getting sicker each day and I have a strong urge to use, just to stop this misery."

"Why don't we take a few days and go someplace," he suggested. "Maybe it would do you good to get your mind off this."

"I'm sorry," she said. "I'm not up to traveling. I just want this agony to be over. Oh, Chris. I had no idea it was going to be this horrible. And it keeps getting worse. I wish there was some way I could get some relief."

"I called Carlos this morning," said Chris. "He said that we have to keep in mind that the symptoms will go away as soon as the brain readjusts to being without heroin or methadone. We have to keep that in front of us. It will go away and every minute we're getting closer to that."

"I know. I know." she said. "I'm trying to keep that in mind. I'm going to go lie down."

"Do you want me to come with you?" he asked.

"No. I just want to try to quiet myself down a bit."

She lay down on the bed with her clothes on, but felt a chill so she pulled a blanket over her. She tried to relax, but was too anxious. Her body seemed unable to find any position of comfort. The pain in her back and legs had increased; a constant, deep ache. She was unable to keep her legs quiet. As soon as they were in one position, they jumped to another. Despite the chill, she began to sweat profusely.

There was no escape. There was no relief. Her entire body seemed to be committed to contributing to her misery. The onslaught was relentless and exhausting. She crawled to the bathroom and vomited repeatedly until she collapsed on the cold tile floor in tears.

In the dark center of her torment was the terrifying realization that she could end the misery herself. All she had to do was to inject heroin into her body and all this would go away. That knowledge mocked her misery and made it worse.

She called the methadone clinic. "My name is Erin Leahy. I was just on a detox program. I'm really having trouble. Terrible withdrawal symptoms."

"Well, you should ask for some medicine to help you," came the answer.

"I have the clonidine, but it's not working. I need to get back onto the program. I think I need to be on the long term program. Please help me."

"I'm sorry, Erin. You're not eligible for the long term program. You have to be addicted for two years before you can get on the maintenance program."

"Two years," she moaned. "My god, I'll be dead before that. Well then let me back on the detox program. Please."

"I'm sorry, Erin. You have to wait ten days before you can get back on."

"Oh my god. What am I going to do? Are there other programs in the area. Please."

"All the programs are hooked up by computer so if you try to get on another program before you're eligible, they would notify us. I'm sorry. You're just going to have to be strong."

She was becoming more desperate when she hung up. Things were closing in on her and she was becoming more agitated and anxious. She put in a call to Carlos and waited for his return call.

When he called, she said, "You've got to help me. Can't you please give me some more methadone. You prescribed it for me before. Why can't you do it now?"

"I'm sorry, Erin. I would if could, but its illegal. You can only get methadone from licensed programs. I can prescribe methadone for pain, but not for addiction. That's the law."

"But can't you admit me to the hospital and give me methadone again." she sobbed. "I'm really trying, but I just don't think I'm going to be able to make it."

"I can't admit you and treat you with methadone for addiction. I could do the last time because you had ODd. but I can't just do it for treatment of addiction because we're not a licensed in-patient addiction facility. I know that doesn't sound like a very good reason to you at this time, but it is the reality. I'm very sorry. Please, try to get through this with the clonidine and don't use again."

She hung up the phone and moved woodenly back to her bed.

She fell in, with a deep, aching foreboding. She felt helpless, frustrated that all her good intentions seemed to be in vain. She was facing a force that was more evil, more powerful than she could have ever imagined. Her will to resist had been badly eroded by the fact that those who wanted to help her, could not, and if they couldn't, no one could. Without effective help, she felt doomed.

By taking several clonidine pills, she was able to finally fall into an exhausted sleep for a few hours. But in the morning, she was again under terrible assault and her resolve was weakening further. Her misery made her desperate for relief.

"I'm going out to get some groceries and some other stuff I need," said Chris. "I shouldn't be gone long. Is there anything I can get you now, or while I'm out?"

"Yeah," she said wearily. "A new body and a new brain. Come here and hold me before you go."

He embraced her and she clung strongly to him for a long moment and then said. "Thanks. I needed that more than you can know."

He kissed her and left.

She knew she couldn't hold out any longer. She took the remaining clonidine pills and collapsed on the bed to wait for them to take effect. When she began to feel better, she quickly showered, dressed and gathered her things. She then took a pen and wrote:

"Dearest Chris

I thought I could do it, but I can't. I'm not strong enough, even with your love which I treasure and trust. I have to fight this through myself. Don't look for me. Know that the thing I want most in the world is to be with you and that my love for you provides the one chance I have to beat back this monster. I won't come back until I'm well and we can resume our lives together.

I adore you.   Erin."

She took a cab to the BART station and caught the next train going to the East Bay. When she reached the Berkeley terminal she took another cab to her apartment.

She was feeling sick again when she entered. She quickly went to the drawer and took out the locked box. She prepared the solution and injected it into the plump vein in her left arm. She closed her eyes and fell back across the bed as the warm comfortable feeling of relief began to spread through her tortured body. She drifted off into a warm, welcoming high that transported her to a place where there were no cares, or concerns and no withdrawal symptoms, only pleasant, drowsy oblivion.

The sound of the ringing telephone brought her out of her reverie. She heard Chris's frantic voice speaking into the answering machine, pleading with her to call him and not to do anything precipitous.

She got up quickly, tried to shake herself out of torpor, and began to gather most of her remaining clothes and personal effects. She loaded them, including the locked box into the trunk of her car and locked up her apartment.

She drove to her bank, withdrew the balance of her money and closed the account. She was feeling hungry, but decided not to take the time to eat yet. She headed the car toward the freeway, taking the interchange to Interstate 580 which intersected with Interstate Five, the main north/south route in the state.

Her time in northern California had ended, at least for now. She would head south, down to the other part of the state. There, she would try to find her way back; to this place, to Chris, to the rest of her life. She was traveling downward into an unknown from which she could only hope to return.

Chapter Fourteen

Erin drove south on I-Five through the central valley. She had never felt so isolated. The green, exuberant fertility of the vast fields made her feel even more barren and devoid of life.

Her life had always seemed to be as well directed as the freeway she was traveling, heading directly for success, happiness and fulfillment. Now, there was no direction, no hope, no confidence, no optimism, just the overpowering weight of futility and failure bearing down on her shoulders and chest. Dread and the nausea that seemed always to be with her now, were her companions as she drove south.

She had come so close to having her dreams fulfilled. And then, cruelly, at the moment when she met her Prince Charming and everything was within her grasp, she was cast into this hell and he was lost to her. She wanted to believe she could find her way out of the terrible labyrinth and back to Chris, but the uncertainty was vast and frightening. She knew she would have to fight through the maze of compulsive heroin use one tormenting day at a time.

The nausea grew stronger and she realized she had begun to sweat. As she was looking for the next exit sign that promised a motel, she felt a chill and the nausea became stronger.

She found a motel, a solitary link in a national chain, and checked in. She went to the room and immediately fixed. Then she fell into a long unconscious interlude. When she awoke she showered and then ate at the diner which was attached to the motel.

After dinner she returned to the room. She looked at the four bleak walls, made more dreary by the insipid prints that had been placed there as a part of the "decor." She turned on the TV and scanned through the channels with the remote control. There was nothing that even vaguely appealed to her.

Her mind was leaden; heavy and gray, unable to attach itself to anything. She couldn't even force it to engage in the plot of one of the simple stories the screen presented that might provide a brief interlude of escape. She was left with herself, unprotected and plodding through the numbing misery of her abject loneliness.

Her heart was aching and she could barely swallow. Tears formed in her eyes and ran down her cheeks until she was overcome by her misery and self-pity. She succumbed to the weight of it all and slumped on the bed, her body racked by convulsive sobs.

The next morning she headed out early, driving steadily down the monotony of I-Five, trying to keep her mind occupied. She tried listening to music but found that whatever she heard bought Chris painfully to mind. So she listened to talk shows and NPR.

Below Saugas she began to see the signs that indicated that she was nearing the turn-off for Simi Valley, which brought up another source of pain and recriminations. "I'll do this, Mom and Dad. I'll break this habit. I'll do it for you two, also," she said out loud peering at the road through the tears that had formed in her eyes.

She drove through Los Angeles and all the way south to San Diego, where she turned east on I-Eight. Leaving the green foliage of the coast, she headed doggedly into the desert. Stopping only for gas, she made it into El Centro, a city in the middle of the California desert, only a few miles north of the Mexican border. The landscape was bleak and uninviting.

"This is about as far from everywhere as I can imagine," she said, stepping into the warm, dry air at the motel parking lot. "This is where I'll figure out how to beat this thing," she told herself as she walked to the office. She checked in and immediately fixed and fell into a drugged sleep.

The next morning she sorted through her clothes. "I need some blouses with long sleeves," she said to herself, noting the bruises that were appearing on her arms.

After she bought some clothes, and changed, she bought a paper and looked through the want ads. She looked at secretarial positions, in which she had done summer work and felt well qualified, but decided that the constant pressure and scrutiny of an office job might be too intense for comfort. She had also spent some time as a waitress, so she decided to answer those ads.

She was hired at the third place she tried. It was a truck stop that had a diner and a bar.

"You look too high class for this place," said Roy, the manager, a portly man in his fifties with a shining receding forehead. "But if this is what you want, we'll give you a try. Just pick out three uniforms from the shelf in the back. There should be some to fit you. We'll launder them for you but you're responsible for your blouses. We're short on evenings now so we'll break you in there. You'll have to be willing to rotate shifts. That a problem for you?"

"No problem at all," said Erin, greatly relieved to find a job.

"All right," he said. "Be here at three-thirty."

She went back to the motel and did an inventory of her other things, including the contents of the locked box. In her mind, she was still committed to breaking her habit and getting back to Chris, but the agony of her failure in San Francisco had convinced her that she couldn't do it alone. She would have to figure out how to do that, but in the mean time, she knew she would have to continue to use.

She still had some packets of heroin, and some syringes and needles. She calculated that she had enough for a couple of weeks, if she were careful, but she would have to make a local connection before she ran out. That prospect terrified and mystified her.

In the next few days, Erin rented a detached room behind a larger home and settled into her new routine. Her mind floated back to northern California and Chris whenever she wasn't occupied but she held herself together emotionally.

A constant wind blew through the town. Hot and dry, it desiccated everything, extracting the moisture from her skin and leaving her with the feeling of being dehydrated. There was no moisture in the soil to hold the surface particles together, and so they contributed a dusty, brown residue to the swirling air.

The sun rose early and encountered no obstructing cloud cover to retard the baking impact of its rays. Its bright, yellow glare overwhelmed all other colors, washing them out and reducing them to insignificance.

The work in the diner was straightforward. Truckers flirted with her, but she was experienced enough to handle the advances firmly without insult to the customer.

During the second week, Myra, the other waitress on her shift came over to her during a slow period. "Let's go have a drink when we get through.

Erin was a bit reluctant, but decided to accept the invitation because of her loneliness and some mild curiosity.

When they ended their shift, Myra said," We can both drive. Just follow me. I know a quiet place."

They both pulled into the parking lot outside a small bar. The temperature had cooled, but it was still warm and dry. Inside, the air conditioner was still running. Soft music was coming from a sound system.

"They don't have a juke box," said Myra. "This way they can control the sound level. They don't get as many dancers but they do get the quiet drinkers." She was in her late thirties or early forties. She was still pretty, with big brown eyes and a quick, easy smile. The regularity, symmetry and flawless whiteness of her teeth revealed that they weren't hers. Her make-up softened the wrinkles that attested to the hard life and many miles she had traveled. Myra ordered bourbon. Erin asked for white wine.

"So where you from?" asked Myra.

"Up north," said Erin. "Bay Area."

"I've been through there a few times," said Myra. "It's O.K. but it doesn't suit me. You look like a college type."

"I've been there," said Erin. "It was time to get away for a while."

"I've been watching you. You seem to be pretty comfortable doin' this kind of work."

"I've done this sort of thing before," said Erin. "It's always about the same. Where're you from?"

"L.A.," said Myra. "Actually Long Beach."

"Have you been here long?"

"A little over a year," said Myra. "I had to get away from a bad thing I had going with a sailor. I figure sailors don't like the desert. What about you? Is there a guy involved?"

"Isn't there always?" said Erin.

"You got that right," said Myra. "Look, I don't want to pry, but I noticed you look a bit strung out toward the end of the shift."

"What do you mean?" asked Erin, immediately on alert.

"Well, I notice you wear long sleeves," said Myra. " Like me. That's kind of unusual in the desert."

Erin said nothing. She just continued to look down at the table.

"I don't want to bum you out," said Myra. "I just thought you might need a local connection. No stash is big enough forever."

"I don't want any trouble," said Erin.

"Don't worry. This guy's all right. I've been dealing with him for six months. He's got a good steady source from Mexicali. He knows what he's doing and he stays away from trouble."

"I was hoping I wasn't so obvious," said Erin.

""Don't worry about that," said Myra. "Nobody that's straight would have noticed. You've just got to make sure you use enough to get you all the way through the shift."

"I was trying to stretch what I have," said Erin. "I didn't know how I was going to find a connection here."

"You haven't been using long, have you?"

"Just a few months," said Erin.

"O.K. Don't you worry. I've got plenty for now," said Myra. "I'll pull you through and, if you want, I'll put you in touch with this guy."

"Thanks, Myra," said Erin. "I really appreciate this. I don't know anybody else. I didn't know what I was going to do."

"Don't mention it," said Myra. "I've got some stuff in my car that I can give you tonight. You better get going. You look like you're getting a bit sick."

"I'll be O.K.," said Erin. "By the way, is there a methadone program here?"

"Naw," said Myra. "You don't want to mess with that stuff. The short detox program doesn't work for shit. And the long program, maintenance, is just a way of getting you hooked on that stuff for ever. I wouldn't go near it."

Days turned into weeks, proceeding in numbing similarity. The arid heat of the desert surrounded her, extracting the fluid vitality from her body at the same time the heroin was desiccating her mind and soul. There was no pleasure to be found in the injections, just a numbing sedation that robbed her of any animation or imagination. Everything in her existence became parched and dry. Even the pain of her losses faded into a dry past, the memories of which lost their color and texture and became tedious and uninteresting, like the landscape.

In an ironic way, the flat, dull, numbness of her psyche produced by the heroin protected her from the depression that would certainly have seized her had she been forced to endure the three dimensional reality of being separated from everything she valued.

She was wandering through a wasteland of infinite size, in which color, texture and rhythm were absent, replaced by the bland, endless repetition of actions and events that were without tension or passion and were devoid of any capacity to bestow rewards by their occurrence. Monochromatic and monotonous, the time passed, divided into meaningless segments by the need for regular injections of heroin.

Chapter Fifteen

When Chris returned to the apartment and found her gone, the hair on the back of his neck bristled and a wave of panic spread through his body. He knew she was suffering but it had never occurred to him that she would bolt.

He knew that calling her friends in Berkeley would be futile. They would be the last people she would turn to. She wouldn't want the story of her addiction spread around campus. She wouldn't go to her parents. She was too ashamed to be able to tell them.

The dark fear that began to seize him was that she would really disappear. She was bright and resourceful and she had some money. She could go any number of places that he couldn't even imagine.

When he called her apartment and she didn't answer his fears increased. Then he found her letter, which confirmed what he had dreaded. She was gone and was unlikely to resurface until she was ready, or some disaster befell her.

The protective feelings she always evoked in him were frustrated to the point of torment. He should never have left her, he told himself. His highest priority should have been to stay with her.

But what could he have done? Maybe there were other treatment programs he could have found. Maybe he should have explored the possibility of having her admitted to one of the specialized hospitals that advertise on TV. He reproached himself for not having exhausted all the possibilities.

He went to their bed and lay face down, drinking in the last remaining remnants of her scent before they, like she, faded into his memory. He remained silently there, unable to think of anything but her face, and form, and the myriad aspects that comprised the reality of her. He was not experiencing the pleasure of the memories, rather the physical torment of his loss.

Part of him felt numb and unreal, hoping to wake up from the nightmare of all that happened. Another part was experiencing the churning in his gut and the ache in his chest that were the bitter results of her absence. His mind went only to her, to their joy and the horror of her loss. There was no room for music in his brain or his soul.

Feeling more lonely than he ever had in his life, he slowly cleaned up the apartment, packed his things and loaded them into his car. He threw out the flowers that she had brought home, locked the door and drove back down the peninsula to Portola Valley.

He no longer awoke to music playing in his brain. His sleep was troubled, intermittent and not refreshing. Erin dominated his dreams which were unpleasant, sometimes terrifying fragments of adventures in which he was trying to protect her from some shadowy menace. At other times it would be he who was under attack, fleeing, but unable to escape the vague, relentless pursuit. Seized with terror, he would be unable to scream or even to raise his hands to ward off the shattering, destructive blow that descended but never arrived before he awoke, agitated and perspiration-soaked.

He would pick up his guitar, or sit at the piano, trying to escape from his pain by immersing himself in the soothing, protective cloak of his music. But his efforts were unsatisfying and provided no comfort. The most significant, central, consistent force in his life, his music, had been muted. It held no joy. It provided neither relief nor escape. Ultimately, in pain and frustration, he stopped trying.

At the lab he went through his tasks in a perfunctory manner. His mind was distracted. He had always been able to focus intently and that focus made it possible for him to analyze complex problem quickly and accurately. Now, relatively simple problems were elusive and frustrating. He couldn't concentrate his mental powers long enough to make headway.

After a week, he went to his mentor. "Jack, I need to talk to you. I have a personal problem that's really messing with my head. I just can't concentrate well enough to get any good work done. It's frustrating the hell out of me."

"It's been noticed that you don't seem to be your usual carefree self," said Jack. "Anything you want to tell me about?"

Chris sighed deeply and his head dropped. He slowly raised it. "I don't think I can right now. I feel a lot of conflicting emotions inside me that I can't sort out. Believe me, you're one of the people I really want to confide in, but right now, I just can't. I feel honor bound to secrecy. Maybe that's stupid, but until I can resolve it I can't say anything more."

"I won't push it," said Jack. "I don't want to pry. You know how I feel about you. You do what you have to do to take care of yourself. Do you want to take some time off?"

"No," said Chris. "I don't think that would be good for me. I need to stay in contact with things that're important to me. I don't want to become reclusive. I just want you to know I'm not being very effective."

"You're more effective at half speed than most others are at full," said Jack. "I'm glad you told me. Have you thought about seeing someone?"

"You mean a shrink?" asked Chris, surprised.

"I mean a counselor. Someone you could talk to without feeling you were betraying a trust."

"No, I hadn't," said Chris.

"Well, think about it," said Jack. "Think about it seriously."

"O.K. I will," said Chris.

"I'm going to keep my eyes on you, but I won't say anything. Maybe we should get together for lunch, or dinner, or whatever, from time to time. I won't crowd you. You know where I am."

They both stood. Chris held out his hand. "Thanks," he said. Jack took his hand and pulled him in for a strong embrace.

"Take care of yourself," said Jack as Chris left and walked back to his cube.

That evening, Chris was fixing himself some dinner when the phone rang. It was Rick.

"Do you have the TV on?" he asked.

"No."

"Turn it on to channel four. Quick. I'll wait," said Rick.

Chris went to the set, turned it on and selected channel four.

"Police are investigating all possibilities but the shooting appears to be a gangland style execution," said the reporter. "The question of illicit drugs is a prominent possibility although the police refuse to comment further. Now on to sports."

"What's the deal?" asked Chris. "Who was killed? I didn't hear that part."

"It was Cal Martin," said Rick.

"Jesus," said Chris. He paused for a moment and then said, "Look, I've got to talk to you. Can you come over?"

"Sure," said Rick. "What's this all about? Do you know something about him that I don't?"

"Just get your ass over here," said Chris. "I need to talk to you."

"You've got it," said Rick. "I'll leave right now."

Thirty minutes later, Rick arrived. "So what's up?" he asked as Chris showed him in.

"Let's sit," said Chris. "You want a beer?"

"You gonna have one?"

"I think I need something stiffer," said Chris. "I'm gonna have a scotch."

"You're the one who knows," said Rick. "If you're gonna need scotch, I'm gonna need scotch."

Chris made the drinks and the two sat down in the living room.

"Now what's this all about?" asked Rick. "What was going on with Martin?"

"It's Erin," said Chris, struggling with the words.

"What do you mean, 'it's Erin'? She chose you and right now that looks like a damned good choice."

"God, this is hard to say," said Chris. "Even to you. I'm really struggling here." He took a drink of scotch, took a deep breath and began. "You predicted it. That miserable son-of-a-bitch. In order to get back at me, he got her hooked on heroin."

Rick's mouth fell open. "Oh, no. No! No one, not even that prick could do something that low," said Rick angrily. "That asshole. Wait a minute. You didn't off him, did you? I wouldn't blame you if you did."

"No. But I'll tell you, I would have very cheerfully strangled that cocksucker. Erin convinced me not to because it would mean that I'd spend the rest of my life in the slammer. So I just sat on it.

114

It wasn't easy, but she was right."

"I'll say," said Rick. "They'd be talking about you on TV now. Wow. I can't believe that mother-fucker did that. Man, he deserved to die. But where's Erin? What's going on? How did you find out?"

"She kept her addiction hidden because she was so ashamed. Then one night she screwed up on her dose and OD'd. I called 9ll and they took her to the hospital."

"Where?" asked Rick. "In Berkeley?"

"No," said Chris. "We were in the city. You know who took care of her?"

"No clue."

"Carlos. Jimmy's brother,"

"Really," said Rick. "Was he good?"

"He was great," said Chris. "He helped me get her into a methadone program."

"So she's O.K?" asked Rick.

Chris was silent. He couldn't speak. His throat was constricted and his chest was aching. Tears began to run down his cheeks. He sat there silently, slowly shaking his head.

Rick was stunned. He went to his friend's side and put his arm around his shoulder. "Take your time," he said.

Finally, Chris was able to blurt out, "She's gone." He began sobbing.

"Let me get you some water," said Rick. "Here. Use this," he said handing him a napkin.

Rick brought a glass of water. Chris slowly drank it and gradually was able to compose himself.

"What do you mean, 'she's gone'"? asked Rick. "Where has she gone?"

"She tried, Rick," said Chris. "Jesus, she tried so hard. I've never seen anybody go through something that miserable. I had no idea how hard it was to kick. God, I feel so awful. It's all my fault."

"Now wait," said Rick. "What do you mean by that?"

"If I hadn't come along and made my big play for her, she'd be fine now."

"Oh, sure." said Rick. "Just fine. Dating a sociopathic drug dealer that gets himself killed. She'd have been just great. Where is she?"

"She's gone," said Chris. "I don't know where she is. I don't even know how to start to find her. She wrote me a note that she doesn't want to be found until she figures out how to get herself off heroin."

"Wait a minute," said Rick. "I'm missing some stuff here. I don't understand what happened."

"I'm sorry. I'm not my usual self," said Chris. He related the story of the period after the hospitalization and the methadone experience.

"Man, that's tough," said Rick. "For both of you. Christ, that goddamned heroin really fucks up your whole life, doesn't it?"

"I had no idea how powerful it is," said Chris. "I mean, she's really a bright, strong, squared away, no-bullshit person, and she just couldn't handle it."

"What are you gonna do?" asked Rick.

"I don't know," said Chris. "I want to talk to her folks, but I don't feel I can since I don't know what she's told them, if anything. She must have contacted them to tell them that she was dropping out of school, but I don't know what reason she gave them."

"You really love her don't you?"

"Completely," said Chris. "After going through this with her, I admire her even more for the courage she showed. She wasn't whining or blaming anyone. She's really tough.

"We were so good for each other. Being with her was the most natural, invigorating, nourishing experience I've ever had, and I know that it was the same for her. And now, it's gone, for both of us. I know this must be tearing her up as much as it is me."

"Jesus, Chris, this is the saddest story I've ever heard. I mean it. I know it's not the Christian way, but I'm really glad that piece of shit Martin got his."

"I just hope the son-of-a-bitch suffered," said Chris. "You can't imagine the torture he's already caused her. And this thing is far from over."

"Well, I don't know what more to say," said Rick. "You know I'm here for you if there's anything I can do, but I sure don't have any bright ideas right now."

"Listen," said Chris. "It's really done me one hell of a lot of good just being able to talk to someone about this."

"You haven't told your folks?" said Rick.

"No," said Chris. "I don't think I can. They really fell in love with her, too. They could see how great we were together. I just don't think I can tell them."

"You're gonna have to tell them something," said Rick. "Better the truth than any lame bullshit you could come up with."

"You're probably right," said Chris. "I'll have to think about it some more. Listen, there's another thing I have to lay on you."

"Shoot," said Rick.

"The band," said Chris. "I just can't do it right now. I can't even play around here."

"Man, I never thought I'd hear you say that," said Rick. "It's like hearing you say you can't breathe."

"I know," said Chris. "It's something that's always been so much a part of me that I took it for granted. It's gone, too. It'll probably get better when the shock of this experience wears off. But for now, I'm sorry. I just can't do it."

"Well, I've been putting them off, the way you were putting me off about it," said Rick. "I'll just continue. You've carried us for a lot of years. I know they'd want to cut you all the slack you need. I'm sorry I can't tell them but I understand. I'll think of something."

They embraced and Rick left. Chris felt better after the conversation but the center of his being was empty. There was a huge void where his soul had been. But the dark chamber that had been filled with hatred and the desire to wreak vengeance on Cul Martin was closed. He would spend no more energy on the slain man's evil act.

Chris was at his parents home for Sunday dinner. His mother was finishing up some work in the garden, so he took the opportunity to talk to his father.

"Dad, do you ever see any drug addicts in your practice?"

"A few," said his father. "I've had a couple in my practice and I've done a couple of consultations on addicts, about other problems they were having."

"What was your experience with them?" asked Chris.

"Well, these weren't the kinds of poor souls that they see at the large city and county hospitals. The ones I saw were mostly ex-addicts who had gotten their lives back together. I guess a couple of them were still using and still having problems."

"Did you know any that had been on methadone?" asked Chris.

"None that were on methadone when I saw them, but at least two who had been on it."

"So you think methadone works?" asked Chris.

"I've certainly seen examples of its success," said his father. "I knew two executives in large firms who were quietly taking methadone and functioning perfectly well. No one at their companies knew. Why all the interest?"

"I'll wait until Mom gets here." he said. "Oh, here she is." He rose and embraced her.

"Good to see you, darling," she said, patting his cheek. Then she looked around. "Where's Erin? I thought she'd be coming."

"Sit down, please. Both of you," he said. "I have something very painful to tell you."

"Oh, no," said his mother. "I hope it isn't about Erin. She's such a wonderful young woman."

Tears glistened in his eyes. "Yep. That's the way I feel about her."

He told them the story of her becoming addicted, her treatment and her disappearance. With tears running down her cheeks, his mother came to him and embraced him. "Oh, Chris. That's horrible. What an evil man. I'm glad he's not going to be able to harm any more innocent people. Poor Erin, and poor you. What you two must be going through."

"My god, son," said his father. "That's just awful. I sensed that something was troubling you, but this is tragic. What are you going to do? How can we help?"

"I don't know," said Chris. "I'm completely stymied and frustrated. I really don't know where to start, except that I'm going to learn more about addiction. I feel completely ignorant."

"I feel the same way," said his father. "As I told you, it really doesn't come into my practice very often so I tend not to learn about it. I know they're learning a great deal about neurobiology and neuropharmacology, but I haven't pursued any of it, until now. I suppose, like most of my colleagues, I just keep the whole issue at arm's length and let other people deal with it. It's such a terrible problem.

"It's strange. It's a part of medicine that seems to have become separated. So much of addiction medicine seems to take place under the aegis of the law and the criminal justice system. We 'main stream' physicians just really aren't involved so we remain less than fully informed and vaguely uncomfortable with the whole area.

"But, you know, there's a guy at the medical school that you should talk to. Bernstein. He's one of the real pioneers in methadone research. He's a wonderful guy. Very caring, very compassionate, and smart as hell. You should talk to him."

"Good idea," said Chris. "I've got to start someplace. I've got to find a way to get her back and get her cured. She's my life, and I feel so responsible for this terrible mess."

"I'm sure you do, honey, even though it isn't really your fault," said his mother. "Please keep trying and let us know if there's anything we can do to help."

Chapter Sixteen

Chris walked up the stairs and turned down a long hall, following the directions he had been given. He followed the ascending numbers on the doors until he came to the one he was seeking. "Department of Neuropharmacology--Office of the Chairman".

He entered a small ante-room. An elderly woman was at a table sorting reprints. She looked up when he spoke. "Hi. I'm Chris Childs."

'Welcome, Dr. Childs," she said. "Dr. Bernstein had to step out for a moment, but he'll be right back. He asked that you wait in his office. Can I get you some coffee?"

"Some water would be fine, thank you," he said as he followed her into the inner office. It was the typical office of an academician. Shelves were lined with books and journals, mostly medicine, science, and pharmacology of assorted editions. Surprisingly, there were also some legal books and some governmental codes. There were also some works of philosophy and history, a leather bound collection of Shakespeare and some other collections of assorted English and American poets.

On the walls were diplomas, licenses and certificates of membership in numerous distinguished scientific societies. There were proclamations and awards. Also prominently displayed were an assortment of photographs. Some color pictures of Yosemite and a number of black and white portraits of distinguished looking people, autographed to Gavril Bernstein.

Chris knew the story, almost a legend. Bernstein was the distinguished professor and head of the department, whose laboratory mastery had played a major role in the early developments in addiction biology and fundamental neurobiology and neuropharmacology. His early successes included his seminal works on the identification of the endogenous opiates, the chemicals that the body needs to control the internal pathways of reward, the endorphins.

These works alone, completed before he was thirty, had placed his name on the lists of those being considered for the highest awards in the biological sciences. They had also led to his coming here to head the department when the medical school moved from San Francisco to Palo Alto. He had joined that distinguished faculty along with other pioneers and Nobel Laureates, all eager to lead the bright, young students into the majestic world of molecular biology.

But it wasn't only the world of the abstract, the cloistered cerebral temple, in which Gavril Bernstein had made his contributions. More than an investigator, more than an inspiring teacher, he had spent much of his life and his indefatigable energy actively involved in treating heroin addicts. He had started out in New York, working with the pioneers of the methadone movement, who were taking their theories and their calculations out of the warm safety of academia into the cold, dark, putrid world of the inner city heroin addicts.

There they did their early, courageous work, shining the light of their curiosity and their compassion into the shadowy world of the desperate, frightened, hopeless wretches whose lives had been destroyed by their addiction. At the same time they had had to battle with the federal drug bureaucracy which was horrified at the thought of putting an addictive material like methadone into the hands of addicts. But they had persevered and won.

Convinced by his experience that substitution therapy with methadone and other similar compounds was effective, he had been a pioneer in founding clinics for treating heroin addicts in California. He was still very active, carrying out experiments, writing, lecturing and consulting all over the world.

Chris heard the outer door open, and then an exchange between male and female voices. Then the door opened and the professor entered the office with energetic dignity. He was a tall, thin, almost gangling man with graying hair and beard. His brown eyes were quick, yet soft and kind. He looked like the conventional picture of a rabbi.

"I'm sorry I kept you waiting, Dr. Childs," he said, offering his right hand as he read the card in his left. "'Post-Doctoral Fellow in

Immunobiology.' One of Jack Current's boys. I think I've heard of you. Are you the musician? Oh, sure. I've met your father, John Childs. He's a fine physician. He took care of one of our faculty member's wives. Welcome. What can I do for you? Please, sit down."

"Thank you," said Chris. He sat down and was silent for a moment. "I don't know anything about heroin addiction. I know I could go to the library and the internet and get a lot of information, and I will, but I wanted to have a chance to talk to you and get your perspective first."

"Is this an academic interest?" asked the professor quietly.

Chris paused again. He was unable to lift his eyes to meet Bernstein's gaze. "No."

"Someone very important to you?" asked the professor.

"Very," said Chris.

"I won't pry, but it would help if I knew a few details," said Bernstein gently. "How long has the addiction been present?"

"Only a few months," he said. "Only a few months," he repeated as though he didn't believe that it could be true. He sat quietly.

Bernstein left his chair and came and put his hand on Chris's shoulder. "Heroin addiction is a terrible problem. But it can be licked, particularly if it's still early in the course."

"I feel that it's my fault, that it wouldn't have happened if it hadn't been for me. So, I feel that I have to do whatever I can to help her get out of this terrible mess."

"Whatever knowledge and experience I have is at your disposal," said Bernstein. "Do you feel up to telling me the story?"

"Yeah," said Chris. "I can, if you think it would help. I've told it to my parents and my best friend, so I can get through it."

"O.K.," said Bernstein. "Let me clear a couple of things."

He left the office and Chris composed himself.

Bernstein was gone only a few minutes. When he returned, he said, "We have plenty of time, now. Tell me what you think I should know."

Chris related the entire story to him. When he had finished Bernstein shook his head. "Hawthorne says that the definition of evil is 'the violation, in cold blood, of the sanctity of the human heart'. That man clearly qualified. He used her innocence to try to destroy her and hurt you. Monstrous. So you don't know where she is, but you presume that she's using heroin?"

"Unless she's been able to get herself into some kind of a treatment program," said Chris.

"Let's hope that's what's happened," said Bernstein. "The other part of what you told me that infuriates me is the fact that she wasn't able to get appropriate methadone treatment."

"You mean the twenty-one day detox?" asked Chris.

"Yes," said Bernstein. "It's idiotic and frustrating that this state has laws which make us ineffective in rendering what treatment we do have. Both California and the Federal Government require that persons have to fail two detox episodes before they can get long term treatment. Twenty-one days is too brief. It's rarely effective which means that the reputation of methadone treatment as a whole is damaged in the eyes of other addicts, the criminal justice sector and the public."

"Why is there such a law?"

"I really don't know," said Bernstein. "I suspect that it may have something to do with the influence of the criminal justice system which has never understood nor accepted methadone treatment. But the effect is that people who need long term treatment have to jump through these idiotic hoops and continue using heroin. Well, enough of that, for now. As you can see, I won't hesitate to expose you to my own beliefs on this subject. I know that you're a good enough scientist to see through my distortions. Did you ever study neurobiology or neurphysiology?"

"No," said Chris. "I've stayed pretty much with immunology."

"That's fine," said Bernstein. "I'll be talking a lot about receptors and ligands which are analogous to your antigens and antibodies. Let's see. Where to begin? The nervous system is so overwhelmingly complex that it's difficult to know where to start, even for me." He looked around the room and then back at Chris. "You're a musician. Do you compose music?"

"Yes," Chris answered.

"Have you ever given any thought to that process? I mean, have you considered that it's all biochemistry? I'm asking you to think about your own creative processes in biochemical terms; in terms of enzymes, chemical messengers and the flow of ions."

"I can't do that," said Chris. "It's too overwhelming."

"Good." said Bernstein, his face lighting up with energy and enthusiasm. "Now, let me make it even more abstract. When you compose or when you hear beautiful music, do you have an emotional response?"

"Of course," said Chris. "Those are some of the most treasured moments in my life."

"Have you ever thought of that in biochemical terms? Have you ever stopped to consider the biochemistry of profound joy? It's all biochemistry. We scientists intuitively know that, but when you try to become specific about certain aspects of the processes we take for granted, it becomes very exciting."

"You're right." said Chris. "I never have thought of it in these terms. I'm overwhelmed. It seems too vast to encompass, like the universe."

"All right," said Bernstein. "One more. Even your recognition of that vastness and the sense of awe it inspires are biochemistry. Just keep that in mind as we consider these things--it's all biochemistry.

"Now, think of a computer--a complex set of switches and relays sending electrical information very rapidly in a highly coordinated fashion. For it to work, you have extremely precise pathways for the electricity to travel. All this precision is contained within the engravings on the microchips, right?"

"Right."

"In a computer or an electrical circuit there has to be an uninterrupted flow of electricity from some source to whatever component is functioning. In the nervous system there are some similarities. There is also electrical flow. Signals flow from one part of the brain to another or from the brain to the spinal cord or vice versa. Now, as you know, that electricity does not depend on a generator, but on the flow of electrically charged particles."

"Sodium, potassium and chloride ions," said Chris.

"Exactly. The flux of these ions across the membranes of the cells in the nervous system, the neurons, creates electrical differences which cause current to flow along the membranes of the cells, sometimes for considerable distances."

"Like in our arms and legs?" asked Chris.

"Yes, and some which go all the way from the brain to the spinal cord," said Bernstein. "Another major difference in biology is

124

that electricity doesn't flow from cell to cell in an uninterrupted fashion. At the junctions between nerves, or nerves and muscles, there are small packets of chemicals called neurotransmitters which are released from the end of one nerve. These chemicals flow into the microscopic space that separates the nerves.

"When they reach the second nerve they come in contact with structures on the surface of that nerve called receptors. The neurotransmitter fits into the receptor like a key fits into a lock. When it does, it sends a biochemical message into the second nerve that causes changes in its internal chemistry and another message is composed and sent on.

"All this takes place extremely rapidly, in milliseconds. Then the neurotransmitter is biochemically taken apart, removed or deactivated and the receptor goes back to its resting state, ready to receive another transmission."

"Are these junctions called synapses?" asked Chris.

"When the transmission is from nerve to nerve they're called synapses. When the transmission is from nerve to muscle, the structure is called the motor end-plate, but the process is the same. The motor nerve releases the neurotransmitter which interacts with the receptor on the motor end-plate which causes the chemical changes that result in the contraction of the muscle fibers."

"And these neurotransmitters and receptors fit together like antigens and antibodies?" asked Chris.

"They're similar in that the interactions both depend on three-dimensional geometry. Only certain molecular structures can fit. If a molecule is similar, it may be able to attach to a receptor, but may not bind completely; or it may bind so completely that it disables the receptor and prevents the nerve from functioning in a normal way."

"So there are other molecules, other than the ones produced by the nerves that can bind to the receptors?"

"That's what pharmacology is all about," said Bernstein. "Finding and understanding molecules that will bind to specific receptors, not only in the nervous system but in other organ systems as well, such as hormones. Medicines don't have their effect directly, but by binding and altering receptor function. That's true for almost all medicines--heart medicines, high blood pressure pills, cancer medicines, you name it. It's a game of finding receptors and the chemicals that react with them.

"It's fascinating to realize that our species has been using plants as sources of such molecules for as long as our history has been recorded. You can imagine what disasters must have taken place as our ancestors went through the trials and errors of figuring out which plants were safe to eat and which would cause illness or death.

"Think about the members of some tribe stumbling onto some new mushrooms, eating them and watching each other die a horrible death from liver failure. Can you imagine the terror of those people thinking they had incurred the wrath of one of their gods by eating a sacred plant. But you can be certain that the culture of that tribe then evolved a prohibition against eating those mushrooms to protect their members."

"But maybe they could use that plant as a weapon against their enemies," said Chris.

"An excellent point," said Bernstein. "You probably know the story of the use of curare by the primitive Indians in South America. Early western explorers, including Sir Walter Raleigh, brought back the story that the Indians put a poison on their arrows which paralyzed the animals they hunted. Scientists tried for centuries to isolate and duplicate the substance. Only in the last part of the 19th century was any headway made. Now it's known that the substance comes from several plants of the Chondrodendron family. The active ingredient binds to the receptor of the motor end-plate, preventing the normal neurotransmitter, acetyl choline, from getting there. The animal, or human, suffers total paralysis and dies of asphyxiation."

"That's interesting," said Chris. "We've just been able to figure it out recently but the Indians were probably using it for centuries. And I thought that chemical warfare was something new."

"On the positive side, the use of herbs for medicinal purposes is certainly as old as our species," said Bernstein. "As is the use of mind-altering plant compounds. Alcohol use is as old as history. The Egyptians and Romans used fermentation to produce alcoholic beverages."

"I've read a little about the use of mind-altering plants," said Chris. "Peyote was used in some Indian tribal rituals that must have had ancient beginnings."

"One of the fascinating aspects about this," said Bernstein, "is that in all the eons of our existence, after all the generations that have gone through evolutionary pressures, only a handful of compounds have been discovered to have these special, mind-altering qualities. Further, those compounds which effect human beings have similar if not identical effects on all vertebrates that we have tested. This speaks volumes about the fact that metabolic systems that are effective in primitive species, such as bacteria, are found in much more highly evolved species. Evolution modifies them and improves them, and makes them more complex, but the fundamentals remain the same. For those of us interested in addiction, this means that we can use animal systems to obtain answers that are applicable to the human problems we face."

"Can you give me an example?" asked Chris.

"You can addict rats to cocaine," said Bernstein. "You create a system in which the rat receives some cocaine in a fluid or a tablet each time he presses a lever. They quickly learn how the system works. They begin to press the lever more and more rapidly and will continue to do so until they die of exhaustion and hunger. This behavior is analogous to the cocaine binges humans experience. They'll continue to use until there's no more left or they collapse in exhaustion. By way of contrast, rats only self- administer opiates to the point of mild sedation and then they stop, returning only after the effects of the first dose have worn off, which mimics the way humans use heroin."

"How do you study hallucinogens like LSD?" asked Chris.

"Animal models can't tell us everything about human behavior," said Bernstein. "Unfortunately, you can't interview a rat, so that kind of investigation has to be carried out on human volunteers. Since the substances tend to have nasty side effects and long term consequences, not much research can be done.

"I want to go way back into evolutionary time and consider with you some of the imperatives of the nervous system. If we think about what was going on in that primordial soup, with single cell organisms being the among the earliest expressions of life on this planet, we can suppose that a nervous system wasn't necessary since all the control and communication took place within that single cell. All the functions of life, absorption of nutrients, metabolism, excretion and procreation took place within that cell.

"But more complex, multi-celled organisms would have survival advantages over the more simple ones, and once you have more complexity, and specialization of function into more evolved tissues and systems, then, you need to have a system for communication and control. The relentless, cruel pressures of survival would eliminate those solutions which didn't work, or worked less well. What is absolutely astonishing to me is that some of the systems that are found in extremely primitive organisms such as snails and slugs, are also present in human beings. Neurotransmitters that are found in primitive forms are very similar to the dopamine that is so important in our brains."

"The same molecules?" asked Chris.

"Virtually the same," samd Bernstein. "Which means that they also had the same metabolic pathways to produce them and the receptors that they fit into."

"That is astonishing," agreed Chris.

Now let's presume that we understand the process completely, and that survival and "fitness" in the Darwinian way of thinking is the ultimate goal of the evolutionary process. Since primates appeared so relatively recently in evolutionary history, and seem to be gifted with capacities not present in other species, we would have to assume that the systems present in our species have been tested and honed by the entire time and pressure of the evolutionary process. You could say that the human brain is the jewel in the crown of evolution. All the systems have been tailored to ensure that our species is as perfectly fit as is evolutionarily possible for life on this planet. And just consider how our species is able to survive and live in climates as diverse as the rain forests of the equator to the frozen lands of the Arctic. It really is marvelous."

"That's right," said Chris. "I'd never given that any thought. Humans can survive huge changes in temperature."

"External temperature," said Bernstein. "That's the amazing part. The mechanisms maintain the internal temperature within narrow limits to protect our metabolic capacity. We can also live from sea level to over ten thousand feet in the Andes or Himalayas which covers a huge range of barometric pressure and oxygen tension. In addition to all the ways in which our higher centers in the cerebral cortex can dazzle us, there is an incredible amount of energy and attention given to monitoring and managing the minute complexities of keeping an organism alive and functioning in diverse circumstances in a competitive environment on this planet."

"The autonomic nervous system?" asked Chris.

"Right," said Bernstein. "Actually two almost opposing systems operating in delicate, precise balance. One accelerates the heart rate, the other slows it. One raises the blood pressure, the other lowers it. All this in second to second responses to changing needs that we never even perceive. I'm sure you remember the concept of homeostasis from your biology and physiology courses."

"I do. Homeostasis is a state of dynamic balance where all the systems are operating in harmony."

"Exactly, and the autonomic nervous system is the command and control system that maintains the homeostatic balance.

"For example, when you arise from lying down, gravity will cause the blood to flow into your legs and feet, when you need it to be carrying oxygen to your brain. But the autonomic systems instantly make the adjustments to force blood out of your legs and back into your cerebral circulation. When it works, you're completely unaware of it. If it doesn't work quite quickly enough, you experience momentary lightheadedness when you stand up. If it doesn't work at all, you pass out."

"My mom has a problem with that," said Chris. She has to be careful when she gets up from bed. She gets dizzy."

"Consider the adjustments that have to be made when you jump up from bed and run up a flight of stairs," said Bernstein. "Not only does the system have to compensate for gravity and maintain the blood flow to your brain, it has to begin supplying the largest muscles in your body with oxygen and glucose so they can do the work of lifting the weight of your body.

"Sensors in your body detect the need to obtain more oxygen and get rid of carbon dioxide so your breathing is speeded up without your having to think about it or make any decisions. Because your efforts are generating heat, other sensors signal the central control mechanisms and more blood flow is directed through your skin, where heat can be exchanged. Your skin also begins to perspire, all of which maintains a constant, optimal internal temperature without your ever having to think about it. Then when you stop, adjustments are again made to restore the normal, resting balance, instantaneously, and precisely.

"These vital adjustments are made continuously, even while you sleep. Your temperature, heart rate and breathing are constantly being adjusted. So that's the autonomic system; a system of sensors and profound, precise, instantaneous adjustments to the most important functions of the organism. No decisions and no awareness is necessary on our part. If we had to make all the decisions involved in maintaining the intricate balances, we'd use all our mental energy doing so. As it is, we're free to focus on other things, such as creativity and language."

"Not to mention what a mess we'd make of the whole thing if we had to make the decisions," said Chris. "So mother nature demonstrates her wisdom as well as her skill."

"Absolutely," said Bernstein. "It's also important to realize that most of the terrible withdrawal symptoms that Erin experienced were caused by the brain's disordered direction of the autonomic nervous system. The terrible cramps, the nausea, vomiting and diarrhea are all under the control of this enormously powerful system. But like many of the most important systems, we only pay attention to them when they're not working correctly.

"I want to switch to considering motivation and how the nervous system deals with motivation. Again, I want to talk in terms of our species, and what forces are necessary to maintain the integrity of the species and keep it viable. If you were going to design such a system what would you think would be the polar extremes?"

"Hmm, " said Chris. "Let me think. You'd have to have both ways to reinforce the things you wanted the species to do, and ways of preventing what would be damaging."

"Excellent. You'd want to be able to manage behavior to achieve exactly that; seeking out the beneficial and avoiding the destructive. Think about pain in these terms. Pain teaches us to avoid certain acts that could damage or destroy an organism. So pain has enormously important survival value not only for the individual, but for the species as well. Can you think of other examples."

"Sure. We have hunger to ensure that we eat. We seek shelter when we're cold."

"Good examples," said Bernstein. "They're also both negative, like pain. All are examples of using negative experience to avoid destructive behavior. What about the positive side? What about pleasure."

"Of course. The pleasure that's derived from eating, from comfort and from sex. But is there a neurological structure for pleasure?"

"Have you heard of the 'reward pathway'? asked Bernstein.

"I don't think so."

"It was first discovered it in animals using electrodes, which, when implanted in certain specific places in the brain, would induce animals to stimulate themselves repetitively with electrical currents. We later discovered that these same locations are the places where many of the psycho-active drugs have their effects. Then we knew we were getting closer to some major advances is understanding this mystery.

"Let me go back to something we touched on earlier. Opium has been used as source of pleasure for thousands of years. Morphine and heroin are directly derived from it. But why does it work? You remember my emphasizing the importance of receptors in understanding pharmacology? Some very bright guys took derivatives of morphine and tagged them with radioisotopes. They then were able to show that these compounds bind specifically to structures in the brains of animals. Do you want to guess where?"

"The reward pathway?"

"Precisely. It was then confirmed that the same is true for humans. But this raised a critical question. Why in the world do vertebrates, including humans, have brain receptors for a compound derived from plants? It didn't seem to make any sense."

Bernstein was quiet for a moment and Chris sat with a puzzled look on his face, Then he brightened. "Unless...unless,.."

"Go on," said Bernstein. "Unless what?

"Unless vertebrates make a brain compound that is structurally very similar to the active ingredient in opium. That's how you discovered the endorphins."

"There were a lot of people who contributed to that work. I was fortunate enough to be one of them. We've been able to learn a lot about the reward pathway, and the variety of ways in which the endorphins play critical roles in everyday life as well as in crisis situations. They modulate our responses to pain making it possible for us to endure pain, within certain limits. They also play an important role in our ability to cope with stress and not become completely undone by what life serves up to us.

"They are an internal source of the chemical substrates of happiness and pleasure. Just think of it. These small molecules are the keys that control some of the most vital, critical forces in our lives, both protecting us and rewarding us. It's truly awe-inspiring.

"But we're a long, long way from understanding all of this. We've learned an enormous amount of very specific information about certain of these systems, but what we still don't know presents a formidable challenge. Locked within the complex circuitry of the one hundred billion or so neurons in the human brain are the secrets of why personalities are different. There are biochemical underpinnings to the different decisions that lead to bravery or cowardice; to charity and humanity or avarice and selfishness; to morality and integrity or deception and duplicity. Thinking about the process by which children learn to make the distinctions between right and wrong, good and evil, is a wonderful challenge. And, what's the biochemistry of wisdom and creativity, of original thought? What about love, longing and loneliness? We have a long, challenging, wonderful road ahead of us."

"Absolutely mesmerizing," said Chris. "And we haven't even begun to talk about the addiction part of the puzzle."

"Let's save that for the next session," said Bernstein. "I have a couple of articles for you to read."

They scheduled the next meeting and Chris left. Nothing had been said specifically about heroin addiction, or the way it begins or can be treated, but Chris was feeling more hopeful. Dr. Bernstein's knowledge, enthusiasm and wisdom had given him some assurance that there were answers to some of the terrible, unanswered questions and the challenges he and Erin still faced.

Chapter Seventeen

Chris was still waking to the absence of music, but his mood had improved. He was reading the material that Dr. Bernstein had given him about neurophysiology and that had given him a positive alternative focus for some of his mental energy. He still spent a great deal of time thinking about Erin, worrying about where she was and the dangers she was encountering in the world of addiction.

He didn't know that world. Despite the understanding that he was gaining about the science of addiction, the ugly reality remained a dark mystery that he could only try to fathom. That Erin had been plunged into that world was a source of unrelenting pain.

He was frustrated by his complete inability to formulate a plan to find her. There didn't seem to be any reasonable first step to take that wouldn't compromise her, such as calling the police. His feelings of utter helplessness added to his grief over the loss. The belief that she was also suffering from their separation was of no consolation to him.

What had initially been a fierce, sharp, wrenching pain, was gradually being transformed into a dull ache which would push through into his consciousness whenever he wasn't intently mentally active. His work at the laboratory was improving and he was finding it beneficially distracting.

His mother called daily, his father less frequently but also regularly. They had stopped asking the questions that were still on all of their minds, but maintained a hovering, solicitous presence.

Rick also called and the two had dinner at least once a week. Their conversations resumed their usual tone and focus. Only occasionally would Rick bring up the subject of Erin and it was quickly brushed aside after Chris confirmed the painful facts that there had been no contact and that no plan had been evolved.

It was a beautiful, warm day when Chris returned for his second appointment with Dr. Bernstein. He walked through the campus which was filled with students. Some lay on areas of lawn studying in the shade of live oaks. Others sat in intense discussion, their books open and papers spread. Bicycle riders wove their way among the walkers. Couples drifted in and out of the book store or the student union or just sat at the edge of the large iron fountain, talking quietly. The innocent happiness caused a deep pang of loneliness to fill his chest.

When he reached the office, Dr. Bernstein suggested that they get out of the office. "It's too nice a day to spend inside," he said. "I know a quiet little courtyard where we can hold forth without any interruptions. Let's stop at the vending machine and get a couple of drinks to take along."

They walked to a small inner courtyard which had three empty tables with shading umbrellas. Carefully tended shrubs and flowers decorated the periphery and the faint scent of jasmine floated in the warm air. They chose their seats, opened the sodas and Bernstein began.

"We talked about the survival value of pain and how it helps us avoid self-destructive acts. But pain itself ultimately becomes confining, enervating and destructive. So, the use of techniques or materials that are effective in alleviating pain has been an important part of the history of our species in general and of the practice of medicine.

"In some cultures, herbal medicines have been used. In China, acupuncture was developed to a high degree of sophistication. The poppy has had a two sided history, being used both for pleasure and to alleviate pain. There's evidence that extracts from the poppy were used as early as 4000 BC. by the Sumerians. The ancient Greek physicians also used poppy extracts for pain and were apparently aware of its addictive potential. Arabian traders understood of the power of the poppy and introduced it into the orient, although the Chinese only used it to control diarrhea."

"I thought the Chinese had smoked opium for many centuries," said Chris.

"No," said Bernstein. "Not at all. Opium for non-medical purposes was introduced into China in the middle of the 18th Century
by the British, who brought it from India. The Brits were desperate
to find something that the Chinese wanted so they could trade for
their silks, tea and porcelains.

"The emperor outlawed the import, sale or use of opium but
corrupt officials made fortunes trading in the contraband. Canton
was the only Chinese city into which westerners were permitted to
sail and ply their trade. Since Canton was so far from Peking, it was
difficult to enforce the law. Finally, in a fury because he was being
openly disobeyed, the Emperor sent his troops to seize the opium
and close the port of Canton to the westerners. The British were, of
course, indignant over the insult to her majesty's honor and the first
opium war ensued. The frail Chinese boats were no match for the
British fleet and China suffered a humiliating defeat which ultimately opened all of China to western trade.

"In Europe, Paracelsus, the great Swiss physician from the 16th
Century was the first to use tincture of opium, which he named 'lau-
danum'. The name 'morphine' was first used by a German chemist
in the early 19th Century who purified the active molecule in the
complex poppy juice. He named it after Morpheus, the Greek god
of sleep and dreams, recognizing a third aspect of these compounds,
depressing consciousness. By the middle of the 19th Century,
chemists were extracting more of the pure alkaloids from the
mixture that was contained in the crude poppy juice. Codeine was
one of those that was discovered this way. Heroin was also derived
from opium in the late nineteenth century. Ironically, it was first
marketed as a cure for morphine addiction."

"The Germans certainly do seem to have a knack for chemistry,
don't they," said Chris. "I remember all the contributions they
made to organic chemistry."

"There's another big contribution that they made that will be
coming up soon," said Bernstein. "In this country, our tragic Civil
War spawned the first large mass of morphine addicts. Many of the
soldiers who had suffered terrible, disfiguring wounds and under-
gone battlefield amputations were treated with this new substance
which left them addicted."

"As if that war wasn't horrible enough," said Chris.

"After the war, the addiction became much more common in

this country," said Bernstein. "But remember, at that time, these drugs were not illegal and they were incorporated into myriads of tonics and patent medicines, which led to further addiction. Coca Cola was named for the cocaine it originally contained. Sigmund Freud advocated the use of cocaine as a tonic. The typical American addicts early in this century were middle-aged, middle to upper class females who had been given tonics for vague symptoms. When they became addicted, opiates were prescribed by physicians, and addiction was considered exclusively a medical problem. And some very prominent people were included among those with the problem."

"I think I read that Jack London was an addict," said Chris.

"Yes. He became addicted because of the pain associated with his kidney disease," said Bernstein. "Of course, Poe and Oscar Wilde were only a couple of the literati that used opiates.

"Another technical change had a major influence on addiction in a quantitative sense. When taken orally, opiates only slowly absorbed from the intestines, so the doses that get to the brain at any one time are relatively small. With the invention of the hypodermic syringe, intramuscular and ultimately intravenous injections made it possible to get very high doses to the brain, which meant that the effect, the high, was greatly magnified, as was the physical dependence that was produced.

"In 1914 there was a major change in the way our society dealt with addiction. Because of the growing numbers of addicts and international concerns about drug use, the Harrison Act was passed by Congress. Under this law, physicians were prohibited from supplying opiates to known addicts under penalty of losing their license. So the issue of addiction passed from being a medical problem to being a criminal justice problem. Faced with the stern penalties, physicians turned their backs on the problem and, for the most part, on the addicts."

"I've already had a little exposure to the effects of that," said Chris. "Some of the regulations in the methadone clinic seem completely counterproductive."

"Always remember that the regulations are a reflection of underlying attitudes of society. The Harrison Act wasn't the only attempt to legislate morality. Remember, the Volstead Act, Prohibition, was also a product of those times and mores. The regulations won't change until the attitudes do," said Bernstein.

"Actually, in the nineteen thirties, the federal government did make some attempts to understand and treat addiction. They recruited volunteer heroin addicts, mostly from New York City, who were admitted to the Public Health Service Hospital in Lexington, Kentucky, located in a lovely rural setting. After going through the miseries of withdrawal, the addicts were isolated from heroin for six months to a year and underwent a valiant attempt at rehabilitation. The investigators were confident that they had been successful. But within one year of returning to New York, over ninety per-cent were again addicted to heroin."

"How discouraging," said Chris. "Not only for them, but for me."

"It's one of the things that most people don't appreciate about addiction," said Bernstein. "You can get an addict through the short term misery of withdrawal. The real questions are the mid and long term ones. How do you keep them from relapsing? While much of society believes that it's simply a matter of character---'just say no'-the scientists and physicians in the field of addiction medicine know that addiction is a disease in which the chemistry of the brain has been dramatically altered. Real, lasting cure can only take place when
these changes have been reversed and the systems normalized. Unless that fact is taken into account, our success will be no greater than it was in Lexington. Relapse is the hallmark of addiction."

"So, when does methadone get into this act?" asked Chris. "I need to hear some good news."

"In the years of World War II and following, physicians had gained knowledge and experience with other opiate drugs which were used for pain control. The question then emerged, 'are there other compounds that can be substituted for heroin that will permit addicts to get free from the ravages of heroin?' If there were such drugs, the argument went, it would permit programs to help addicts regain control of their lives first and then deal with the secondary addiction under far better circumstances. This was important because after World War II there had been an enormous increase in the amount of heroin brought into New York from Turkey, via Marseilles."

"The French Connection?" asked Chris.

"Right. In the sixties, some scientists at the Rockefeller Institute in New York City were admitting volunteer heroin addicts to a research project designed to test the 'substitution' thesis. On the wards, they were given free heroin, chemically pure, and sterile, or one of the other compounds under investigation. One of the compounds they tested was methadone which had been synthesized during World War II by the Germans who needed a substitute analgesic, since their access to the poppies to make morphine had been cut off."

"Those German chemists again," said Chris.

"I told you they'd pop up in our story," said Bernstein. "Methadone has two characteristics that made it attractive. First, it could be taken orally and didn't have to be injected. Second, it was metabolized more slowly than heroin. Because heroin is rapidly metabolized, addicts need to inject it three or four times a day to avoid withdrawal symptoms. With methadone, a single daily dose was found to be sufficient.

"One of the aims of the study, was to gain some understanding of the minute-to-minute and hour-to-hour aspects of the life of an addict. What the investigators observed was that the heroin addicts spent all of their time submerged in heroin. Either they were completely focused on their next dose--when they would get it, how big it would be, and whether they would have to suffer any withdrawal symptoms---or they were numbed out from the effects of their last dose."

"Not much of a life," observed Chris.

"Hardly a life at all," Bernstein agreed. "When the volunteers were put on sufficiently high doses of methadone, they began to broaden their focus. They began to spontaneously talk about baseball, the weather and politics. In short, they began to behave normally."

"Did they get high?" asked Chris.

"No, they didn't," said Bernstein. "If the dose was too high they would become over-sedated and nod off. If the dose was too low, they'd experience withdrawal symptoms. But when the right dose was achieved, they had no withdrawal symptoms, no craving for heroin and they behaved normally."

"That was the experience Erin had," said Chris. "She said that after a few days on methadone she began to feel like her old self.

Are there any long term side-effects?"

"No, other than the fact that it, too, is addictive. Since the sixties, literally millions of doses of methadone have been given, all around the world. It's a very safe medicine. You hear anecdotes that it rots the bones or it destroys the liver, but those stories are completely untrue."

"Then why has it been so controversial?" asked Chris.

"I'll come to that in a moment," said Bernstein "Because of the way methadone seemed to work, the investigators postulated that there were receptors in the brain to which heroin is bound. Since methadone is chemically similar, they reasoned, methadone also binds to the same receptors. As long as the receptors are occupied by the methadone, there is no craving for heroin. After twenty-four hours, enough of the methadone has been metabolized to open up some of the receptors and withdrawal symptoms begin as does craving for heroin.

"They published the results of their early successes in substituting methadone for heroin, plus the theories on which it was based. There was enormous enthusiasm among the scientific community, probably too much. The lay press also became enraptured and talked about a 'magic bullet'."

"I'm not surprised," said Chris. "It must have been very exciting."

"Too good to be true, one might say," said Bernstein. "I can still remember that excitement. It really did seem like we had made a major breakthrough."

"You were a part of that, weren't you?" asked Chris.

"Yes. I was there." said Bernstein. "But enthusiasm from the scientific community was more than equaled by the horror from the law enforcement sector."

"I don't understand," said Chris. "I would think that they'd be thrilled to think that there might really be a way to treat addicts."

"Ah, but you see, that's the response of a biologist and a scientist like you. The law enforcement people saw it as an irresponsible attempt by a bunch of egg-heads to put addictive substances in the hands of dope fiends. They were infuriated and attempted to arrest some of the principal investigators. Only the enormous prestige and respect of the Rockefeller Institute saved the day. The Institute cloaked and protected the work as legitimate science, not subject to their intervention."

"Did that work?" asked Chris.

"Yes," said Bernstein. "It kept the work going, but we were still harassed by the feds who continued to spy and try to obtain evidence of wrong-doing. At any rate, they did prevent the rapid adoption of the methadone strategy in the US."

"That seems so destructive," said Chris.

"I don't think it was the result of malevolence," said Bernstein. "I just think that people with that kind of background and training see the world differently than you or I do. They're selected for their professions by their background and attitudes the same as you and I are."

"So how did you get around all the resistance and hassling?" asked Chris.

"It was the result of one of the greatest ironies I've ever witnessed," said Bernstein. "During the horror of the Vietnam war, as many as forty per-cent of the servicemen in Viet Nam used heroin because it was available and cheap. They would never have done so if they hadn't found themselves far from home, lonely, in a jungle, in the middle of a terrifying war that many of them did not believe in. The estimates are that almost twenty per-cent, or about half of those that tried it, became addicted. But most of those poor soldiers would never have been exposed to heroin if it hadn't been for the war and where it was fought. Circumstances beyond the individual's control can place them in a situation of vulnerability, which is what happened to your Erin."

Chris sat quietly for a few moments, letting that painful truth wash over him. Then he refocused his attention on what was being imparted to him. "So, not everyone that uses heroin becomes addicted?"

"No," said Bernstein. "Many are able to try it and stop there. I'm certain that must be painful for you to hear."

"Very," said Chris. "I just don't understand it all. I guess in some ways I still can't believe it."

"We'll come back to the question of the range of vulnerability to addiction and some of those mechanisms," said Bernstein. "Now, let's see. I was talking about the experience in Viet Nam. The Nixon Administration was under a lot of pressure about that war and the issue of heroin addiction in the services was becoming a serious embarrassment. They had to quickly put together a program for drug treatment so they seized on methadone as the answer, to the great amazement and chagrin of the criminal justice types."

"That must've really floored them," said Chris.

"For a while," said Bernstein. "The opponents couldn't reconcile the fundamental conservatism of the administration with such an outrageous idea. But Nixon was adamant. They were going to treat our boys and methadone was going to be the centerpiece of the strategy."

"So the narcotics bureau had to accept it," said Chris.

"They were able to strike a bargain with the administration," said Bernstein. "In exchange for their cooperation, they were given the right to draw up the regulations so they could be assured that their attitudes would be a controlling force in the administration of the program."

"So they were able to make it difficult," said Chris.

"You bet they were," said Bernstein. "They regulated the dosages and the schedules, decisions that should have been made by physicians. They made it difficult, if not impossible, to keep people on the program long enough to achieve meaningful rehabilitation."

"What do you mean?" asked Chris.

"People who become addicted to heroin, as you well and painfully realize, often lose the best parts of their lives. They are so focused on getting their next fix that the rest of their lives collapses. They often become involved in criminal behavior to support their habit. They abandon their responsibilities for family and employment. They spend increasing amounts of their time in jail or prison.

"Methadone is not a cure-all. What it does is turn off the compulsion to inject heroin and permits addicts to rebuild their lives. But to be successful, they need time and good counseling. It's a slow, painful process of rebuilding, often with a lot of relapses and set-backs. The point I'm trying to make is that it can take a long time to be successful. Some times the regulations or other forces prevent the patients from staying on the program long enough to get their lives back together."

"And the patients actually become addicted to methadone, don't they?" asked Chris.

"Yes they do," said Bernstein. "And withdrawal from methadone is not easy. But if they've become successful in the program, they have their lives and their families back, they're working and they have a lot of support systems in place. They've hopefully broken the strong contacts they had with the addiction community. And most important, the withdrawal from methadone can be done very slowly and carefully under medical control and guidance to give the brain a chance to reequilabrate and reestablish its balance. Also, other medicines can be used to assist with the withdrawal."

"Do some people just stay on methadone?" asked Chris.

"Yes," said Bernstein. "Some try to get off methadone and stay clean but are unable to, so they come back to the program. Others, for whom methadone has become the glue that holds their lives together, aren't willing to risk coming off and relapsing, and would rather continue taking methadone daily, much as a diabetic takes insulin, or others take heart medicines.'

"Does that bother you that it's so difficult to get off methadone?" asked Chris.

""'Diseases desperate grown are by desperate measures treated---or not at all' said Shakespeare. Sure. I wish it were easier. But I think it just emphasizes that addiction is an incredibly complex, powerful affliction. Maybe when we learn more about the fundamental mechanisms we'll be able to do better. That'll take more research which will require financial support. For now, being addicted to methadone is far better than being addicted to heroin; better for the addict, for his family and for society."

"What do you mean 'for society'?" asked Chris.

"All the data show that when heroin addicts are on methadone, criminal behavior plummets to only about ten per-cent of pre-treatment levels," said Bernstein. "Not only the direct costs are saved, but the secondary costs like those for the criminal justice system.

"Health care costs also decrease dramatically and the spread of HIV and Hepatitis B and C are decreased. Society also benefits by having these people become contributing members, rather than roaming the streets in pursuit of heroin and the means to buy it. A study in California showed that for every dollar spent on methadone treatment, the state saved seven dollars. That's a huge a return on the investment of society's money."

"Why is it so difficult to stop taking these drugs?" asked Chris.

"We don't know the exact mechanisms but we're getting

closer," said Bernstein. "Part of the difficulty appears to lie in the fact that those parts of the brain that are disordered by addiction are so basic, so fundamental, and so powerful that once damaged, it takes a long time to restore their balance. And when most addicts finally decide that they need treatment, they have been addicted for years, day in and day out exposing their nervous system to this injury."

"And all of this starts in the reward pathway?"

"That's right. In the place that's responsible for the survival of the species by ensuring that those certain acts we talked about be carried out at regular intervals; such as eating, reproducing, staying warm and dry, the sorts of things that give us a feeling of peace, contentment and primal satisfaction. These primitive functions are about the only processes we possess when we're born into the world.

"The endorphins are released from specific parts of the brain, like the pituitary to control this pathway. They bind to receptors located on the surfaces of neurons in the reward pathway. When they do, they activate other chemical pathways within the cells, which cause them to perform other functions, including the release of a neurotransmitter called dopamine. The dopamine then binds to receptors of other cells in the circuits which can lead to changes in our state of mind, or even our state of consciousness. '

"It sounds very complex," said Chris.

"It's enormously complex and it takes a great deal of research to uncover every tiny step in the whole, long process. But we're getting to the point of unraveling some basic molecular biological truths and, equally exciting, of being able to relate these biochemical changes to our behavior and the occurrences of our daily lives."

"What do you mean?" asked Chris.

"The entire nervous system is like a biochemical gyroscope, struggling to protect its equilibrium in a world where life and its stresses are always threatening our balance. Complex systems are involved in the way we deal with stress, helping us maintain our equilibrium in difficult times, such as you've recently been through. In terms of maintaining the viability of the species, that's obviously critical. We have to have the ability to respond quickly to threats, a system that prepares us for 'fight or flight.' What could be more fundamental?

"These very complex, basic circuits are the ones we compromise when we use addictive drugs. The precise balance of these systems is phenomenal, because any over-reaction or malfunction can be disastrous. For every 'up' adjustment, there's an instantaneous counterbalancing 'down' response so that the system rarely permits us to stray far from the balance point.

"So here is this marvelous delicate but complex system which provides protection, rewards and the most fundamentally satisfying moments of our lives, like falling in love, experiencing the birth of our children, experiencing the majesty of the ocean or the sky, the most profoundly joyful moments in our lives. It's like a deep river flowing through our minds and bodies, hidden, subtle but enormously powerful.

"And along comes man with his poppy juice, naive and uncomprehending, stumbling into this system like a child stumbling into a fireworks factory with a box of matches. When someone first injects heroin into his arm, he experiences an enormous rush and an unbelievable high. The heroin that's injected binds to the opiate receptors and releases an enormous amount of dopamine into his system, a system built to accommodate to tiny adjustments and minuscule amounts of neurotransmitters is overwhelmed by a tidal wave of chemical pleasure that's too large to be controlled.

"The system is sent spinning out of control, trying to restore balance, trying to compensate for an event that not even eons of evolution prepared it for. Balance is only achieved when the drug is metabolized by the liver and removed from the body. As the blood level falls, the receptors in the brain give up the molecules that had been bound and the brain returns to normal."

"Is the first dose addictive?" asked Chris.

"There's no simple answer to that," said Bernstein. "It depends on a complex set of variables, including genetics. Typically, the person returns to feeling normal after the drug is metabolized, which gives him a false sense of security. He believes that he's going to be able to use without becoming addicted, so he does it again.

"As he does, he begins to notice some changes. He doesn't get as high as that first unbelievable time, even though he injects more. The brain, caught unaware the first time is already learning and making changes. It's now on guard against similar onslaughts. It will be better able to restore the balance without permitting the pendulum to be swung as far as that first time.

"The other thing he begins to notice is the feeling of being ill. He begins to have stomach cramps. He feels feverish and anxious. At first he may believe he has a case of stomach flu. But what he's experiencing is the result of what they has done to the opiate receptors all over the body, in the autonomic nervous system, and in the GI system, not only in the brain. The system has become reset at a different level that now demands the presence of more opioids in the system. In other words, the system now needs heroin to be balanced. Without it, the unbalance leads to the terrible symptoms of withdrawal; incapacitating abdominal cramps, vomiting, diarrhea, bone and muscle pain, sweating, anxiety. It's as though the brain is using everything at its disposal to drive that human being to inject heroin, fill the receptors and restore the balance.

"It's such a terrible, tragic irony," said Bernstein, "that this magnificent system, carefully crafted by cons of evolution to reward, guide and protect us has been converted into a voracious, insatiable monster that demands this chemical and will relentlessly drive that human beings to self-destruction to obtain it. It will destroy their families, their lives, and ultimately cause their death."

Chris had been listening silently, remembering the agonies that he had witnessed as Erin struggled with her withdrawal. He stood up and said, "Could you give me just a moment? That was painful to relive." He walked away, pictures of Erin painfully vivid in his mind. It was one thing to intellectualize about receptors and neurotransmitters, but when it was replayed as the pitiful human tragedy that he had witnessed, his recall was purchased at the price of deep emotional pain. After a few moments of silence, he returned to the table and sat down.

"I'm sorry, Chris," said Bernstein. "I know it must be very painful for you."

"Not as painful as it was for her," said Chris. "I can certainly demand that I endure some discomfort if it will mean that I'll be better able to help her. I still don't completely understand why the brain gets so out of balance."

"Let me try this metaphor," said Bernstein. "Let's change the system from pain and reward to one of temperature balance for the purpose of illustration. Our model supposes that the experience of warmth is pleasurable and that of cold is very disagreeable. The first time someone injects heroin into their body, the temperature rises dramatically, and he experiences enormous pleasure. But the system realizes that to have so much heat is damaging to the organism, so it adds cold to restore the normal temperature. In doing so it builds up some additional reserve of cold, so that the next time the heroin is injected, the temperature doesn't go up as high.

"Over the next period of days and weeks, the person continues to inject heroin, and the system builds up more and more cold defenses so that finally, no matter how much heroin is injected, the temperature barely moves. Furthermore, when the heroin is metabolized, the system is completely out of balance because of all the cold. So now, the best the person can do is inject heroin just to avoid the cold which causes enormous suffering."

"O.K." said Chris. "That was helpful. Now I think I get it. And the system doesn't care whether it's heroin or methadone which is used to maintain the balance."

"Exactly. With the balance maintained by methadone the person can go on with his life, even though there's still a major imbalance. One of the problems that remains, using our model, is that being so far out of balance, there is no longer any flexibility left in the system and when the person is stressed, it feels like an excess of cold, or craving for heroin."

"But can the system ever get back to normal?" asked Chris.

"Yes," said Bernstein confidently. "It can. But you need enough time to gradually decrease the amount of opiates so the system can be in balance without them."

"All right," said Chris. "Now I think I understand. But what about genetics? Is susceptibility to addiction inherited?"

"I believe so," said Bernstein. "Although there is not much data about heroin or other hard drugs, the pathways by which they operate are very similar. I believe we'll find that what applies to one of these drugs will be at least partially applicable to others.

"We have learned that the synthesis of opiate receptors is under genetic control. We have also discovered that there are differences in the structure of those receptors in different populations, and in different people within the populations. If those differences cause a stronger or weaker binding of the opiates to the receptors it could have a profound effect on the way a person responds to opiates. More research will be necessary, but these differences could explain differences in pain tolerance as well as susceptibility to addiction."

"That could really be exciting," said Chris.

"Here are some references that you can read," said Bernstien. "But the other question is what you're going to do about Erin? Can you find her?"

"I'll have to," said Chris.

"As you learned from the detox experience, the state law wouldn't permit her to get into a long term, maintenance program, which is what she needs. However, I have a few strings that I can pull. If you can find her, I can get her into the program."

"I really want to thank you," said Chris. "This has meant a great deal to me."

"Thank me?" said Bernstein. "Haven't you been listening? This is what I do, what I am. It's how I justify my taking up space on this planet. Keep in touch. I want to know what happens. Now go. Find her."

Chapter Eighteen

Chris called information in Simi Valley. He dialed the number he had been given and after a few rings, he was greeted by a gentle, female voice.

"Mrs. Leahy?" he asked.

"Yes," said the voice.

"We've never met. My name is Chris Childs."

There was a short pause. "Oh, Chris, have you heard from Erin? She wrote us and told us all about you. We had so looked forward to meeting you. We talked about trying to reach you--we didn't have your phone number--but we felt awkward about intruding. We're so worried about her."

"That's why I'm calling, Mrs. Leahy. I'd like to come down and talk to you and Mr. Leahy. I don't think I should do it over the phone."

"Does that mean that you have bad news?" she asked.

"Only in that I have no news at all," he said.

"We're so desperate. When can you come?"

"How about tomorrow evening?" he asked. "I could get a plane after work and be there by seven-thirty or eight."

"Could you come for dinner?" she asked. "We'd love to have you."

"You're very kind," he said. "But I'll eat on the plane."

"We wouldn't hear of it. Don't eat. We'll feed you. You're very important to us." She gave him directions.

The next afternoon he caught a five o'clock plane from San Francisco to the Burbank airport. He watched the Bay Area fall away beneath the wings. He watched the cars streaming up and down The Bayshore Freeway and 280. He found the Portola Valley and remembered the first time Erin had come to his house. The beaches at Santa Cruz, Monterey Bay and Big Sur also evoked painful memories of times spent there with Erin, or trips they had talked about and planned for the future. "Where could she be?" he asked himself as he had so many times.

After landing, he rented a car and followed the directions to the 405 where he quickly became entangled in the commuter traffic heading north. Turning west on 192, the freeway was still crowded with returning commuters. The freeway flowed between the rolling hills that lead down toward the coast beyond.

Following the directions, he took the second Simi Valley exit and made the turns at the indicated points, following a diminishing amount of traffic through the quiet, wide streets. He found the address and pulled into the driveway. A man was working in the flower bed in front of the windows. He stood up and came toward the car as Chris got out.

"I'm Dave Leahy, Chris. Welcome." He was a big, solid man who moved slowly, seeming to favor his right hip. He had a broad brow, with receding gray hair. His eyes were brown and his smile was warm. He shook hands firmly and said, "Come on in. We've been eager to meet you."

As they walked toward the door he shouted, "Jean, Chris's here."

A middle aged woman came bustling out of the house to meet him. Her gray eyes were glistening with tears. "Oh, Chris. Welcome. I'm so glad you could come," She embraced him warmly, without hesitation.

"There I go," she said. "Getting all emotional." She stepped back and wiped the tears from her eyes and cheeks. "Come on in and sit down. Let me get you something to drink. Would you like some iced tea?"

"Or something stronger?" asked Leahy. "I usually have a little Irish whiskey before dinner."

"I'd like that." said Chris.

There was a feeling of sincere welcoming, but at the same time the room was charged with mutual self-consciousness. They went through the social amenities, each realizing that they were circuitously heading toward a subject that was very important, powerful and painful. They were each held by a hesitation to move toward

149

that subject, not only avoiding their own pain, but feeling protective of the other two.

Dave Leahy returned with glasses of Irish crystal. "Some people like Bushmill's or Jamieson's but I prefer good old Paddy's," he said, offering a glass to Chris. "Slainte," he said, raising he own glass. "Cead mile failte---a hundred thousand welcomes."

"Slainte," echoed Chris. "I think I heard that your family is from Cork."

"My father's side," said Leahy. "My mother's people are from Limerick."

"And you, Mrs., Leahy?"

"You must call me Jean," she said.

"And me Dave," said Leahy.

"My mother's family was from south of Sligo," she said. "My father was Dutch. They met in Chicago."

"She's a mongrel," said Dave. "But she's all Irish at heart."

"It makes him happy to believe that," she said.

` "Erin told me that she felt as though she'd been raised in Dublin with all the Irish music and lore," said Chris.

"I'm afraid it gets a bit thick around here at times," said Dave. "But, God help me, I do love it, and Erin was always a good sport."

They had touched the subject, but backed away and endured a moment of awkward silence.

"And your parents, Chris," Jean finally said. "Tell us about them. We do so look forward to meeting them."

"My mother's family is from France," said Chris. "Her grandparents settled in the New York area. Dad's family is from England. They gradually moved from New England to the Midwest and then to Southern California."

"And where did they meet," asked Jean.

"My mother was giving a concert in Los Angeles. Dad was in the audience. He was doing his residency at the time. According to him, he became so enchanted with her music and with her that he made up his mind in an instant that he was going to marry her."

"It wasn't quite as elegant for us," said Dave. "Jean was working in a bank and I came in to make a deposit. I just stayed at the window and stared at her. I didn't want to leave. Look at that. She still blushes when I tell the story."

"It's true," she said with a laugh. "You'd think I'd grow up.

And, Chris, Erin said that you two hit it off instantaneously."

Now they had arrived at the subject.

"It was amazing," said Chris. "I'd heard my folks talk about their first meeting and had read about those 'thunderbolt' experiences, but I'd never had one nor knew anyone who had. And there she was, the most perfectly beautiful woman I'd ever seen, smiling at me. I was riveted to the floor."

"And she felt the same way," said Dave.

There was a pause as each fought to control the emotions that had quickly taken control of them. The silence was prolonged.

"I've got to find her," said Chris, trying to clear a dry throat. "Have you heard anything from her?"

"She leaves messages on the answering machine," said Jean. "She knows our schedules too well and calls when she knows we're unlikely to be here. She won't even hint about where she is. She only says that she's all right and that we shouldn't worry. She says she'll come back when she works things out. What can you tell us, Chris? Why did this happen just when she was so happy? What could have caused her to leave school, and you? Do you know?"

"I'm really in a tough place," said Chris. "I do know more but I feel that if I tell you something she hasn't, I'll be betraying a trust."

"I can appreciate that," said Dave.

"Is it about drugs?" asked her mother.

Chris was astonished by the question. "Why do you ask?"

Dave and Jean looked at each other.

"You know, of course, that Erin was adopted," said Jean. "We knew her mother, god rest her tormented soul, but not her father. He was no good. He got them both into all kinds of trouble, including drugs, and then left her with that little baby."

"How did she die?" asked Chris.

"Of a heroin overdose," said Dave. "The poor thing was so depressed. She was just trying to escape from the pain of his leaving her. She was very strong in many ways, but very fragile in others. He broke her heart."

"Does Erin know this?" asked Chris.

"We never told her," said Jean. "We know so little about drugs and addiction. We didn't know whether it's something that's passed on, like that blood disease. What's it called?"

"Hemophilia," said Chris.

"Oh, yes. Well, you would probably know about these things since you're a scientist."

"I wish I knew more" said Chris. "I'm trying to learn. They do believe that there is a genetic component to susceptibility to drugs, but it's not well understood."

"We just kind of put it out of our minds," said Dave. "Erin was such a bright, healthy child. We just never thought about it again even when she left school, and you, in such a hurry. We've just been racking our brains trying to find an answer. The notion of drugs just popped into my head the other day and I haven't been able to get rid of it. Is that what happened?"

"Yes," said Chris, nodding his head quietly. "But I have to tell you that it's really my fault."

"Your fault?' asked Dave sternly. "Did you get her addicted?"

"No, no," said Chris. "It's not that. I never used drugs. Well, I've never used heroin or any hard drugs."

He told them the story of Martin's revenge and his death.

Dave's face was twisted in anger as he learned what had happened. He got up and slammed his fist into the wall.

"That dirty, low-down bastard," he shouted. "It's a good thing he's dead or I'd go after him myself. I'm glad you didn't, Chris. Erin was right to keep you from destroying your life, too. But me? I'd have strangled him with my own two hands. That miserable son-of-a-bitch. Oh, poor Erin. Our poor baby. God, how she must be suffering."

He went to his wife who was crying quietly. They embraced and then he broke down into convulsive sobs.

"I'm so sorry," said Chris. "I'd do anything to get her back. I'd even stay completely away from her if that would undo this incredible nightmare."

"No, Chris," said Jean. "You mustn't blame yourself. You had no control over that beast. How could you have known? How could anyone believe that someone could deliberately destroy an innocent human being? Particularly one that he has some feelings for. And all for a sick kind of revenge. You couldn't have known."

"She loved you, Chris," said her father. "I'm certain that she still does. You know, she was always popular. She had a lot of dates. But she had never really fallen in love. She was always looking, though. She never found that right person until you. She

152

just raved about you and about your music. She said you're a genius. So brilliant and yet so gentle and caring. Your music must be a great comfort to you now."

"Music has always been a central part of my life," said Chris. "I treasured it even more because it had brought us together. But since she's been gone, it's just dried up. It's as though there was a chamber in my soul where the music came from. She became an intrinsic part of that place, and with her gone, the music has gone too. The chamber is closed. It's silent."

"We'd love to hear you play, Chris," said Jean. "Perhaps later when this nightmare is over."

"I'll send you a tape if you'd like me to," said Chris.

"That would be wonderful," said Jean. "Now I should get dinner."

"I'm sorry," said Chris. "I don't think I can eat anything. I apologize."

"We understand," said Dave. "What are you going to do? What can we do?"

"That's one of the reasons I came here," said Chris. "I feel so frustrated and completely helpless. I don't know what to do. I was hoping you might have some ideas."

"We've talked to her Berkeley friends and they're completely mystified," said Jean. "She hasn't talked to or contacted any of them. We had been paying the rent on her apartment. To stop just seemed like it would be giving up. But now, I suspect we'll drive up and close it."

"We've talked about hiring a private detective to try and find her," said Dave. "I think we'll go ahead now. I think it's important that we try to find her quickly before she undergoes any more damage. I'm sure they'll want to talk to you."

"I'll be happy to talk to them," said Chris. "God, I hope it works. "I'll be going now. I can't tell you how much this has meant to me. Here's my phone number in case you want to set up an appointment for the detective, or for any reason."

"It's meant a lot to us, too, Chris," said Dave. "We have always trusted Erin's judgment. It's obvious that you are the perfect man for her. Now we just have to find her."

On the plane, heading back to San Francisco, Chris' mind kept reproducing the picture of the double helix of DNA, thinking about the millions of molecules of nucleic acids, all in perfect sequence, guiding the synthesis of proteins and enzymes that are the essence of all life, each molecule a perfect product of the genetic template.

And now the question which had exploded in his brain with the new information about Erin's parents. Does a predilection for drugs reside somewhere in the coiled sequence of nucleic acids? Are the minds of some persons more susceptible to the lure of mind-altering drugs? Once exposed to these drugs, are some people able to turn away while others are trapped at the first exposure, unable to release themselves from the tightening grip of biochemical tentacles that relentlessly drag them down to their death? The chilling mystery absorbed him throughout the flight.

When he arrived back in Portola Valley, he went out onto the patio and stared up into the dark sky, gazing at the familiar constellations, trying to find comfort in the vast promenade; so ordered. so beautiful, so magnificent, so distant, so silent. But what he experienced was the profound sense of loneliness caused by Erin's absence. It seemed incomprehensible that he should be able to locate the distant stars and planets, and not have any idea where the woman he adored was. Where could she be? How could he find her?

Chapter Nineteen

When she left Berkeley, Erin had believed that, alone, she would be able to find a way to resist her craving for heroin. She viewed it as a test of her will, her moral fiber and integrity, in all of which she had great confidence. She believed she would be able to find a solid foundation where she could make her stand and fight her battle. That had not happened.

She had planned to gradually reduce her heroin use until she was free of its torment. She had not anticipated the phenomenon of tolerance. Rather than being able to diminish the amount she was using, her brain continued to escalate the amount it demanded to keep free of the torture of withdrawal symptoms. Every week she had to use larger doses to remain functional enough to work so she could continue to pay for the heroin, and her living expenses.

Her salary and tips were inadequate, and she had begun to use her savings, which were disappearing at an alarming, steady rate. In addition to growing panic about finances, there was the vague, shadowy but powerful feeling of helplessness. It was as though she had entered into another dimension in which time and space were thick and disordered. She couldn't move with her customary agility through either. Rather, she found herself slogging through confusing days in which the clock's movement was effectively replaced by her predictable need to fix to avoid suffering.

She was not only immersed in this all-pervasive fluid, she knew that she was slowly, steadily, sinking deeper. She tried to reaffirm her goals and intentions to remove herself from the gel of her prison, but she couldn't even concentrate enough mental focus to do that.

Her memory of Chris was still present and painful, but the pain was less distinct. As the sharp lines of her losses grew hazy, their capacity to inflict the sharp, lancinating bolts of anguish and remorse diminished. More and more of her intellectual capacity was being eroded by her need to focus on her next fix.

She had kept the tapes of his music and played them constantly. They provided the one oasis of spiritual uplift in her existence which was otherwise a desert of deprivation. His music was like a slender tether to her previous life. There were times, after listening to a tape, that she would want to pull on that tether, to contact him, to ask for his protection. But even in her terrible isolation and need, she would not do that.

There were two elements that kept her committed to her isolation. The first was her still strong desire to protect those she loved, knowing that the reality of seeing her in this condition would cause them hideous pain. The other was shame. The revulsion she had always felt toward drug addicts was now turned inward and it was a searing, pitiless beam.

The weeks trudged by in numbing procession, each draining her of more energy, hope and resolve. Each seemed to provide further evidence that she was on a one-way trip to oblivion. While that future held vague terrors, they were no more horrifying than the dehumanizing reality of her present.

Myra came up to Erin while she was taking a break, standing outside the door to the kitchen, smoking, which she had never previously done, and leadenly looking at the dark sky, oblivious to the stars.

"Hi, sport," said Myra. "What's up? You ain't looking so good."

"Hi," said Erin. "I'm O.K., I think. I'm just not making enough here to pay all the bills. I had some savings when I got here, but I'm going through that very quickly."

"Believe me," said Myra. "I know the feeling."

"I even thought about selling my car," said Erin. "but I don't have the pink slip, so I can't."

"Just as well," said Myra. "When you lose your wheels, you're really screwed. Speaking of which, that's what you might have to do to supplement what you're making at this place."

The words initially passed by her without making any impact. She paused and inhaled from the cigarette as the meaning of what Myra had implied began to make itself more clear. She felt an uneasy lump begin to form in the pit of her stomach.

"What did you say?" asked Erin. "Or rather, what did you mean?"

"Well, it's a way to make some more money, if that's what you need," said Myra.

"You're not serious," said Erin, stomping out the cigarette.

"Look, honey," said Myra. "There comes a time when you're faced with the reality that virtue is a luxury you can't afford. You get used to it."

"You?" asked Erin in disbelief.

"Sure," said Myra with a laugh. "What do you think? That I'm too good for that? I've been turning tricks on and off since I was seventeen."

"You're kidding me," said Erin, still unable to make Myra's admission of this reality fit with her own presumptions and expectations.

"Why would I do that?" Myra asked. "I'm just giving you another dose of reality. What are your choices? Theft? Are you going to go out and start stealing? I don't think so. So what are you gonna do? Handicraft? I don't mean to be insulting, but unless there's something about you that I don't know, you're fast running out of options."

"No!" said Erin, resolutely "Never. Not that. No way. I know you're trying to help, but I---there's no way that I could, or would, ever do that. I'd rather die first."

"That's what I said," said Myra. "Actually I bet it's what most everyone says. But then you find that it's not so bad. Like everything else, like your life here, you get used to it. Let me know," she said and went back into the diner.

Erin was badly shaken by the exchange. She had considered her descent into this hell to be one dimensional, related only to drugs. That she was perceived as being so close to criminal alternatives, theft and prostitution, stripped away the thin veil of respectability that she had unconsciously been clutching around herself.

Part of her knew that Myra was right. The cruel, indifferent arithmetic of her finances made that clear. But she had not been ready to take the last step downward or even to acknowledge that she was so close to the bottom.

She felt dizzy and nauseated, as though she had suddenly come to the edge of a precipice and had been forced to look down into a great void. She suppressed her symptoms and completed her shift in silence. By the time she got to her room, she was sweating and anxious. The nausea had increased and she vomited several times before she could fix.

The heroin calmed her down and she drifted off into an uneasy sleep.

When she awoke, it was three in the morning. The conversation with Myra returned with full force, evoking dread and agitation.

She dressed and got into her car. She drove through the deserted streets and out into the desert. She pulled off the main highway and onto a side road that she followed up to the crest of a small ridge. She pulled off the road, and turned off the motor. She pushed one of Chris's tapes into the tape deck.

His voice and the mellow tones of the guitar surged out of the speakers, filling the car with the familiar, caressing sounds. She closed her eyes and tried to concentrate only on the music, trying to obliterate everything else from the arid wasteland of her tortured existence. She desperately wanted to affix her soul to those sounds and let them transport her out of her nightmare and back to the life and the man she loved.

But as beautiful as they were, the sounds did not possess the magic of transport. For one of the few times in her recent past, she was experiencing the full amplitude of her emotions; the soaring beauty of the music and the wrenching agony of her plight and its futility.

She turned up the volume and opened the car door. She stood and looked up into the cold, dark night. She saw the stars that Chris had cherished and loved to tell her about. She couldn't find the order nor the patterns that were so familiar to him. She saw only disorder and distance.

Unable to endure the pain, she stopped the tape and sobbed for a long time. When she was able to compose herself she started the car and drove back to the dark, empty loneliness of her room.

158

Calculating how much heroin to use and when to fix was proving to be complicated and difficult. She had to dose far enough in advance of when she started her shift that she would be over the heaviest sedating effects by the time she arrived at the diner. If she miscalculated the time or dose, she was still high when she started work which was very uncomfortable.

She also had to be certain that she would take enough so that she wouldn't begin to experience withdrawal symptoms before the shift ended. Her anxiety and the shakes made her awkward, which made her more self-conscious and more anxious.

One night, at the end of her shift, Roy, the manager, asked her to come to his small office in the back. He pointed to the chair and she sat down nervously. He sat down lit a cigarette and offered her one, which she declined.

"Erin," he said, looking at her steadily, "I like you. I want you to know that. I don't know why you're here. That's none of my business. And, as long as you do your work, I'm not gonna bug you about your habit."

She started to protest but he waved her off.

Shit," he said. "I ain't stupid. I seen you getting sick at the end of your shift. Them long sleeves is a dead giveaway. But I really don't care about that as long as you do your job. Hell, Myra does just fine. She's a good worker.

"I know you ain't experienced like she is so I've been willing to cut you some slack. But lately, I've been getting some complaints. Nothing big, but some of the drivers, some of our regulars, say you been messing up their orders. They like you, too, so they don't want to cause no trouble.

"The long and short of it is, I can't have complaints. People get to talking and that's bad for business. Bad for our reputation. I know you're kind of in a bad situation, but you gotta know that if I keep getting complaints, I'm gonna have to let you go. You understand what I mean?"

She was silent, stunned by the fact that he knew her secret, and how precarious her situation had become. If she lost this job she couldn't work anyplace in town because too many people knew that she worked here and she'd have to ask for references. The word would be out that she was an addict. She's have to move again and that meant making new connections and facing new risks.

159

"I really appreciate your being so honest with me and giving me another chance," she said. "I won't let you down. I promise."

"O.K." he said. "That's all I have. Good luck."

For several days after the conversation with Roy, she did well. She was on constant alert, and the adrenaline that was surging through her system increased her vigilance. It also increased the speed with which the heroin was being metabolized, so she was having more difficulty avoiding withdrawal symptoms at the end of her shift. She was reluctant to take more heroin because she wanted to avoid the drowsiness.

One evening, she went through her routine of fixing. All went well until she began to inject the heroin and then the vein just seemed to disappear before her eyes. She felt the sharp sting as the heroin solution filtered into the tissues surrounding the vein. She withdrew the needle and flung the syringe on the floor.

She grabbed at the site of the injection and rubbed it with an alcohol sponge which caused more stinging. She knew that some of the solution had entered the vein, but she didn't know how much. She waited for the rush that told her that heroin had reached her brain. After a few seconds she experienced the tell-tale sensation: it was definite, but it was weak.

Now she faced another dilemma. She knew that the heroin that had leaked into the tissues would be absorbed by small vessels and eventually reach her brain. Therefore, if she injected too much more now, she could overdose when the effect of the two injections combined. If she didn't inject enough, or it was delayed too long, she would start to have withdrawal symptoms at work.

She began to panic. She decided to inject a smaller dose, hoping it would be enough to ensure that she didn't come apart at work. But, because of her anxiety, her hands were unsteady and she ruptured another vein and infiltrated most of the solution into the tissues.

She stopped the slight bleeding at the injection site and pondered her alternatives. She thought about calling in sick, but she knew they needed her and doing so would be further evidence of her unreliability. It was risky either way.

She tried to calm herself but wasn't successful. She took a long shower but the warm water was unable to help her sort out the frantic options that were surging through her brain.

By the time she arrived at the diner, she was beginning to experience a second wave of heroin effects, a numbing sedation which was mild. It would not have been unpleasant under different circumstances, but now it was alarming.

The diner was busy and she was feeling pushed to stay up with the pace. It seemed to her that there was more noise than usual and she was having difficulty taking orders smoothly. She found herself asking the customers to repeat themselves.

Several orders became confused in the kitchen, or so she thought. Then she mixed up the orders for adjacent tables. Then she switched two checks and had difficulty sorting out the error.

She was aware that some of the customers were displeased and tried to explain herself but couldn't do so. She was feeling increasingly numb and was able to connect that to the third wave of heroin being absorbed from her arm.

She went toward the kitchen, but toward the wrong door. Another waitress was coming out with a full tray and the two collided and fell to the floor among the shattered dishes, cups, glasses, silverware and food. She heard the angry cursing of the other waitress and tried to explain and apologize. She was sitting there on the floor, dazed and confused when she heard Myra's voice and then Roy's. They helped her into the back room and sat her down in his office.

"I'm sorry, Erin," said Roy. "This is it. I can't have you coming in here loaded. I'll have your check for you tomorrow. I don't intend to be mean or nasty, but you better not use me as a reference. I got to live with these people."

Myra called a cab for her and asked the driver to help her into her room. She was confused when he opened the door and helped her into the chair. She sat, dazed and numb, and tried to collect her thoughts, but the heroin was still in control. It did keep her from realizing that she had just slipped off the bottom rung of the ladder.

The next day, Myra came to her room. When Erin opened the door, her eyes were swollen and red.

"I'm real sorry about what happened to you, Honey," said Myra.

"Everyone was pullin for you. Even Roy. He really likes you. Can I come in?"

"Sure," said Erin, blinking back the sunlight. "I guess so. The place is such a mess, just like me." The shades hadn't been opened and the yellow light of the small lamp on the night stand was the only illumination.

"God, it's dark. I can barely see. Let's get some light and some air in here," said Myra, adjusting the shades and opening one of the windows. "I know you think this is the end of the world, Honey, but believe me, it ain't. Lots of us have been where you're at. The thing you got to do now is just maintain. Don't collapse. You can pull yourself out of this if you have the will and the guts. You're smart and good looking. You just gotta get your feet beneath you until you get a break. Then you'll be back on your way. By the way, here's your check. I think old Roy put a little extra in there for you to help you keep going."

"I don't think I can make it," said Erin, disconsolately hanging her head, sitting on the side of the bed. "I just don't see any way out. I'm a heroin addict, I just lost my job, I'm almost broke and I don't have anyplace to go."

"Sure you do," said Myra, brightly. "Just turn some tricks until you get back on your feet. Hey, did you hear that? I made a joke. Seriously though, it's not as though you're a member of high society with a reputation to ruin. After this is over you can just put it out of your mind. Every woman's a virgin on her wedding night."

"I just couldn't do that," said Erin.

"Look, all you got to do is get a bit loaded," said Myra. "I got some benzo's you can take. They make you real mellow and you just don't give a shit about anything. Just shut your mind off. Just disconnect your twat from the rest of your body. Men don't give a shit. They just want some place to stick their dick into. It might as well be your arm pit."

"No, no, no," moaned Erin. "It is too hideous, too repulsive to even consider. And what about AIDS and all those other nasty infections?"

"Well," said Myra, "You've got to be sure they use a rubber and you've got to douche with nonoxynol. If you're careful, you'll be O.K. Most of the Johns on this side of the border are truckers and they take pretty good care of themselves. Most of them have wives.

162

The Mexicans mostly use the houses on the other side of the border. Arty does a good job of taking care of us."

Arty?" asked Erin. "The drug dealer?"

"Sure," said Myra. "He wants to take good care of his customers."

"Meaning us?" asked Erin.

"Sure," said Myra. "He looks after us. Look, think it over. I know you already have, but you don't really have many options. It's gonna be tough for you to get a job around here because a lot of people know you was at the diner and they'll want to talk to Roy about you. He wouldn't want to badmouth you but he'll have to level with them. You could go someplace else, but you'd have to find a new connection and you don't have much money, which means you don't have much time. You just have to put all that Sunday School crap behind you, take a deep breath and do it.

"I'll leave you alone to think about it for a while. I'll check back with you tomorrow. Look, there ain't anything in it for me. I just kind of like you and wanna help you get back on your feet. That's all."

Erin took her hand. "I know that and I really appreciate it. You're a good friend, Myra."

"O.K.," said Myra. "So I'll see you tomorrow."

After she fixed, Erin sat on the bed, stupefied by her circumstances. She knew there was no other way out. She knew that when Myra came back the next she would have to agree and that she would become a prostitute. She tried to remember the different levels of Dante's Inferno, but it wouldn't come back to her. What had she done to earn this low place in hell? She tried to follow the thoughts but the heroin was making it difficult to concentrate so she rolled over on the bed, pulled the covers over her and let the drug pull her down into a numb, dreamless sleep.

* * *

The next day when Myra came by, Erin had showered and cleaned up the room. "O.K.," she said. "Let's get this over. Where's Arty?"

"He'll meet us if I call him," said Myra. "He has a pager."

They drove to a small neighborhood shopping center that had a public phone. Myra placed a phone call, hung up and waited for the call-back.

"He's gonna meet us here," said Myra when she returned to the car. "He'll be here in a few minutes."

After a brief wait, a black Pontiac Firebird drove up and the driver's window glided electrically down. The male face said, "Erin, you come with me. We're going to take a ride. Myra, wait here. We'll be back in about fifteen minutes."

Erin got into his car and they drove away. Her stomach was churning nervously. She tried to study his face. Since the first time she had seen him she had been fascinated by the fact that he didn't appear to be what he was. He could have been an insurance salesman. He appeared neither sinister nor evil.

"So," he said, not looking at her. "According to Myra, this'll be your first time."

"Yes," she answered leadenly.

"Well, you'll do fine," said Arty. "I think I can keep you pretty busy. You've got looks, a body and you're young. It's harder to keep business coming for Myra. That's why she has to work at the diner. You won't have to. But I guess that's over anyway. Open the glove compartment."

She did.

"Take out that pager," he said. "You know how to use one?"

"No."

"Take the little booklet, then," he said. "It's simple. Keep it in your purse or someplace where it's close by. When I page you, you call me on my cell phone and I'll tell you the name and the time. You'll always go to the same motel. I'll give you the room number. The John will be waiting for you. Make sure he puts on a rubber. Don't stay more than thirty minutes, tops. You be the one to leave. When you leave, just let the guy at the desk know so he can get the guy out of the room.

"The guy will pay you in cash. I'll tell you how much when I call., You keep thirty per cent. We'll meet once a day so you can give me the money, and I can give you the smack if you need it. It's that simple. You got any questions?"

"I don't think so," she heard herself answer, not completely believing where she was or what she was doing.

"If you have to get away for a couple of days or you want some time off, let me know ahead of time so I don't book you. But don't do that very often. Like I said, I'll be able to keep you pretty busy. Just remember, it's all business. I treat my girls good because it's good business. Take good care of yourself. Keep yourself looking good and remember, don't stay long. They'll want you to, but don't do it. Thirty minutes tops. I'll have some business for you tonight."

"All right," said Erin.

They had returned to Myra's car. Erin got out of Arty's car and put the pager in her purse.

"You all right?" asked Myra when Erin got back into the car.

"Yeah," said Erin resolutely. "I'm fine."

Chapter Twenty

That night Erin prepared to start her life on the lowest level of her inferno. She was sedated by a combination of the heroin and a street version of clonepin, a benzodiazepine, the class of drugs that includes valium and librium. When the pager beeped its mechanical message, she called Arty's number and was given terse instructions.

At the appointed time, she drove to the motel, knocked on the door and entered a life that she would never have believed possible. She was determined to treat the customer the same as she would have in the diner. Just be pleasant, and provide him what he wants. It's just business.

Despite her inner revulsion, she found that Myra was right. With the help of the drug, she was able to maintain distance, to detach the physical act from any moral or spiritual consequences. She was relieved that she was capable of performing what was required in order to survive and refused to deal with moral self-recriminations. She was determined to keep going, to put one foot in front of the other, until, in Myra's words, she got a break.

Over the next several weeks she woodenly went through the passive process of being fondled, groped and entered by a dull succession of males with alcoholic breath, unshaven faces and primitive expectations. Despite her minimal responses, the lack of even a pretense of enjoyment, her looks made her popular, and as Arty had predicted, kept her busy.

The financial crises had receded into a murky pool of heroin, benzos and vague repulsion. Her life had been reduced to the numb acceptance of a hazy world of personal degradation made more dehumanizing by the lack of defining dimensions and contrasts. It was a bleak, formless, colorless, empty place that offered neither nourishment nor the morally affirming consequences of pain.

It was on another such night when she answered the pager and went to the motel. The John was leering at her aggressively when he answered her knock. The smell of hard liquor on his breath was pungent and strong. She noticed a half-empty quart of Old Crow on the dresser.

It crossed her mind that this might be one of the situations from which she should retreat immediately. Arty had advised her to do so if the customer was drunk, but she didn't do so immediately, when she was close to the door, and the opportunity faded.

He began kissing and fondling her roughly. She told him to disrobe and took off her own clothes. When she returned to the bed and sat down, he came at her again, clumsily thrusting his body on top of hers, unsuccessfully attempting to achieve an erection.

"Come on, honey," he said. "Make it hard." But she was unable to do so even with vigorous manipulation. He became more frustrated and then angry.

"God damn it," he snarled. "What kind of pro are you if you can't even give me a hard on. You ain't doing it right, that's for damned sure. Now come on. Let's get it on." But despite his and her best efforts he was unable to become hard enough to penetrate.

"God damn you," he said. "What are you some kind of a drug addict that you can't do it right? Look at your arms. You're nothing but a God damned junkie. No wonder it ain't working for me. You're disgusting."

He slapped her across the face. Stung by the blow, she struggled to get away from him. She was able to get to her feet, but he grabbed at her arm with his left hand. He swung his right fist and it delivered a glancing blow to the side of her face.

She was knocked backward and fell, hitting the back of her head on the corner of the dresser. She was unconscious when she landed on the floor.

He panicked when he saw her lying helpless on the floor. He dressed as fast as he could, fled the room and sped away in his pick-up.

The clerk on duty in the motel had been watching the timer that he always set in motion when the girls came in. He looked up to see the pick-up drive off. He phoned the room but there was no answer.

167

Concerned, he ran to the room and found Erin lying unconscious on the floor.

He called 911 and the paramedics arrived quickly and moved her by ambulance to the county hospital. The motel man then called Arty and told him what had happened. Arty then telephoned Myra.

There was an insistent tone that kept occurring at regular intervals. Gradually, the sound became more clear and Chris recognized it as the ringing of his telephone. He switched on the light by his bed, noting that it was three in the morning.

"Hello," he said sleepily.

"Is this Chris Childs?" asked the female voice.

"Yes," he said, rubbing his eyes. "Who is this? What do you want?"

"It's not important who I am," said the voice. "You know a woman named Erin?"

Instantly he was wide awake. "Where is she? Do you know where she is?"

"She's in the hospital," she said. "She's been hurt but they don't think it's serious."

"What hospital? Where is she?" he asked frantically.

"El Centro, California," she said. "The county hospital. The doctor's name is Phillips. They're keeping her for observation. She got slugged."

"Slugged? What do you mean?" he demanded.

"There was a fracas in the diner," she lied. "She got hit accidentally. You should get down here. She needs help. She doesn't belong here."

"How did you find me?" he asked. "How did you get my number?"

"I went to her place and went through her things," she said. "There was some tapes with your name on them in her car. Your phone number was in a little book she had.

"Listen," she continued. "There's some things you should know. She's been doing a gram and a half of heroin a day and she's also had a lot of benzos--mostly clonepin. I don't know if they'll give her any in the hospital so she'll probably go into withdrawal and be sick as shit. She'll be a mess. You better get down here and help her. They sure as hell ain't gonna listen to me."

"O.K." he said. "Thanks. I really can't tell you how much I appreciate this. I'll be there as soon as I can get a plane. What's your name?"

"Myra," she said. "But that don't matter. I won't be around when you get here. Just hurry. She's a sweet kid. She don't belong here."

The phone clicked and Chris closed his eyes as he replaced the receiver. His mind was racing with the adrenaline surge caused by his fear and excitement. He sorted through the information she had given him. El Centro. Dr. Phillips. Benzos. He stopped for a moment to gather himself and plan his actions. He dialed the number for Carlos Garza and reached his exchange.

"Dr. Garza's exchange."

"This is an emergency," he said anxiously. "Have Dr. Garza call this number."

"Dr. Garza is not on call."

"This is a personal emergency. Tell him to call Dr. Childs."

"Oh, yes, Dr. Childs," she said. "I'll tell him right away."

While he was waiting for the call, he picked up the phone book and sorted through to find the section for airlines. The phone rang, startling him. He grabbed the receiver. "Carlos?"

"Chris, what's up?" said Carlos. "Did you find Erin?"

"I just got a phone call. She was taken to a hospital in El Centro, the county hospital. The gal that called me said she had been hit accidentally in some fight in the diner where she was working."

"Did she tell you anything else?" asked Carlos.

"Yeah," said Chris. "She said the doctor's name is Phillips. She's been using a gram and a half of heroin a day and some other drugs, benzos she called them. I think she mentioned another name but I can't remember it."

"Clonepin?" asked Carlos.

"Yeah, that's it," said Chris.

"O.K. That's important," said Carlos. "They won't want to give her any sedatives if they're worried about trauma to her brain, but she'll start withdrawing if they don't. I'll call Phillips and see what's going on. Are you planning to go down there?"

"On the first plane I can get," said Chris.

169

"I'll call down there and get back to you as soon as I learn something," said Carlos.

After he put down the phone, Chris walked nervously around the room. He was frightened about the extent of her injuries but despite that, felt joyful that he knew where she was and that he would be seeing her again in a few hours if everything went well. Then another concern occurred to him. She might not be willing to come home with him.

He was fairly certain that Myra would not have told her about their phone conversation, so his appearance was going to be a total surprise. What if she didn't want to see him? What if she were angry at his intrusion? What if---The phone rang again.

"Carlos?"

"Yeah. Look, she's gonna be all right. She got hit by some guy. She has a minor concussion but the MRI is negative for any serious damage. They would normally release her in the morning, but he's agreed to keep her until you get there. I told him before noon. Can you do that?"

"I think so," said Chris. "I'll get the first flight for San Diego and rent a car. I should be able to make it."

"O.K.," said Carlos. "He's gonna give her enough methadone and valium for a couple of days. That should give you time to get back here, even if you drive."

"What are we gonna do when we get her back here?" asked Chris, submerging his own questions about whether she might not be willing to return with him.

"Didn't you tell me that Dr. Bernstein had talked to the people in the methadone program about getting her on the long term program? I'll check it out. If there's any problem, I'll call him. Do you have his number?"

Chris rifled through his rolodex and read the number.

"O.K. my friend," said Carlos. "Go to it. I'll take care of things back here. Together, we'll pull her out of this mess. One more thing, Chris."

"What is it?"

"Drive carefully."

"Absolutely," said Chris. "Carlos, I can't tell you how much this means to me."

"You don't have to. See you in a couple of days."

Chris parked the rental car in the visitor's parking lot and walked into the hospital through the automatic doors. He followed the signs to the information desk. He explained who he was and the receptionist paged Dr. Phillips. When the page was answered, he was told to pick up the phone on the desk.

"Hello," he said. "This is Chris Childs. I'm here to see Erin Leahy."

"Oh, yeah," was the response. "You're the guy Carlos Garza said was coming. You made good time. Come up to third west. I'll meet you at the nurse's station."

He followed the signs to the elevators and went to the third floor. He walked to the nurses station and saw a physician in his late thirties writing in a chart at the counter.

"Dr. Phillips?"

"Chris Childs," said the doctor. "Let's go sit down." He led the way to a small lounge.

"I don't know exactly what happened in that fracas. She has a bump on the side of her face. Just superficial. Didn't break the skin but she'll have a bruise there. She also has a lump on the back of her head. That's what knocked her out. She has a mild concussion as a result. Neurologically she's fine and the MRI is negative. So she should be fine.

"She'll have a headache and a small amount of temporary memory loss about the incident which should improve over the next few days. If the headache becomes more severe, make certain that someone sees her immediately. It could indicate that she has something more serious going on, but I don't think that's going to happen.

"The other thing to look out for is somnolence, getting sleepy. That's going to be a bit more tricky since she's going to have some valium. Normally I wouldn't give her anything like methadone or valium. We see a lot of addicts here. We just let them go their own way and they get back on heroin and get their benzos on the street.

"Carlos said she's a special patient of his so I already gave her first doses of methadone and valium, as he requested, to prevent her from going through withdrawal or having to use again. Here's a prescription for a few more pills to give you some time to get back to the Bay Area. She looks like a very sweet person--not the kind you'd expect to be involved in this shit."

"She isn't," said Chris. "We're going to get her away from all of this."

"Good luck," said Phillips. "It isn't easy."

"Thanks."

"She's in 316," said Phillips. "I moved her to a single after I talked to Carlos. She can go as soon as she signs some papers. You can pick up the meds at the pharmacy on the first floor."

"Thanks a lot," said Chris, shaking his hand. "I really appreciate everything you've done."

He walked up to the door of the room and looked through the small square pane of glass. His eyes filled with tears when he saw her lying quietly on the white bed. The pallor of her skin was startling. He opened the door quietly and walked in. Her face was turned to the opposite wall.

"Erin?" he said, but the sound caught in his throat and he had to clear his voice and repeat, "Erin?"

She responded with a start. Her recognition of his voice brought her head around quickly, her eyes wide with surprise. Her mouth opened as though she were about to speak. There was a moment of joy that quickly faded as shame and pain distorted her features. "Oh, God," she moaned and began crying, turning away from him.

He walked around to the other side of the bed. He sat down on the bed and put his arms around her shoulders. Lowering his head, he kissed her hair and her forehead again and again.

"I love you so much," he said. "I adore you. You'll never know how miserable I've been without you. I'll never let you go again. There's nothing I wouldn't face with you. Don't you know that? I love you, Erin."

"Oh, Chris." she sobbed. "I wish I were dead. I can't bear to have you see me like this. I just want to die. I don't want to live."

"I'm sorry," he said, caressing her. "I won't permit that. Nor will Carlos. He's waiting for us in the city. We're going to cure this thing. We're going to fight this together. Carlos and another wonderful man that I met are going to help us. We won't fail this time. We can't. I won't permit it."

"But how are we---"

172

"Never you mind about the details now," said Chris. It's all been arranged."

"But how did you find me?" she asked.

"You have a good friend named Myra," he said. "She found the tapes in your car and my phone number at your apartment. She called last night after they brought you here."

"Oh, Chris," she said. "It's been so awful. I'm so ashamed. When you hear it all you won't want me."

"That blow to your head must have messed up your hearing," he said, kissing the tears from her cheeks. "Now listen carefully." He lifted her chin and looked into her eyes.

"Erin, my beloved, I know why this all happened. This was done by an evil human being who tried to destroy us. You talked me out of killing him, which was correct. But now we have to do whatever is necessary to cure you. Then we can continue our lives and be truly rid of him. We can't let him win. I love you and I'll fight for you with every ounce of strength and determination I possess. You've got to let me win this battle with you.

"I know you must have been through unspeakable torture, far more than I know. But I've been suffering my own pain. It's been horrible not knowing where you were; not being able to hold you and comfort you. Darling, I've learned a lot about addiction and I truly believe that we can lick this thing together.

"Please come back with me and we'll make it happen. Won't you try? Won't you give me a chance to help you?"

She was sitting now, with her arms around him and her head on his chest. "I thought I'd never see you again," she said. "I thought my whole life was gone. I'm afraid that if I do come back I'll just lose it again. I couldn't take that. I'd rather die."

"No more of that," said Chris. "This is where we start the rest of our lives together. Right here and now. Right at this moment. We'll do whatever it takes. O.K.?"

"Oh, Chris," she said. "I do want to. I don't want to be apart. Being lonely and separated from you was so terrible."

"Never again, my darling. Never again."

They checked out of the hospital, got her medications, and drove to her room. Her car was parked on the street where Myra had left it.

"I'm so embarrassed to have you see this place," said Erin. "It's the pits."

She opened the door, expecting the dingy squalor from which she had departed. To her surprise, the room was clean. The shades were open. The bed was made and on the pillows was a note and a bunch of flowers. She opened the note and read:

"I tried to help but I guess I got you in deeper. I'm sorry. I know from talking to Chris that he'll be able to take care of you and get you out of this hell hole. You don't belong here. I don't like good-byes. Here's my phone number if you ever need to call. Good luck. Myra

She held the note out for Chris to read and turned away with her nose in the flowers.

"I told you she was a good friend," said Chris after he read the note.

"Can you imagine," she said. "I haven't even seen or smelled a flower for months. I'm so eager to get my life back."

"That's the spirit," said Chris. "Let's get your stuff into your car and get going."

They loaded her car and then drove his rental car back to the local office and returned it.

"How are you feeling?" he asked, when he returned from the rental office to her car.

"I feel a little shaky," she said. "I'm not having any strong withdrawal symptoms but I feel kind of spaced out. Just a little headache."

"Do you want me to drive?" he asked.

"Please," she said. "I want to just sit beside you and watch you. Will that bother you?"

"Are you kidding?" he laughed, leaning over and kissing her.

Driving out of town, they passed Roy's diner. She watched the familiar sign slip away in the mirror and said nothing.

"Would you mind if I played some music?" she asked. "I feel like I want to have as many of my senses stroked as I can. It's like waking up from a long sleep."

He smiled when the tape began playing his voice and his music.

174

"How strange to hear it like this," he said. "I don't listen to these tapes. Did you listen to them often?"

"Not often," she said. "It was too painful. But there were some very important times when I did. They were like a tether that attached me to you."

They drove west to San Diego and then headed north. She had been noticing the changes in vegetation as they approached the coast.

"Could we stop and see the ocean?" she asked.

"Of course," he said. "Great idea."

He began looking for the turn-offs that he remembered. When he saw the sign that indicated La Jolla, he took the exit and followed the signs to the beach. They parked in the public parking lot, took off their shoes and walked down the steps to the beach, hand in hand.

"How are you feeling now," he asked. "Any better?"

"It's very strange," she said. "I haven't felt 'normal' for a long time. Certainly not recently with the benzos. Now I feel kind of like I'm suspended between where I was and where I want to be. I feel tentative. It's not really bad, but hasn't gotten 'good' yet either. But it's tolerable because we're together and I know it'll continue to improve."

"It has to help just to get you out of that place," said Chris.

"I know that many people find the desert magnificent, but I've never been able to enjoy it," she said. "That's why I went there. It was as though I had to punish myself." She closed her eyes and took a deep breath. "Just being near the ocean is so calming and reassuring. It reminds me of our trip to Mendocino. It's so refreshing."

"I know," he agreed. "I can just feel my body starting to vibrate in rhythm with the waves. Really."

The sky was a clear, deep blue, with no clouds in view. Long legged sand-pipers ran along the edge of the water while gulls soared overhead. A gentle breeze nudged against their faces as they walked slowly along the damp sand silently his arm around her shoulder, hers around his waist.

After eating in a small cafe that overlooked the sea, they resumed their drive north.

"Are you tired?" she asked. "I can drive. I'm feeling pretty good. No serious drug sickness. Just a little nausea."

"No. I'm fine," he said. "Do you want to take another nap?"

"No," she said. "I just want to watch you."

He smiled at her and blew her a kiss. "I have some things to tell you. Do you feel up to it?"

"You bet," she said. "As long as you're here."

"First, I talked to your parents." he said. "I called them and then came down and talked to them."

"That was really sweet of you," she said. "They're really worried, aren't they?"

"Of course they are," he said. "Erin, I didn't know what to tell them. I didn't want to break a confidence. The amazing thing is, they guessed."

"About the heroin?" she said, astonished. "How could they? I was always so straight."

He looked over at her then pulled off at the next exit, and stopped the car. "There's something they never told you about your mother."

Her eyes widened. "She was an addict?"

"Yes."

"I always had the strange sense that there was something about her that I didn't know. Wow. You know, it's very strange, but I feel closer to her now. I'm sure I wouldn't have before this all happened. I would have been appalled. But now it's a strange sense of sharing something with her even though it's so terrible." She was silent for a moment and then something else occurred to her. "Oh my God. It's genetic, isn't it?"

"They don't know for certain," said Chris, holding her hands. "It may be. I talked about that with that professor I mentioned to you. He's one of the world's experts in this field and he says it's not certain. But it's not as though you were doomed to be an addict. I'm sure it would've never happened to you if it hadn't been for that asshole Martin. That's something else I have to tell you about."

"What?" she asked.

"He was killed."

"Cal?" she asked, her eyes widened in horror.

"Yeah," he said. "He was murdered. Shot in the head. A gang-type execution."

"Oh, that's terrible," she said. "Poor Cal."

He looked at her in astonishment. "You can feel sympathy for that son-of-a-bitch?"

"Yes," she said. "I can. Isn't that amazing? I feel sympathy for the person I genuinely liked and enjoyed--not the one who did this to me."

"He's all the same to me," said Chris.

"Do they know who did it?"

"No," he said. "But it was drug-related."

"How awful," she said.

"I'm sorry," he said. "I'm giving you a lot to handle all at once."

"No," she said. "That's all right. I think it'll be better for me to begin coping with real world again. I'm going to have to call my folks and talk to them, but I want to wait until I'm feeling a bit more settled. Can I stay with you in the city?"

"I told you. I'm not letting you out of my sight."

Chapter Twenty-One

They spent the night at a motel on the outskirts of Santa Barbara. Before their separation, their intimacy had included a respectful openness with regard to nudity. Now they both felt awkward and shy. Chris also correctly anticipated that sexuality was going to have to be approached very delicately, rebuilding confidence slowly. After putting on pajamas, they slept in a careful, sibling-like embrace.

When they awoke the next morning Chris said, "My internal music had stopped waking me while you were gone. It just started up again. It's a bit faint, but it's back."

"You mean I took away your music?" she said. "That's terrible."

"You've become the center of my soul, whether you like it or not," he said. "I happen to like it. It's just another indication of how important you are in my life."

"What about your band?" she asked. "You've been playing, haven't you?"

"No. I quit a while ago," he said. "I just couldn't do it. But I'll start again. I've already begun to hear some new motifs. I certainly feel more like singing and playing than I have in along time. How do you feel? Any headache?"

"None," she said. "That sleep was the best I've had in a long time. See how therapeutic you are for me?"

They spent the day driving up the coast route so they could enjoy the scenery. Erin experienced some mild withdrawal symptoms which she was able to tolerate. Her mood continued to improve as she let the nightmare of her desert experience fade into a past which already seemed unreal.

They drove over the mountains from Santa Cruz through Los Gatos as it was getting dark, and the lights of Santa Clara Valley twinkled their welcome.

"Now I really feel like I'm getting close to home," she said.

They drove to his place in Portola Valley to spend the night.

"We can move into the city tomorrow," he said.

"That means you're going to have to commute again," she said.

"That doesn't bother me," he said. "I don't mind the drive. There's more for you to do in the city. It's pretty isolated out here. I'm going to call Carlos and find out what he's arranged."

She turned on the music and wandered out onto the patio and began to inhale the fragrant air. She was standing, leaning against a post when he came out.

"It's all set for you to come to the clinic tomorrow morning. Dr. Bernstein, that guy I told you about, made sure there wouldn't be any problems. They want us to be there by seven."

"I just love this place," she said. "Remember that first afternoon? What a thrilling experience you are. Come here and hold me."

Her arms tightly held him to her and he kissed her hair. They stood silently for a long moment.

"When I'm with you like this, I begin to believe that it can happen, that I can be cured and that we can have our life together."

"I can understand why it seemed so impossible for you where you were," he said. "It must have seemed like being on another planet. But we can do it. We have help and we have a lot going for us. Just look up into that sky. Have you ever seen anything more magnificent?

"And we've been given the intellectual power not only to be able to study and understand the universe but also to be thrilled by it. That's what I've begun to appreciate since I've been talking to Dr. Bernstein. It just makes me tingle with excitement. What could be better? A clear, beautiful sky and you in my arms. We'll have a lot of these together."

"Will you teach me about the stars?" she asked.

"Absolutely," he said. "And about the brain. Studying neurobiology is as thrilling and vast as the universe. We'll do it all together."

"To music," she said.

"To our music," he said.

The following morning they left Portola Valley early and drove to San Francisco. Chris dropped Erin at the clinic and then went to the apartment to unload his things. He checked in with his voice mail, answered some messages and left a message with the secretary telling her where he could be reached. Then he busied himself with some work and waited for Erin to call.

After he dropped her off, Erin went to the admission desk and presented her identification card. The clerk sorted through some charts on her desk and retrieved one that had her name and identification number on it.

"You were here for a detox a few months ago, weren't you?"

"Yes," she answered.

"O.K. Now you're scheduled for maintenance. One of the main differences is the counseling. You'll be assigned a counselor who'll meet with you later this morning and explain how the system works."

The administrative processing was completed and she underwent an exam by a clinic physician, Dr. Reynolds, a middle aged, scholarly looking man.

"The detox didn't work for you?" he asked

"Not when the dose got below ten milligrams," she said.

"It usually doesn't," he said. "That program's not worth a damn. It's a waste of time and money, but it's the law. They leave these important matters in the hands of politicians and bureaucrats. No wonder it's all screwed up. Let's see. You haven't been addicted for the required time, but is says you've been granted an exception by the Director. You must know some important people."

"My fiancé does," said Erin, realizing as she said it that she and Chris weren't really engaged, nor had they ever discussed marriage. It just seemed natural to identify him as such, but realizing she had not told the truth, she blushed.

"Well, good," he said. "If you're really motivated to break your habit, this program can change your life. Good luck. We'll start you at forty milligrams, which is what you've been getting on the prescription. Have you been feeling all right?"

"Yes," she said.

"Have you had any withdrawal symptoms?" he asked.

"I had some a couple of days ago, but I'm feeling pretty normal now."

"Well, you're still taking the valium," he said. "When you've finished getting off that you may experience some anxiety and insomnia. Let your counselor know or contact me and we'll adjust your dose. Good luck."

After she dosed, she looked at the slip she had been given. It directed her to the office of Margo Sutherland. She knocked and heard a voice tell her to enter.

The woman at the desk looked up at her, smiled and extended her hand.

"Welcome," she said. "I'm Margo. And you must be---"

"Erin."

"Ah, yes," she said, crossing off the name on list on her desk. "May I have your folder, please."

Erin handed her the folder that contained the papers she had been accumulating.

"Have a seat while I go over these," said Margo.

Erin sat and watched her. She was middle-aged, well groomed and had an air of effectiveness about her. She was attractive, with pleasant features, but lacked the qualities of beauty. Her brown hair was pulled back from her face and was tinged with gray. She put own the file and turned to face Erin.

"Well, now," said Margo. "Where to begin? I see you haven't been addicted long. Why don't you tell me why and how you became addicted."

Erin told her the story.

"My God," said Margo, genuinely disturbed. "That's awful. What a terrible person."

"He was killed rather recently," said Erin. "Shot."

"In Berkeley?" asked Margo.

"Yes," said Erin.

"I read about that," said Margo. "Well, at least he won't be hurting others. So the first time you were here, you came after an overdose. Was that accidental or intentional?"

"Completely accidental," said Erin. "I just panicked and injected too much."

"Who found you?" asked Margo.

"My fiancé," said Erin. "Well, he's not really my fiancé yet."

"And he got you to the hospital?" asked Margo.

"Yes," said Erin. "He called 911. I woke up here.

"And Dr. Garza took care of you?" asked Margo.

"Yes," said Erin. "He's a friend of---of Chris's."

"He's one of the best physicians I know, and I know what I'm talking about. I'm an RN. I was married to a surgeon. Carlos is one of the special ones. So that's when you went through the detox?"

"Yes."

"But it didn't work?" asked Margo.

"I was fine for about two weeks, but then I just began to fall apart when the dose kept getting lower," said Erin.

"If that program doesn't work for someone with as short an addiction history as you, it won't work for anyone," said Margo. "But let's put that aside for now. I need to know more about you. Why do you think you were so susceptible to heroin addiction?"

"I'm not sure," said Erin. "I was adopted, and I just found out that my real mother was a heroin addict."

"And you never knew that until just recently?"

"Very recently," said Erin.

"That's fascinating," said Margo. "Tragic but fascinating. It may be a reason. It may be the reason. But whatever, the important thing for you to know is that you're very susceptible. You might have gone through your whole life and never come in contact with this terrible drug, but the fact is that you did, you became addicted and now you have to deal with it.

"Methadone works. You learned that from your detox experience. It can turn off your body's craving for heroin and permit you to function as a normal person. The price you pay is that you're addicted to methadone. You're trading one addiction for another. Don't make any mistake about that.

"The difference is that methadone, taken carefully, is safe. It has very few side effects. It's taken by hundreds of thousands of people around the world every day. It's been used for thirty years, and that experience has given us a lot of answers about what methadone is and what it is not."

"First," said Margo. "It's not a magic bullet. I like to think of it more as a bridge between addiction and being completely normal.

The ultimate goal is to gradually get you off methadone and back to being completely drug free.

"That will take courage, commitment and patience. Most of the people in this program have been addicted for years--even decades. Their brains have become so accommodated to heroin and other drugs that it takes a long time to get them to the point where they can be completely without heroin or methadone. The brain has to be chemically re-calibrated and re-balanced and that takes time. If they become impatient and try to get off too quickly they'll usually relapse and have to start all over again. It's a difficult road.

"There are a lot of studies that demonstrate that when addicts are placed on methadone, their heroin use drops dramatically. Criminal behavior also decreases, as do the health problems associated with heroin use.

"These studies also show that if skilled counseling is added to the program, there is a further improvement in all categories. So, to be on the maintenance program you have to agree to attend counseling on a regular basis. You'll have both group sessions and one-on-one sessions with me. While you're new, there'll be more frequent one-on-ones so we can get to know each other more quickly. We'll meet for an hour at a time.

"Now, something about me," she continued. "I told you I was an R.N., married to a surgeon. The ideal couple, right? Ideal until we both became addicted to heroin. It destroyed our marriage and our professional lives. I'd be dead right now if I hadn't gotten on a methadone program.

"My former husband wasn't so fortunate. He died of an overdose, leaving our children with the terrible shame and agony of having their father's image destroyed. I tell you this not to elicit your sympathy but by way of providing you with my credentials--not only professional credentials, but addiction credentials and human credentials. I've been there and now I'm back. I was on methadone for three years. I've now been off for ten. I want you to remember that every time you look at me. This stuff works. I'm living proof.

"Here's the schedule of the groups meetings," she said. "I'll see you alone at this same time next week. By the way, some people find Narcotics Anonymous very helpful. You should consider going to a meeting and checking it out. Any questions?"

Erin was still reeling from the power of Margo's revelations. "I

183

don't think so."

"Here's my card," said Margo. "It has my office phone number here and I wrote my home number on the back. If you have any questions, any problems; if you start feeling sick or wanting to use, call me. I can't help you if you don't ask. See you in group. By the way, come to my office fifteen minutes before group and I'll tell you a little about the format."

Erin left the office and went back to the lobby where she phoned Chris. Then she walked outside to wait for him. She watched the people entering and leaving the clinic's several doors. It was the same mix of people that could be seen entering and leaving other clinics around the hospital. There was nothing about them that made them conspicuous as drug addicts. They looked like ordinary people.

She heard the beep of a horn and turned to see Chris waving from his car. She got in and learned over to kiss him. "Hi there," she said.

"How're you doing?" he asked. "Do you feel O.K.? How was it?"

"I feel fine," she said. "Maybe a little heavy, but not bad. No withdrawal symptoms. I think this program is going to be able to help me. I met my counselor. She's really impressive. An RN who used to be an addict, but cleaned up on methadone."

"Wow!" said Chris. "There's some credibility."

"Exactly. I have to go to group sessions once a week and I'm also going to meet with her privately once a week at the beginning."

"Good," said Chris. "So you feel supported?"

"Very well supported, thank you," she said.

"How about physically?" he asked. "How do you feel?"

"Better," she said. "Still a bit uneasy, but the nausea is almost gone. No headache at all."

"Great," said Chris. "Carlos called. He'd like to see you in the next day or so to check up on you. You can call him and make an appointment."

"All right," she said. "I'm looking forward to seeing him. I'm also going to call my folks."

When they got back to the apartment, she went into the bedroom and dialed the number in Simi Valley.

"Hello," said the familiar voice. Erin's throat constricted with emotion.

"Mom," she said. "It's me."

"Oh my God, Erin, where are you? Are you all right?"

"I'm in San Francisco, with Chris," she said. "We just got here this morning. I'm in a drug treatment program and I'm fine."

"Thank the lord," said her mother. "We were so worried about you. Your father was half crazy with worry. I'll have to call and tell him as soon as I hang up. He'll want to talk to you himself. Where were you, Erin? What were you doing?"

"It's a long and painful story, Mom," she said. "I'll tell you all about it when I'm feeling stronger."

"Well, when can we see you?" asked her mother. "Can you come down here?"

"Not right away, Mom," she said. "I need to get more into the treatment program before I can do that. But I'll be talking to you regularly now. The silence is over."

"Oh I'm so relieved," said her mother. "Chris probably told you that he came down to see us. What a wonderful young man. Your father hasn't stopped talking about him. I'm so glad that you're with him. You give him our love."

"I will, Mom. Mom, I'm sorry I put you through this. You shouldn't have had to suffer this way."

"Neither should you, honey," said her mother. "Chris told us about that terrible man. But I know things are going to get better now. I can just feel it. Give me your phone number so your father can call."

Erin gave her the number and they hung up. She went back into the living room where Chris was working on a manuscript.

"It meant so much to them that you went to see them," she said, sitting down on his lap.

"It meant a lot to me," he said, holding her to him. "They're wonderful people, like you."

She moved over on the couch beside him. "Something happened today that I have to tell you about."

"Something bad?" he asked.

"I don't think so," she said. "Maybe you will. I was describing something in one of the interviews, I think it was with the doctor, and I described you as 'my fiancé'. I just couldn't think of what else to call you and it popped out. 'Boy friend' seemed inane and sophomoric and 'significant other' sounds like something out of a sociology text."

He smiled. "So what is this, a confession or a proposal?"

"I'm not sure," she said. "Maybe a little of both. I'm not talking about rushing into anything. I know I have a lot of work to do. But it occurred to me while I was waiting for you that maybe if that was something I could look forward to, to shoot for, it might really be helpful. You know, if and when I can consider myself cured, maybe then. Is it something you want?"

"Of course it is," he said. "But I don't know if I like that way of thinking about it. Getting married shouldn't be a prize you win. It should be something we do because we love each other and want to spend our lives together. Look, what I'm saying is that I don't think I want to wait. I don't know how long this program is going to last but I don't want to be tied to some kind of external landmark. I know it's too soon now, but in a few months maybe it won't be. I want to marry you and I don't want to commit myself to waiting longer than necessary.'

"That's really touching," she said. "You'd marry me even if I were still an addict."

"Erin, I wanted to marry you before this all happened and nothing has changed my mind," he said. "The only question is when is the right time."

She looked at him and shook her head. "You really are wonderful. You're right. Let's see how this program goes and then make a decision."

"Meanwhile, you can keep calling me your fiancé if you want to," he said.

Chapter Twenty-Two

On the appointed day, Erin returned to Margo Sutherland's office and was promptly ushered in.

"Sit down," said Margo with a warm smile. "How's it going?"

"I think it's going well," said Erin.

"No withdrawal symptoms?" she asked

"None," said Erin. "Not even a bit of nausea."

"Are you having any craving for heroin?" asked Margo.

"No. None," said Erin.

"Do you get any sensation of a high after you get your methadone?"

"Just a slight kind of a glow," said Erin. "It's very mild. It doesn't last."

"When does that happen?" asked Margo.

"About noon," said Erin.

"When do you usually dose?' asked Margo.

"About eight o'clock," said Erin.

"The timing's right," said Margo. It's happening right when your plasma level should be the highest. You'll accommodate to it. It'll just disappear. But it's not bothersome?"

"No, not at all," said Erin. "It's very soft and brief."

"Well, we'll keep track of that as we go along," said Margo. "Have you seen Dr. Garza?"

"Yes," said Erin. "I saw him a couple of days ago. He said that there are no after effects from the concussion."

"Great," said Margo. "It sounds like everything's going well. The real reason I wanted to see you now is to tell you a few things about the way I run my group counseling sessions. First, and most important, everything that's said in group is confidential. You signed a form on the first day saying you would maintain confidentiality, but you need to know that I take it very seriously. We can't accomplish anything if everyone doesn't feel comfortable about exposing some very difficult and painful things about themselves. So we all have to have a reverence for that trust and a deep respect for the confidentiality it's built on.

"Second, these groups aren't like AA or NA groups. They're not at all confrontational. You don't have to speak at all unless you want to. No one will question you. Mostly what happens is that members of the group have some issues that are bothering them, that they want to discuss. That leads to getting others involved and the exchanges just happen.

"It's not very structured. I try to keep things going, but avoid being too controlling or intrusive.

"I've made the decision to put you in an all-women's group. That's not necessarily permanent. I have some good co-ed groups that you could change to if that becomes interesting to you. I just have a feeling that it would be better to start you in a women's group and I wanted you to know that it was my decision. Any questions?"

"I don't think so," said Erin.

"O.K., then. Let's go."

They went down the hall and entered a conference room in which chairs had been placed in a circle.

"Good morning, group," said Margo. "We have a new member. Her name is Erin. Do you have anything you want to say, Erin?"

"Not today," she said.

"All right," said Margo. "Who has some issues to get us started?"

"I've got one," said an angry middle-aged Hispanic woman.

"Why don't you introduce yourself," said Margo.

"Oh, right. I'm Elvira, Erin."

"Pleased to meet you," said Erin.

"O.K. I'd like to talk about that prick Dr. Carter."

"Why so mad?" asked Margo.

"That son of a bitch took one of my steps away."

"For your understanding, Erin, steps are take-home privileges which you can earn by complying with all the rules and being fully engaged in recovery. The higher the step number, the greater the

188

amount of freedom you're permitted and the fewer times a week you have to come to the clinic to dose. When you get to step six, you only have to come to the clinic once a week. So what's your beef, Elvira?"

"I was on step four and my urine came up positive for codeine. I had a prescription from my doctor. I was coughing and he gave · me some cough syrup that had codeine in it."

"So what's the problem," said another woman about the same age as Elvira. "They should excuse the dirty urine if you had a prescription."

"Even though I brought in the bottle, Dr. Carter wouldn't excuse it," said Elvira.

"Why not?" asked Margo.

"Because he says I didn't register the prescription," said Elvira. "Jesus Christ. So I forgot to register the goddamn thing. It's a valid prescription. I asked him to call my doc and verify it and he says it didn't matter. He says that if I didn't register it it's not valid no matter what my doc says. Jesus. What an asshole."

"Elvira," said Margo, calmly. "What's the rule?"

"I know. I know," said Elvira, rolling her eyes at the ceiling. "You have to register the fucking prescription as soon as you get it. But for Christ's sake, I was sick or I wouldn't have had to get the fucking prescription. Why can't that asshole ever cut me some slack? Dr. Reynolds would have."

"The point is you can't count on somebody cutting you some slack," said Margo. "You've got to play by the rules or pay the consequences."

"But you know I was sick 'cause I called you," moaned Elvira.

"I know," said Margo. "But he'll probably say that since you were able to come in for you dose, you should have been able to register the prescription."

"Come on, Margo," said Elvira. "I worked hard for those steps. You should go to bat for me with that prick."

"Since you did call me, I'll talk to him about it," said Margo. "But don't count on it. What I want you to do is to stop with the anger and frustration. It's not going to do you any good. Swallow it. Get on with your life. Don't let it rock your boat so bad that you lose it and go into a tailspin. This is a set-back, but you've got to deal with it. Focus on getting that step back. Work on that. This's part of your recovery and it's too important to let it mess you up."

"Yeah, Elvira. Margo's right," said a young black woman sitting next to Erin. "Oh, yeah. My name's Sandy. It's the shits that he did this to you but you've got to put it behind you."

"I know," agreed Elvira sullenly. "I'm not gonna let that asshole ruin me. But I had to blow off some steam. Man, he's a nasty prick. I think he really gets off on nailing people. Especially addicts. Why does a guy like that work in a place like this."

"Because he gets off on it," said a woman named Cheryl.

"Look," said Margo, calmly. "That's life. You meet all kinds. You're gonna run into people for whom the letter of the law or the regulation or the rule, is more important than the reason or the intent behind it. They like to get between reason and the law and use the law to support whatever they do. Did any of you see *Les Miserables?*"

"I did," said another woman. "My name is Gloria. Welcome, Erin. I really liked the music and singing."

"I did, too," said Sandy.

"O.K.," said Margo. "Do you remember the cop, Javert?"

"Yeah," said Elvira. "He was a mean mother-fucker."

"Yeah," said Sandy. "He ran that poor dude down. He was on his ass, big time, even though the dude cleaned up his act and was doin' good and all."

"Do you remember what happened to Javert?" asked Margo.

"I think he was killed in battle," said Cheryl.

"No," said Elvira. "He committed suicide. He jumped off the fucking bridge."

"That's right," said Sandy. "He jumped off the bridge."

"Why did he commit suicide?" asked Margo.

"Wait a minute," said Elvira. "It was because the main dude let him go. The cop thought he was going to get his ass killed, but the good dude let him go."

"That's right," said Margo. "So what did that mean? Why did he jump?"

"It was because the good guy had cut him some slack," said Sandy.

"I don't get it," said Gloria. "Why did that make him kill himself?"

"Because," said Margo. "He realized that his life had been

190

empty. He had spent it chasing this man, Jean Valjean, because he had broken the law. Now, at this moment, he realizes that Valjean was, in fact, a better man than he was. Even though he'd always followed the letter of the law, Javert realizes that he's a failure. He had wasted his life."

"Wow!" said several people simultaneously.

"So think about that," said Margo. "It's important to follow the rules and the regulations, but you've also got to be building your strength as a decent, honest person. So, Elvira, even though you've been guilty of breaking the letter of that regulation, you should focus on the fact that you didn't really do anything wrong in a moral sense. You're a strong, good person. Build on it. O.K.? Who's got something else they want to deal with?"

"I do," said a plump, pasty woman in her late thirties. Her hair was in disarray and she looked as though she hadn't had time to complete her personal preparations before leaving home. "I'm Carla. Welcome, Erin. I've been clean for nine months. I've got a job and my sister's been taking care of the kids. Everything was really coming together. Then, my old man gets out of the joint. He comes back with all this macho shit that he's running things now. He wants me to quit my job and just take care of the kids. But even worse than that, he's using and I think he's dealing. All these asshole friends of his are hanging around the house all the time and I'm afraid I'm gonna start using again."

"I'd run him off," said Elvira. "I'd hit the mother fucker over the head with a frying pan and run his ass off."

"I'd like to," said Carla. "But I'm not strong like you. He'd mess me up."

"Has he been abusing you?" asked Margo.

"No," said Carla. "Not so bad. He just shouts a lot and threatens me. It doesn't bother me so much, but I know it bothers the kids."

"You ought to take those kids and leave," said Sandy.

"I thought about that," said Carla. "But I know he'd come after me. I could go to my sister's but they really don't have any room and he hates her anyway. I don't want to get her involved."

"Carla," said Margo. "I better talk to you about this after this session. Be sure you stay. I don't want this to get any worse. There are some things we need to go over. O.K. What else is going on?"

"I've been clean for a year," said Sandy. "I just got another step."

There was applause from everyone.

"That's great, Sandy," said Margo. "You've come a long way. All right. That about does it. We'll see you all next week. Carla, meet me in my office."

As they were walking out, Sandy came up to Erin. "Welcome, Erin. I seen you was kind of quiet. I was too at first. But you kind of get to know the other girls and all. They're really great. So's Margo. She's the best. They've really helped me a lot. Listen, I just wanted to tell you that this program really works. It's working for me. So if you got any question, just call me. I wrote down my phone number on this paper. Any time. Just call. See you next week."

Erin would drive into the clinic between 7:30 and 8:00 o'clock and line up for her dose. She began to recognize the other people who also received their methadone doses at about the same time. Some she didn't see every day. They could be recognized by the small locked boxes they carried, into which they would receive the plastic bottles each containing one daily dose.

Because the people in her group were all women, she began to be curious about the types of men who attended the clinic and began to observe their variety. There were men in overalls, men in suits. There were men in ragged clothes and men in silk shirts, prominently displaying gold jewelry.

There were small, delicate looking men, and powerful, muscular men. There were young men, barely out of their teens, looking like they might be on their way to a college class. Others looked forbidding and walked with the swagger of power carried conspicuously.

There were black men, Hispanic men, a few Asians and some men who looked Arabic. There were tall, blond Nordic-looking men and short, swarthy Mediterraneans. There were clean-shaven men wearing the uniforms of the company whose truck they drove. There were bearded men who looked like poets or academicians.

There were middle-aged men who were still strong and muscular and others whose bodies bore the tell-tale signs of the wear and tear their addiction had inflicted--who walked with a hesitant gate and stood with stooping shoulders and sagging chests.

There were older men, a few of whom still walked with confident, powerful strides, but most of the older men looked weary and concerned. They moved slowly, lacking vigor and energy.

There were men who looked as though they could have been friends or associates of her father, and others who appeared to inhabit worlds that he would never know, nor want to.

She realized that the men she was observing had come to this place by pathways as varied as their appearance and that the roads they would travel from here to their final destinations were as uncertain as her own.

Chapter Twenty-Three

In response to a phone call from the secretary, Chris walked down the hall and into the outer office of Dr. Bernstein.

"Hello, Dr. Childs," said the secretary. "Go right in. He's expecting you."

Chris walked into the now-familiar office. "Good morning," he said.

Bernstein turned around from the arranging he was doing at one of the book shelves. "Ah, Chris," he said, turning and offering his hand. "Good to see you. Sit down, please. How are things going? How's Erin?"

"She's doing very well, as you predicted," said Chris. "She's on fifty milligrams of methadone and feels essentially normal. She's still tapering the valium. I can't tell you how grateful we are."

"Grateful?" said Bernstein. "For what? I did nothing."

"You got her into that program," said Chris.

"Well, it shouldn't have been necessary for me to intervene," said Bernstein. "The system needs repair. We have a lot of work to do."

"Some of the things we're learning about the program bear that out," said Chris. "It's pretty rigid and bureaucratic."

"What can you expect when the rules are made by bureaucrats and politicians who have had no experience in drug addiction or its treatment? It's very difficult to get things changed. Treatment of addiction isn't a very high political priority. Addicts aren't a very powerful constituency."

"Nevertheless," said Chris. "She really enjoys her counselor. She's an RN. and an ex-addict."

"Margo Sutherland?" asked Bernstein.

"Yes," said Chris, surprised. "You know her?"

"I was consulted during her illness and that of her former husband," said Bernstein. "What a tragedy. But now I see Margo at professional meetings."

"She really seems to know her stuff," said Chris. "Erin has nothing but good things to say about her."

"Good," said Bernstein. "So is Erin learning about addiction?"

"About addiction and addicts," said Chris.

"And you," said Bernstein. "Do you still find this subject interesting?"

"Absorbingly so," said Chris. "I'll confess to you, and I'll hope you won't tell Jack, I've been spending a lot of his time learning more about neurobiology and neuropharmacology."

"And?" asked Bernstein.

"It's a marvelously complex field," said Chris.

"Have you gotten into any of the immunology?" asked Bernstein.

"Yes," said Chris. 'As a matter of fact, I'm reading a series of articles now about using antibodies to treat cocaine addiction."

"Do you think that approach has any merit?" asked Bernstein.

"Well, the animal models look promising. It seems to me to open up a whole to field of investigation. I'm also fascinated about the prospects of using antibodies as catalysts."

"I agree," said Bernstein. "Tell me. Do you find yourself in any way drawn to such a field?"

"Why do I get the feeling that you're leading me down a certain pathway?" said Chris, laughing.

"Ha," laughed Bernstein. "And I thought I was being so subtle. All right you caught me. Chris, I got a copy of your resumé from Jack Current's office. I hope you don't mind. I was very impressed.

"I've had a faculty position open in this department for a couple of years. I haven't actively pursued the process of filling it because I wasn't certain which direction I wanted to take. But recently, I've also become convinced that immunology has an exciting role to play. This just happened to coincide with my stumbling across an ideal candidate with an outstanding background in immunology."

"Me?" asked Chris, completely taken by surprise.

"Who else?" said Bernstein. "I'll have to go through the motions of posting the position, but it will be so crafted that you'll fit the description to a 'T'. Are you interested?"

"Absolutely!" said Chris enthusiastically. "Of course." Then, more cautiously he said, "I'd love to look it over. But, I'm very flattered and I want to seriously consider it."

"Good," said Bernstein. "It'll be a full tenure track position. Nothing less would be appropriate for you. I have some grant money and several private sources in the wings, so I can guarantee that you'd have plenty of support to get a research program off the ground. There's one other thing I'd ask. I'd want you to begin helping me with the lectures at the medical school on neurobiology and the biology of addiction."

"I'd love to do that," said Chris. "I'd have to do a hell of a lot of preparation but I always enjoy being on a steep and challenging learning curve. You really caught me off guard. But you can see how excited I am about this."

"Excellent," said Bernstein. "I was hoping you'd feel that way. Here's the prospectus that I've prepared describing the position, the scope, the career implications and the commitment that will be made by the department and the university. Read it over and get back to me about any questions or suggestions. When you're completely comfortable with it, I'll submit it and get things rolling. By the way, I had a brief talk with Jack Current so he knows what I have in mind and would be delighted to support this. He thinks the world of you and wants to keep you around even if it can't be in his shop."

"He's been a good friend and a wonderful mentor and colleague," said Chris.

"If you decide to do this, we'll put it on schedule for you to move over here when you finish at Jack's," said Bernstein. "Let me know what you decide."

"I'll let you know within a week," said Chris, shaking hands again.

The rest of the day, Chris's mind was absorbed with his new prospects. He was yearning to discuss it with some of his colleagues but didn't feel comfortable doing so until he was closer to

196

his decision.

That night he burst into the apartment, startling Erin who was sitting and reading quietly. He ran to her and picked her up by the waist and swung her around.

"Something wonderful has happened," he said kissing her on the neck.

"Well, tell me," she said.

"Dr. Bernstein called me in. He has a faculty position in his department and he's offered it to me."

"But he's in pharmacology, isn't he?" she asked.

"He wants to bring in an immunologist to work on some newer aspects of addiction and he thinks I'm the guy to do it."

"Oh Chris, that's wonderful, but what does immunology have to do with addiction?"

"The connection is very new," said Chris. "But there have been some recent studies that are very provocative. One line of investigation, using animals, indicates that you can immunize them and produce antibodies that render them indifferent to cocaine."

"I don't understand," she said.

"You can construct an animal model in which you can train rats to become addicted to cocaine," said Chris. "You can train them to depress a lever that gives them cocaine. When they learn to do it, they'll continue to press the lever until they collapse, ignoring food or exhaustion."

"Just like human beings," said Erin.

"Exactly," said Chris. "But if the rats are first immunized with a compound that causes them to produce anti-cocaine antibodies, they become completely indifferent to cocaine and won't even depress the lever."

"Wow," she said. "Can they do that in humans?"

"That's the question that's being investigated," he said. "You can see how exciting that approach would be since there's no pharmacological equivalent of methadone to use for cocaine addicts."

"That would be wonderful if it works," she said.

"There are a lot of ways that antibodies can be used to explore the physiology of the normal opiate receptors," he said.

"How?"

"You could produce antibodies to one of the receptors and then inject them into the animals. The antibodies would prevent the normal functioning of those receptors so you could then figure out what happens to the animal when those receptors are knocked out. And you could use the antibodies as radioactive probes to map the position of all the receptors. The possibilities are endless."

"You're really excited about this, aren't you?" she said, smiling at him. "It's just shining in your eyes."

"Yeah," he said. "I'm really flying. I'd never considered it. It's a complete surprise, but it's an absolutely ideal academic slot. It has a lot of organizational protection and I'm sure this field is really just taking off."

"I thought you had reservations about the academic scene," she said.

"There are parts of it that I don't like," he explained. "There's a lot of personal infighting and petty backstabbing that goes on. I suspect it's worse at the lower levels where the insecurity is rampant. There's a lot of pressure to get on a tenure track and build a solid foundation for your career. But that's probably true in any high pressured organization filled with competitive people. The wonderful thing about this opportunity is that I'll be isolated from most of that.

"Dr. Bernstein has sources of grant money to get me started. And in that department I'll be the only immunologist, so I won't be invading anyone else's turf."

"Won't it be isolating for you to be out of the mainstream of immunology?" she asked.

"That's a good point," he said. "If it doesn't work out, it might be difficult to swing back into more conventional immunology. But that's just a chance I'll have to take. I won't lose track of the main field. I'll still keep in close touch with Jack and his people.

"The other thing that was hanging me up about staying in academics was that I'd have to leave this area. Now I won't have to. We can stay right here and have it all. What do you think?"

"You mean you want my opinion?" she asked.

"Of course I do," he said. "I'm talking about our lives, not only mine. You certainly get to have your say."

"I'd go anywhere with you," she said. "I'd even go back to El Centro if that's what you wanted. You're the center of my universe. Looking at how excited you are, I can't imagine your making any other decision, unless you know or find out something bad. I want you to know how important it is to me that you're back with your music and your band. I know you feel responsible for my addiction, but I feel responsible for your loss of your music. Now the picture will be complete."

At her second one-on-one session, Margo began by asking, "How are you feeling? Are you having any disturbing symptoms?"

"I'm not sleeping as well since the valium dose has decreased," Erin admitted.

"Sleep is very important," said Margo. "I'll arrange a meeting with the doctor so you can get an increase in your methadone to compensate for the valium. How did you feel about the group session?"

"I found it very interesting," said Erin. "It was very intense. I was particularly pleased that Sandy came up and made a point of offering her help after the session."

"Good," said Margo. "She's worked very hard to get her life back together and she's being successful. She's come a long way, believe me. Tell me, how are you spending your time now that you're feeling so much better?"

"Mostly reading," said Erin. "And I go for walks."

"That's good, but it's not enough," said Margo. "Don't you need to get a job?"

"Well, sure," said Erin. "I guess I do. There isn't any immediate financial pressure, but yeah. I should."

"You seem a bit hesitant," said Margo. "What kind of work were you doing in El Centro?"

Erin blushed. "I was working in at a restaurant," she said self-consciously.

"And what else?" asked Margo.

Erin's head was down and she didn't answer. Margo let the silence prolong. Erin started to say something, and then her eyes filled with tears. She put her hands over her eyes.

"What else, Erin?" Margo repeated gently but firmly.

Erin took several moments to compose herself. "I was a prostitute," she said, almost inaudibly.

"It's very painful to say and to admit, isn't it?" said Margo.

Erin shook her head.

"Have you discussed this with your fiancé? What's his name?" asked Margo.

"Chris."

"Have you talked about this?"

Erin shook her head negatively. "I just couldn't."

"Don't you trust him?" asked Margo. "Don't you trust his love?"

"That's not it," said Erin. "I'm just so ashamed."

"I understand that," said Margo. "Believe me, I do. But you must realize that as long as you're carrying and hiding this secret, you can't get beyond it. It's like a huge weight holding you down.

"Erin, many of the women in this clinic, including your counselor, have faced the same repugnant dilemma that you did, and made the same choice for survival. That's an example of the power of heroin addiction. It eliminates many of your choices and most of the ones you're left with are bad.

"In some cases, I'd say that it would be better if the partner weren't told and never knew because the revelation would be too destructive. But from what I know about you and have inferred about Chris, I really don't think you should keep it from him. It'll continue to eat you up from the inside until you let him help you by sharing this truth. Use it as something that can bring you together. Don't let it keep you apart.

"Secondly, I think that your not wanting to get a job, or rather, your reluctance to do so is somehow related to that whole painful sequence. You must get a job, even a volunteer or part time job. You must normalize your life in every way that you can. I cannot emphasize this too strongly."

"You're right," said Erin. "I can see that I've been hiding. The truth is I'm still terrified."

"Look," said Margo. "It doesn't have to be a high-pressure position. Along the way through your education you've acquired a lot of skills that are valuable to others. Just find something to do that fits, even if it doesn't fit well. Believe me, it'll be more beneficial than you can imagine."

"All right," said Erin resolutely. "I'll start looking today. And I'll talk to Chris tonight."

*   *   *

200

That evening, after dinner, Erin came into the living room where Chris was reading. "I have something to talk to you about. Something important." she said.

He put down the journal he was reading and smiled at her. "Sure. What's up?"

"There's a part of the El Centro experience that I haven't told you about," she said.

"You don't have to if it's painful," he said. "If you'd rather not."

"It is painful, but I must tell you," she said. "I must tell you even though I know it's going to hurt you. This all came up today with Margo and I'm convinced that she's right. This has to be dealt with."

"O.K.," he said. "So let's deal. I'm up to it if you are."

She sat next to him on the sofa and was silent for a long moment while she composed herself and gathered her thoughts. She reached over and took his hands and held them firmly.

"When I first got to El Centro, I got a job in a diner, a truck stop. It wasn't a great job but I really needed it. Roy, the manager, was a decent guy and that's where I met Myra. The pay was adequate and with the tips I could have done all right.

"The problem was my habit. I couldn't believe how expensive the heroin was. I was rapidly going through all my savings. I was using more and more and spending more and more. I really got panicked.

"Roy figured out that I was a junkie. Myra did too. She was also using and she got me hooked up with her connection. Anyway, I was getting more and more strung out and started making mistakes. Roy told me I'd have to shape up or he'd have to let me go.

"That really panicked me. One night I missed my vein and ended up taking too much, way more than I could handle. I was really loaded at work. I dropped a bunch of dishes and made a real mess. Roy had to let me go."

"He fired you?" asked Chris.

"Yeah. He didn't want to," said Erin. "He was a real nice guy. But people were beginning to complain about my screw-ups, so he had no choice. Then I really panicked. I had to have money, not only to live but also for the heroin. I was afraid to go to another town where I didn't know anybody and wasn't connected to any source of heroin."

She paused again to compose herself. Then she continued.

"Myra had talked to me earlier when I complained that I was having money problems. She knew I didn't have many alternatives." She took a deep breath and let it out slowly. "She did occasional tricks for some extra money."

"She was a prostitute?" asked Chris intently.

"Yes, occasionally," said Erin. "You can figure out what happened." She took another deep breath. "When she first suggested that I do it, too, I was so repelled by the notion that I became physically ill."

Chris moved closer to her. As he began to realize what she was telling him his eyes filled with tears.

"But that was before I got fired," she said, tears running down her cheeks. After that, I didn't have, as she put it, 'the luxury of virtue'."

He put his arms around her and held her tight. "You don't have to go on," he said softly.

"Yes, I do," she said resolutely, trying to maintain her control. "I was doing as many as four or five tricks a night. Mostly truckers. The only way I could make myself go through with it was by taking benzos and getting numbed out.

"Between the heroin, the benzos and doing tricks, it was as though there was just the slimmest remnant of the real me that remained and that part was filled with shame and disgust for what I had become. The only way to avoid the pain was with drugs.

"I made enough that money was no longer the problem. The problem was that I lost all hope and direction. I completely gave up the dream of ever seeing you again, knowing that if you ever did see me you'd be as disgusted with me as I was. I was getting very near the bottom and I barely even cared."

Chris sat with his head down. His eyes were closed and he was shaking his head back and forth. He was struggling to control the emotions that were tearing through his body; the enormous sympathy, the fury and the frustration. " My God. How could this have happened to you of all people?" he shouted in anger.

"It happens to a lot of people like me," she said. "One false step or a series of bad decisions and there they are. There I was. If that trucker hadn't hit me I'd still be there."

Chris took her in his arms for a long moment. "Has it helped to tell me?" he asked softly.

"I don't know," she said. "I certainly don't feel any release or exhilaration. What I is feel exhausted, and dirty."

"Dirty?" he asked.

"Of course 'dirty'," she said with a hard edge in her voice as she pulled away from him. "Come on, Chris. Be honest. You can't feel the same about me as you did before knowing this. I'm dirty."

He was quiet for a moment while he examined his response. "I can honestly tell you that the feelings I have right now are pain and sympathy for what you've been through. I also feel anger and indignation," he said quietly but firmly. "Erin, look at me. Do you think that I'd abandon you or feel different about you if you were raped?"

She considered that for a moment. "No. I guess not. I'm sure some men might. But no. You wouldn't."

"This is no different," he said. "You were the inocent victim of a terrible violence that was inflicted on you. You were literally bludgeoned by those circumstances into doing something that was completely repugnant to you. I can understand that you might have believed that it would bother me. But, for Christ's sake, it doesn't change the way I feel about you."

"Even sexually?" she asked.

He paused for a moment and thought. "Neither of us were virgins when we came together, but to me, our sex life has been as pure as if we had been. I've been curious about why you were being physically remote since El Centro, but with all you've been through, I was more than content to be patient. What I wanted most was just to be with you; to see you; to smell your fragrance; to hear your voice. Just to touch you is a wonderful thrill after not knowing whether or not I was ever going to see you again.

"But I still have very strong sexual feelings for you," he said kissing the back of her hand and then looking steadily into her eyes.

"Even now," she asked. "After what I just told you?"

"Even at this very moment," he said and kissed her gently but ardently.

"You are truly amazing," she said, brushing back the hair from his forehead. "Just amazing. Now I am feeling relieved. But you're going to have to continue being patient.

"If you say so," he said. "But why?"

She took another deep breath. "They did some laboratory tests at the clinic. It included a test for AIDS. I won't have the results for a few more days."

"Oh my God," he said. "That's right."

"And I think I better see a gynecologist and get a complete check up. I'll call Carlos and find out who he would recommend."

"So, you've been carrying all these terrible concerns around in silence, haven't you?" he asked.

"Yes. I just couldn't face it until Margo insisted that I do so."

"I'm very impressed with her and thankful you have her for a counselor," he said. "She's a good and wise person."

"You've got that right," said Erin. "She was right about the importance of telling you and she was also right about another thing."

"What's that?" he asked.

"She said you could handle it," said Erin. "As much as I love, admire, and respect you, I was still concerned that this would be asking too much."

"Ain't no such thing, my darling. You are worth every bit of it and more."

When Erin called the office of the gynecologist that Carlos had recommended, she was told that he was not available for the next month.

"We always recommend Dr. Collins," she was told. "He's a very nice man and we have never had anything but praise from those we send to him."

Erin called the number she was given, and scheduled an appointment for the next week.

When she arrived at the office, she filled out the forms, and was then taken to an examining room where she waited, a bit nervously. After a short interval, a middle-aged, balding man entered the room. "Miss Leahy?" he asked, and extended his hand in greeting. "I'm Dr. Collins. I'm pleased to meet you. May I call you Erin?" he asked with a warm smile.

"Please do," she responded, feeling herself relaxing.

"That's a pretty name. Rather unusual. Irish, I suspect."

She explained the origin of her name and provided the information about being adopted.

"And it says here that you're a graduate student. So your adoptive parents must be very proud of you."

"Well, I hope they are," she answered, a bit nervously.

"Let's go through your medical history." He went through a series of questions and then asked, "Are you taking any medicines?"

"Yes, I'm taking methadone," she answered without hesitation.

Instantly, the warmth she had felt vanished. He visibly stiffened and paused before he asked his next question.

"For pain control?" he asked, looking at her carefully.

She became aware of the dryness in her mouth. "No. I'm in a treatment program. I take it for heroin addiction."

He put down his pen and after another pause he looked at her sternly. "I think we better get something straight right now, Miss Leahy. I will not prescribe any opiates for you. I'm not going to feed your habit."

She was completely taken back. "I have no intention of asking you for any prescriptions, except, maybe birth control pills. The methadone has completely taken away any craving for drugs. I'm not here for that—for what you said. I don't want any more opiates—ever." She knew she was stammering.

"Fine," he said. "Just as long as we understand each other."

The rest of the exam was completed in a cool atmosphere with no further pleasantries.

That evening she discussed her experience with Chris.

"It was astonishing," she said. "He had been so pleasant. It was as though, when I said the word 'methadone', I had been transformed from being a patient into something loathsome and disgusting. He didn't even ask whether I was doing well on the program, or was now clean. He just presumed that I was there to dupe him into providing opiate prescriptions."

"That really is appalling," said Chris. "My dad told me that most physicians don't know much about addiction and actually try to distance themselves from it. So I knew they were likely to be uncomfortable, but this—this really sounds cruel and inappropriate."

"Margo told me to be upfront about being on methadone, and

being and addict, because if you're not and they find out later, they will usually dismiss you. But after this, it's going to be difficult to put myself in that position again. I'll just stay with Carlos for everything."

Chapter Twenty-Four

Because of the difficulty Erin was having with her sleep as the valium was being tapered, Margo made an appointment for her to see a physician in the clinic to discuss an adjustment in her methadone dose. She expected to talk to Dr. Reynolds and was a bit surprised to be called in to see another physician, Dr. Carter.

"Come in, Ms. Leahy," he said. He was very neatly and impeccably dressed. He had silver gray hair and dark, penetrating, cold eyes that watched her carefully.

"Sit down, please," he said curtly. "Your counselor tells me that you requested an increase in your methadone dose."

"Yes, that's right," she said.

"And why do you think you need an increase?" he asked.

"My counselor said it was likely that I'd have trouble sleeping when the valium dose was lowered. In the past week I have been waking in the early morning and feeling uneasy "

"Uneasy?" he repeated. "How do you mean uneasy? Are you craving heroin?"

"No," she said. "That's not a problem. I just don't feel completely comfortable."

"We're not here for your comfort, Ms. Leahy," he said. "We're here to treat your addiction. I don't approve of counselors recommending changes in methadone doses. That's something for the physician to decide."

"Oh, I'm sorry," she said, feeling flustered. "I didn't mean---"

He cut her off in mid sentence. "However, since Ms. Sutherland is an RN, I do grant her a bit more latitude. I will increase your dose by five milligrams. If you should have further problems, you should make an appointment to see me.

"I've been looking through your chart. You aren't really qualified to be on this program according to state regulations."

Now she was more shaken. "Yes. I know," she said. "An exception was---"

"I don't approve of these sorts of exceptions," he said coldly. "The laws are there for a purpose. If we make an exception for you, we should make it for others and then we might as well have no regulations at all. I realize that this isn't your fault, but I feel it only fair to warn you that I intend to take this up with the director."

"What will that mean?" asked Erin.

"I'm not certain anything can be done now since you've already been admitted and have received treatment. It should have been dealt with before you were admitted--and it would have been if I had been the one to do your evaluation. However, I do intend to seek clarification with the director. I think it's wrong to break regulations for trivial or political reasons, whatever the case may be. You may go. Oh, by the way, your laboratory results are all normal."

She paused for clarification. "All of them are normal?"

"Yes."

"That includes the AIDS test?" she forced herself to ask.

"Yes. But if you have had a recent known exposure you should be retested in six months."

"Thank you," she said, her relief over the test results completely eclipsing the concerns he had raised about her admission.

That evening she prepared a special meal. She had a bouquet of fresh flowers on the table and a bottle of champagne cooling in an ice bucket. The CD was playing a collection of Chopin pieces when Chris walked in. She greeted him with a strong embrace and a fervent kiss.

"Woah," he said, stepping back. "Are you trying to tell me something?"

"Yes," she said. "We have something to celebrate. Actually two things. My AIDS test was negative and the gynecologist found no evidence of any infection or abnormality."

He picked her up by the waist and whirled her around. "Erin, that's wonderful. Piece by piece we're shoving this whole nightmare into the past. Are you feeling as terrific as you look?"

"I'm feeling wonderful," she said twirling around. "I had a moment of uneasiness this afternoon when I talked to the doctor. It wasn't about the test results but about some regulations. I asked Margo about it and she assured me that it was nothing to worry about. Anyway, enough of that. I'm in the mood to celebrate. And you?"

"Count me in, my fair lass," he said with a brogue. "I've always been a sucker for sexy Irish women and you qualify on all three counts."

After dinner they went to the bedroom. Released from her fears and inhibitions, Erin was eager and ardent. Chris was a bit hesitant, mostly out of concern for her, but the hunger of their passion overcame any remaining self consciousness. It was swept away in the growing flood tide of their love. For the first time in many months, they felt that they were completely reunited.

The following week Erin answered an ad and took a part time job working in a book store. It was a small, quiet place that had been operating in the same location since after the second World War. It was owned by Frances, a widow, the survivor of one of the prominent San Francisco poets of the sixties, whose powerful anti-war feelings found expression in the haunting verses he had poured out in a steady, passionate stream.

His long struggle with cancer had eroded much of the money they had put aside, and so she had to try to keep the store afloat despite the capsizing competitive waves created by the new chain book stores.

Frances was able to work in the mornings when she felt fresh, but by afternoon, her weakened heart began to produce symptoms that clearly told her that she should cut back on the amount of time she spent in the store. She was a frail, thin, delicate woman, whose remaining vitality was concentrated in her alert, inquisitive eyes and charming smile.

"I'm so pleased to have found someone who enjoys and appreciates books," she said to Erin when her offer was accepted. "That would have meant a lot to George, too."

"Well, I'm happy to have found a place like yours to work in," said Erin. "It's a treasure."

"A museum you mean," said Frances. "With these new chain stores and the internet, I don't think you'll be finding these kinds of places around for much longer. I know I couldn't survive if I had to pay rent. That was the best decision we ever made, to buy the store and the apartments above it. So at least I have a little something coming in. I'm sorry I can't pay you more. I'm sure you're worth it."

"The pay is fine and the hours are perfect," said Erin. "I can get some things done in the morning and be here so that you can leave at one. Earlier if you prefer."

The pace was very slow. There were some steady customers who were usually alarmed to see Erin behind the counter, presuming it implied failure of Frances' delicate heart. Having come, they tended to linger and share their reminiscences about the history of their relationship with the shop and its owners.

There was a lot of time that she was able to fill with her own reading. She chose those classics that were outside her field or favorites that she wanted to revisit.

She wasn't ready to resume her pursuit of a degree or even think seriously about it. She was content to let her mind sink into the rich, dense prose of Conrad, Henry James, Melville, Crane and Dreiser. She had rarely experienced the joy of reading when she wasn't pursuing an academic deadline. Now she could wander slowly, thoughtfully, through the carefully constructed phrases, savoring the nuances and textures of the beautiful language, rereading passages to capture the subtlety of the shadings. She discovered humor which she had missed on previous, time-pressured readings.

After the intellectual desolation of her experience in El Centro, she was delighted to be able to immerse herself in luxuriant self-indulgence and enjoy the infinite variety of the literature at her disposal. More than the mental challenges she set for herself, her reading also contributed to her spiritual rebirth, further pushing the nightmare into the past.

* * *

Erin went to her group meeting, feeling more positive even considering sharing some of her recent success. She was no longer taking any valium. The only drug she was taking was the methadone which had provided the adhesive to assist her in pulling the pieces of her life together.

"Does anyone have any issues to discuss?" asked Margo.

"Yeah," said Gloria. "I want to talk about my daughter. She's really pissing me off. Her old man left her without no money so she moved back in with me. She said it was only gonna be for a few weeks, but it's been four months now and I can't get her to leave."

"What do you mean you can't get her to leave?" asked Elvira. "If you want her to leave, you tell her to leave. If she don't leave, throw her ass out, throw her stuff out and lock the door."

"I can't do that," said Gloria. "Not with the two young kids. I love them. I can't throw them out. It's not their fault."

"Is she using?" asked Elvira.

"I don't know," said Gloria.

"What do you mean you don't know?" said Elvira. "Are you giving her money?"

"Well, she needs some money," said Gloria.

"She's living at your house," said Elvira. "She's eating your food. You're taking care of her kids and you're giving her money so she can score drugs. Are you crazy?"

"What about that?" asked Margo.

"Well, I don't want her to be using, with the kids and all," said Gloria. "But I'm afraid that if I don't give her money she'll get in trouble."

"What you ought to do is tell her if she's using you'll turn her in to the Children's Protective Services and have her kids taken away from her," said Sandy. "Isn't she on parole?"

"Yeah," said Gloria. "But I couldn't rat her out."

"Wait a minute," said Sandy. "You're supporting her habit. How can you do that? What chance do these kids have if she don't clean up her act? Man, you're way too lenient with her. You always have been. You got to come down hard on her. Make her clean up."

While they were talking, Cheryl, another member of the group, came in quietly. "Sorry I'm late," she said in a breathless voice as she carefully slid into one of the chairs.

"Excuse me," said Margo walking hurriedly toward Cheryl "Let's stop for a moment. "Are you feeling all right? You don't look well."

"I think I've got an infection," she said between labored breaths. "An abscess or something."

"Have you been using?" asked Margo quietly.

Cheryl kept her eyes down, but nodded affirmatively. Margo took her hand and counted her pulse. Then she put her hand on Cheryl's forehead.

"You're burning up," said Margo, clearly concerned. "How long have you been sick like this?"

"A few days," said Cheryl. "I'll be all right. I just need some antibiotics for this abscess."

"You need more that," said Margo. "You're going to have to go to the hospital."

"Oh no, Margo. Please," she said trying to catch her breath. "They really treat you like shit. I'll be O.K."

Margo turned to Sandy. "Go get one of the nurses. I'm going to put her in one of the treatment rooms. Come on, Cheryl. Can you walk?"

"I think so," she said, barely audibly.

With the help of two other members of the group, they assisted her into the treatment room and onto the examination table, just as one of the clinic nurses came in.

"She's really sick," said Margo. "I didn't take her temp but she feels hot. All right, ladies," she said to the group members. "Back into the room. I'll be there in a minute."

"Her pulse is one twenty and her temp is 103," said the nurse. I'm going to call the Emergency Room. They can send a gurney over here and take her right in. Will you stay with her?"

"Sure," said Margo. "Cheryl, hon, would you feel more comfortable lying down?

Cheryl shook her head. "I can't breathe lying down."

Margo propped up the folding back of the table and took some pillows out of the cupboard to help her find some comfort. "I think you may have a bad infection," said Margo. "You must have known. You should have gone to the hospital"

Cheryl shook her head. "I told you," she gasped. "When I go to the ER they always treat me like crap. Once they know I'm a junkie and I'm on methadone, they don't do anything for me."

"That's not true," said Margo. "There are some very good doctors over there."

"And some real assholes," said Cheryl.

"O.K.," said Margo. "You take it easy. Don't try to talk anymore. I promise you I'll make certain that they give you their very best."

The nurse returned and began to repeat the vital signs. As she did so, attendants from the ER arrived and assisted Cheryl onto the gurney and wheeled her the short distance to the ER.

Carlos Garza was in the physician's dressing room, changing into his working scrub suit. He had just returned from a painful trip to Watsonville, to attend the funeral of his uncle Luis. He was still carrying the heavy emotions of his loss, and his thoughts were wandering through the memories of their times together. The reverie was abruptly terminated by the jolt of his pager. He pressed the button and read the message. The number was that of the Emergency Room.

The clerk who answered asked him to wait while she summoned the resident who had called.

"Carlos," he said. "We've got a real sick one. I think you should see her."

"I'll be right there," said Carlos.

"What you got?" he asked the resident walking into the E.R.

"Heroin user. On methadone, but she's been skin popping. She's been feeling sick for several days, but she refused to come in. Her temp's 103.5 and she's hypotensive."

"Sepsis?" asked Carlos.

"I'm sure of it," said the resident. "We already got the blood cultures so I started the antibiotics."

"O.K.," said Carlos. "So what's the problem?"

"She says that she's been getting short of breath in the last twelve hours. Can't lie flat in bed. Her lungs sound wet clear up to the inferior margins of the scapulae. She's got a loud systolic murmur. I checked her chart. She had a soft Grade one to two murmur the last time she was seen here. This sounds like a train going through her chest."

"Jesus," said Carlos. "Let's take a listen."

"That's not all," said the resident. "She's got a bad headache and her neck is a bit stiff."

"Did you do a spinal tap?" asked Carlos.

"I couldn't, she couldn't tolerate lying down. Even with oxygen running full bore she gets too short of breath."

"Get another tray ready," said Carlos. "I'll do it sitting up."

They walked into the patient area and the resident introduced him to the sick woman. "Cheryl, this is Dr. Garza. He's the chief of the ER. He's going to help make you well again."

"Hello, Cheryl," said Carlos. "We need to understand what's going on before we can make you better. I'm going to listen to your heart and lungs, and then I'm going to perform a quick procedure to remove some fluid from your back."

He loosened her gown and listened to the labored sounds of. her breathing, moving his stethoscope quickly over her back. Then he moved to the front and listened to her heart, again moving the stethoscope quickly to several positions and switching the head from the bell to the diaphragm position. He then quickly noted the color of her skin and nail beds. Then he walked away from the bed and conferred with the resident. "I can't hear an opening snap or a second sound. I think she's wide open."

"That's what I was afraid of," said the resident.

"Have you called the surgeons?" asked Carlos.

"I wanted to wait until you heard her," said the resident.

"I'm sure you're right," said Carlos. "She's ruptured her mitral valve. They're going to have to do surgery and put in a prosthetic valve."

"Will they be willing to do that as sick as she is?" asked the resident.

"They don't have any choice. She can't survive unless they do. Let's do the tap."

With Cheryl sitting on the gurney, supported by the nurse and the resident, Carlos located the bony landmarks of the vertebral column, found and marked the correct level, then cleansed the skin and prepped it. Then he pulled on his gloves and selected the smallest bore needle.

Sitting on a stool behind her, he anesthetized the skin surrounding the mark he had made. Then he carefully slipped the needle through the skin and along the bony ridges that protect the spinal cord. He deftly advanced the needle until he felt a momentary resis-

214

tance followed by a quick release that indicated that he had penetrated the protective layer of the meninges. He removed the obturator from the needle and permitted a few drops of fluid to flow through the needle and into the sterile plastic containers which were used to collect it.

"O.K. Get these to the lab," he said to one of the clerk. "Now let's make her as comfortable as possible." The resident and nurse helped rearrange the pillows to support her in the upright position. When they completed the arrangements, he said to her, "Cheryl, you have a serious infection. I did the spinal tap because we're concerned that it may have spread to the fluid that surrounds your brain and spinal cord. We've already started giving you antibiotics to fight that infection. But there's another problem. We think the infection has spread to your heart. Have you been having fevers, chills, and sweat?"

She nodded yes.

"We think you have an infection of the lining of the heart called endocarditis. We also think that it's damaged one of the valves in your heart."

Her eyes were wide with terror.

"I'm asking some other doctors to come and see you. You may have to have to have heart surgery to replace the damaged valve."

"Oh my God," she gasped through the oxygen mask. "I'm going to die!"

He took her hands and looked steadily into her eyes. "You have a very serious infection, but we can treat that. We're already treating it. Your heart has been damaged but the surgeons can repair that. You have to fight hard. We're all going to have to fight hard. We'll do our very best. I promise you that. It's going to be tough but we can win."

"Dr., Garza, there's a call for you," said a nurse.

He left Cheryl with the resident and went to the anteroom where a wall phone was blinking. "Dr. Garza," he said.

"Hi, Carlos. This is Margo. I'm glad you're on the case. The clerk told me you'd seen her. What's going on?"

"You don't send us easy ones, do you?" he said. "She's really sick. She has sepsis, endocarditis and early meningitis."

"Jesus," she said.

"Her mitral valve has been damaged by the infection. We've

215

asked the surgeons to see her right away. She's going to have to have the valve replaced."

"Now?" she asked.

"She can't survive unless they do. She's already in congestive failure, and we're having to give her some pressors to support her blood pressure."

"God damn," said Margo. "I feel so bad. So frustrated and angry."

"What's that all about?" asked Carlos.

"She was really doing well," said Margo. "She'd been clean for over a year. Then her family started hassling her about being on methadone. Her parents threatened to take her kids so she gave in and demanded that we lower the dose. She started getting drug sick on the lower dose so she started using on the sly. I confronted her but she wouldn't let us raise the dose. She's been skin popping and got some bad stuff. She wouldn't come to the hospital sooner because of some previous bad experiences, but you know all about that problem."

"Only too well," said Carlos.

"Is she gonna make it?" asked Margo.

"Too early to tell," said Carlos. "We'll know better when we see how well she tolerates surgery and the early recovery period."

There was a pause, then Margo said, "O.K. Well, I'm glad you're there for her. She couldn't have better."

"We'll do our best," said Carlos. "I have to go."

"O.K.," she said. "I'll check with the nurses to see how she's doing. Thanks, Carlos."

He returned to the gurney. The senior resident in cardiothoracic surgery was just finishing his examination. When he finished, he turned to Carlos, and a junior resident began his exam. Carlos sand the senior resident walked a few feet away from the gurney.

"Man, these folks can really get themselves fucked up," he said.

"Yeah. Tell me about it," said Carlos. "So when are you going to do the surgery?"

"As soon as we can get her ready," said the surgeon. "We're going to ask for a consult from Infectious Diseases. We'll move her up to our place to make all the preparations."

"Good luck," said Carlos.

"She's the one that'll need the good luck."

216

Back at the clinic, the other members of the group had been stunned by the seriousness of Cheryl's illness.

"Does anyone want to share her feelings?" asked Margo.

"It's really a downer," said Sandy. "I mean, like she was doing real well before she went on that taper."

"But what could she do?" said Gloria. "They were going to take her kids."

"My parents want me to get off methadone," said Phyllis, one of the younger members of the group. "They say it's just another form of heroin and I should be strong enough to kick. Man, what do they know? When I try to taper, I get down to twenty milligrams and then I start getting sick. I start craving so I have to get my dose raised again because I don't want to use. I want to get off, but I've got to do it really slow or I'll relapse. That really scares me."

"I think most of us have faced this problem in one form or another," said Margo. "People in general don't understand addiction and they don't understand methadone. It isn't easy to get off and that's frustrating. But all you have to do is to look at Cheryl and you know that it's much, much safer for addicts to be on methadone. Please remember that if you ever think about using. It's like playing Russian Roulette."

All afternoon at the bookstore, Erin continued to mentally revisit the scene at the clinic. She hadn't seen many sick people and the experience deeply troubled her. She kept remembering the glitter of Cheryl's eyes, her gasping for breath and the dusky, unnatural color of her skin. She couldn't rid her mind of the thought that she might have been the one in that predicament instead of Cheryl. She was still brooding over the somber events when Chris arrived. She told him what had happened.

"It was really frightening," she said. "I've never seen anyone look that sick. She really couldn't get a normal breath and her eyes looked so frightened and helpless. It was just awful. Poor thing."

"It must have been scary for everyone," said Chris.

"Especially for her. I just haven't been able to get her expression out of my mind," said Erin. "And a lot of other things have been popping into my brain."

"Like what?" asked Chris.

"This whole methadone thing," said Erin. "I don't want to stay on this stuff forever and at the same time, I'd be terrified if I didn't have it. Look at poor Cheryl. She got sick because she was trying to get off methadone. I'm really getting confused. I feel like it's both a protection and a trap."

"That's something you can talk over with Margo," said Chris. "You said she's been through it all."

"I wonder if Margo ever got real sick," said Erin. "Chris, hold me. I've been so terrified. I know that could have been me."

He put his arms around her. "I don't blame you for being scared. Just hold on tight. I've got you."

Late that night, Margo received a phone call.

"Hi," said the voice. "It's Carlos. I'm afraid I have bad news."

"Oh no," she said, closing her eyes and shaking her head.

"There was just too much damage," he said. "They couldn't attach the prosthesis firmly to the heart because of the damage that the infection had done to the surrounding tissues. It continued to leak around the prosthesis. They couldn't even get her off the pump. I'm sorry. They did everything they could."

"I know you all did," she said. "Thanks, Carlos."

She put down the receiver and walked to the window. She looked out at the city lights, blurred by the tears that were welling up in her eyes and spilling down her cheeks. She thought about the fragility of the addict's life, recalling her own and her former husband's brushes with death, before he finally succumbed. "The human organism is endowed with so much strength and flexibility," she thought. "But addiction spends them profligately and, finally, there is no more margin for error, no more elasticity, and the whole system snaps. Tragedy or pathos?" she wondered. "It all ends the same."

Chapter Twenty-Five

Chris was again waking to his internal music. The strains would tug at him and he would smile inwardly, relishing their return He had previously presumed they would always be there but Erin's disappearance had disproved that. Now that they were back he cherished their presence more than he ever had.

As soon as he became aware of the music, he also became aware of Erin's presence beside him in bed and he turned to her and enfolded her in his arms, savoring his two loves simultaneously.

When he embraced her, Erin stirred and kissed his hands. "Good morning, darling," she said. "How are the tunes?"

"Heraldic," he answered. "They're all about you. Just triumphant. I think I'll write a symphony--'The Erin Symphony'. What do you think?"

"I know you're just kidding, but I believe you could do it if you really wanted to," she said, rolling over to face him. "I think you can do anything you want."

"What I want is to lie here in bed with you forever," he said, kissing her neck.

"Even that would get boring after a while," she said, giggling as he nuzzled her breasts. "Not now, but after a while. Maybe in a year or two." She was squirming as his kisses became more serious. The nuzzling and tickling gave way to urgent kisses and strong, tender caresses and then to rapturous, intense, soaring love.

"You're wrong," he said as they rested. "I'll never get tired of that." She snuggled closer to him. "What are you going to do today?"

"Same old same old," she said. "I'll do some things around here, go for my walk, clean up and go to the book store."

"Sounds perfect," he said. "What are you reading?"

"I'm getting into the turn of the century San Francisco writers," she said. "I've read some of Jack London and now I'm reading Frank Norris. I'm also getting interested in San Francisco history. I want to get you interested so we can take some walks."

"I'm in," he said. "I'd love it."

"Anything special for you today?" she asked.

"I think I'll call Rick and have lunch," he said.

"Don't eat too much," she said. "Remember we're going to your folks' house for dinner."

"I did forget," he said. "How could I forget? I set the whole thing up so you all could meet Dr. Bernstein. What an idiot I am. All right. I'll just meet you at the folks."

"If I drive, then we'll have two cars there and we'll have to drive home separately," she said. "I'll take the train and you pick me up."

"A much better plan," he said. "Be ready. When you get off that train, I'm gonna be all over you."

"Well, for decorum's sake, I hope we can make it to the car before we consummate," she said. "I've always been shy about public displays of affection."

That evening they were gathered in the living room at the Childs' home, listening to a piano duet being played by Chris and Mrs. Childs. Also present was Dr. Bernstein, who was a widower. The exquisite music from the two grand pianos filled the elegant room and the listeners applauded enthusiastically at the conclusion.

"It's such a thrill for me to hear you two play together," said Erin. "I look at you and watch your wonderful hands and I know exactly where Chris gets his music from."

"Now wait," said Dr. Childs as he distributed glasses of wine to each. "How do you know that I'm not also musically gifted and that I am, in fact, the source of his extraordinary talents?"

"Because I've told her about your abilities and your genius, Dad, and it's not music," said Chris.

"Ah, well," said his father. "It was worth a try."

"You're right, Erin," said Dr. Bernstein. "It's a perfect example of flawless genetic transmission. Like Leopold Mozart and his two

220

child prodigies, Wolfgang and Nannerl. Someday, when they complete the project of mapping all the human genes, we may be able to know exactly which gene or genes are responsible for the transmission of musical talent."

"And in your work, you'll be able to find out which genes are responsible for addiction," said Dr. Childs. "Oh, I'm sorry, Erin. That was clumsy and thoughtless of me."

"Not at all, Dr. Childs," said Erin. "I find it very fascinating. Chris has tried to explain it to me, but I don't quite get it."

"Let me try," said Dr. Bernstein. "Genes are collections of nucleic acids that direct the synthesis of the molecules that make up the organism. Each gene, as far as we know, is responsible for the production of one molecule, such as an enzyme, or a receptor in your brain. In our species, there may be a variety of similar ways to make these receptors in different people. Though they're slightly different, they all work well.

"It may be that the gene you inherited from your mother which controls the structure of the receptors in your brain is a perfectly workable alternative in most circumstances. But in the unusual event of exposure to opiates, it doesn't function quite as well. Maybe it binds too strongly to the heroin which keeps the heroin in place longer than usual. Maybe the receptor causes too much of a neurotransmitter to be produced. Maybe the enzyme that metabolizes the neurotransmitter isn't as efficient as it should be, so the excess neurotransmitter continues to upset the balance in the brain.

"This is all conjecture on my part. We don't understand the genetics of addiction susceptibility. The only solid human data indicate that the children of alcoholic parents are four times more likely to become alcoholics. Since many of the pathways by which alcohol disrupts the normal functioning of the brain are the same as those for heroin, it's not unreasonable to speculate that the same will be true for heroin.

"One of the problems is that we haven't had enough time to study this, since heroin addiction is a relatively recent phenomenon. But things are moving more quickly now. Maybe someday we'll be able to identify the markers for susceptibility to addiction."

"It seems to me that it might be very dangerous, even destructive, to frighten parents, for example by telling them that their child is likely to become addicted," said Dr. Childs. "Plus there would

221

be all the other problems of who should have access to that kind of information, such as insurance companies or potential employers."

"You're absolutely right," said Dr. Bernstein. "All genetic information and information about disease susceptibility shares those inherent problems. It would have to be used with great caution."

"But addiction would seem to be a particularly sensitive issue," said Mrs. Childs. "I greatly admire Erin's parents who made the decision to adopt her knowing that her mother was addicted. I'm certain that many people would have run from the potential danger."

"I agree," said Dr. Bernstein. "There's no question that the public in general has very little sympathy or tolerance for the tragedy of addiction. I'm not certain that I completely understand why, but the attitude in our country has been to demonize and marginalize addicted people and treat them as unclean pariahs."

"Do you think this relates to the Puritan roots of our country?" asked Mrs. Childs.

"That's a part of it," said Dr. Bernstein. "But then, why are we so tolerant of alcohol abuse which is far more prevalent? In terms of overall costs to society for health effects, crime and violence, alcohol is a far greater problem. A very high percentage of rape, child and spousal abuse cases are associated with alcohol. And yet, here we all are, enjoying our alcohol, just has been done in most societies we know anything about."

"Maybe that's the difference," said Chris. "We tolerate the abuses associated with alcohol because we have personal experience with its benefits."

"Speaking of which," said Dr. Childs, "Chris will you provide our guests with some more wine, please."

"I think you're right," said Dr. Bernstein. "And as we have a certain experience with people who use alcohol to excess, we have none with a heroin addict. Part of it, I think, may be related to the fact that heroin use involves injecting yourself with a needle which makes it more repugnant to most people. So the notion of doing something so unnatural for the sake of pleasure adds a dimension of 'the crazed' to it and further removes it from the experience of most people. But that's only a guess."

"I hate to interrupt this," said Mrs. Childs. "But I've just been told that our dinner is ready to be served. I usually do this all myself, but tonight I was determined not to miss out on any of the con-

222

versation so I'm treating myself to some help. Let's go into the dining room."

They sat down and Dr. Childs raised his glass. "We have a lot to be thankful for, and it all seems to be revolving around our guest. First, in assisting Erin, who has become so precious to us, and now, the wonderful prospect of a challenging and rewarding career for Chris. We're very grateful to you, Dr. Bernstein."

"Seeing Erin doing so well is more gratifying to me than you can imagine," said Dr. Bernstein. "And as for Chris, well, I'm the one who should be grateful to you. So let's all toast to each other."

They all raised their glasses and toasted. As they talked, two uniformed women glided silently around the table, serving their salads.

"Addiction is such an enormous, horrible problem in our country," said Mrs. Childs. "We all know that. But before Erin, we didn't really have to pay much attention to it. It seemed very comfortably remote."

"I think that's a typical experience, and, if you'll pardon me for saying so, a major part of the problem," said Bernstein. "Most Americans don't really want to come to grips with the problem of addiction. It's too unpleasant. They'd prefer that it just go away. That's fundamentally why we spend so much money putting drug addicts in prison, a strategy that's ineffective, inhumane and expensive."

"What do you mean, 'ineffective'?" asked Dr. Childs. "I thought we were winning the 'war on drugs'."

"Not really," said Dr. Bernstein. "We're winning the war on drugs the same way we were told we were winning the war in Vietnam---with inflated body counts and other forms of deception. As I study the numbers, I don't see dramatic decreases in the number of heroin addicts in San Francisco or any other large city. I see increased smoking of heroin by people of college age. I see increasing traffic in methamphetamine made in chemical laboratories all over the state. I don't think we are or can be effective until we admit that addiction to heroin or any other substance is fundamentally a medical problem. By the way, this is a delicious Caesar salad."

"Thank you," said Mrs. Childs. "It's one of our favorites. It was the only way I could get Chris to eat anchovies."

"Mother," said Chris. "You're making me sound not only difficult but a gullible in front of my new boss."

"It's best he know the truth, dear."

"Why can't we get over that basic hurdle of admitting that this is a medical problem?" asked Dr. Childs.

"First, those who are in charge of the war on drugs would have to admit that they've been wrong. Politicians are very unlikely to do so. There's another very pernicious aspect to the problem. The war on drugs has been made into a Holy War---a struggle between the good people and the forces of the devil. Once that characterization has been widely accepted, those who wage the war are absolved from the obligation to win."

"I don't understand that," said Erin.

"If you're in a war with the devil, the mere fact that you're fighting becomes justification for continuing to do so. How can you not, as a good person, fight against the devil? You must continue to fight, even if you're not winning, because to not fight is unthinkable.

"The other terrible consequence is that the addicts become the minions of the devil, the demons. So, what do you do with demons? You put them as far away as possible so they can't do any harm. This, despite the fact that many of the people who are now addicted started when they were teen-agers.

"Again, look at the discrepancy. There's a major, widely supported effort to prevent teen-agers from starting smoking, as there should be. We don't want our young people to be victimized by the tobacco companies. We rise up in righteous indignation to oppose it. But why are those people who became victims of addiction as teenagers not treated with concern and compassion rather than with disgust and disdain?

"Think for a moment about some of the other consequences of teenagers becoming heavily involved in drug use at such a critical time in their development. At an age when Chris and Erin were maturing intellectually, emotionally and spiritually, when they were developing their own sense of integrity, morality and responsibility for their own actions, when they were well on their way to appreciating the beauty of music, literature and nature, these addicted youngsters were spending most of their time and focusing a good deal of their mental energy on where their next fix was going to come from and how they were going to get the money to pay for it.

"Consider what a profound, devastating effect that has on their capacity to become responsible, mature adults. Even if there are no neurologic consequences, the developmental damage is enormous. One of the biggest challenges of the multi-disciplinary treatment programs is to teach the patients how to behave as adults."

"Well, now I can see how enormously important it is to have skilled counselors involved in their rehabilitation," said Dr. Childs.

"And I've certainly seen how difficult their lives are," said Erin. "The women in my counseling group are struggling with more problems than I could ever have imagined."

"There's another, related aspect," said Dr. Bernstein. "Drug addicts live in a parallel universe."

"Whatever do you mean by that?" asked Mrs. Childs.

"Once they become immersed in the drug culture, they begin to think of the non-addicted world as an adversarial place, inhabited by people who are hostile, such as the police and parole officers, lawyers and judges and all the other people who they perceive, understandably, as their enemies. Not surprisingly, they're only comfortable with other addicts, whom they may not completely trust, but at least understand. So when they make the decision to try to clean up, they have to begin by trying to relate to and live in the other universe where they feel like aliens. The stress of that dislocation alone is enormous. When it becomes intolerable, they go back to their other universe."

"And the counselors are left with the task of trying to pull them back into our world again," said Erin. "What a tough job."

"But we make the problem worse by continuing to put addicts in prisons rather than getting them into treatment programs," said Dr. Bernstein. "It costs about thirty thousand dollars a year to keep someone in prison and less than four thousand to treat them with methadone as an outpatient. A study done in California estimated that for every dollar spent on methadone treatment, the State saved seven dollars in the costs of crime, criminal justice and health care dollars."

"That's astonishing," said Dr. Childs. "Chris, will you please refill the wine glasses."

The salad plates were removed and the main course was served.

"I hope you enjoy salmon, Dr. Bernstein," said Mrs. Childs.

"As often as I can get it," he said. "I love it cooked any way but my favorite is poached. You must be clairvoyant."

"Maybe I'm just lucky," said Mrs. Childs.

"Just a few more boring statistics," said Bernstein. "If you follow addicts who start out being HIV negative, in seven years, 51 per cent will contract HIV as opposed to 21 per cent who are in treatment."

"But aren't most addicts in treatment?" asked Dr. Childs.

"Only about fifteen percent of the country's heroin addicts are in methadone programs," said Bernstein. "So you see, Erin, you're really among a select few."

"Why isn't that number higher?" asked Chris.

"One of the most obvious reasons is that the programs are usually full to capacity," said Dr. Bernstein.

"Then why aren't there more treatment programs?" asked Mrs. Childs.

"Probably because the public doesn't care or doesn't want them," said Bernstein. "A few years ago, according to one poll, almost two-thirds of the American public supported treatment for drug addicts. More recently that's decreased to about one-half, while eighty-five per cent of the people believe that tougher criminal penalties are the solution to the drug problem.

"They don't seem to realize that putting people in prison virtually assures that they will become criminals if they aren't already. You take a young kid from San Martin or Gilroy who's older cousin gets him involved in drugs. The kid gets sent to prison. By the time he gets out he has been indoctrinated into one of the prison gangs and is now connected to a web of criminal activity that extends across the state. He can now become a dealer. He can now dispose of stolen goods. He's become a part of organized crime.

"It works like this. When they first go into prison they're terrified. Someone from their home town comes to them and offers them protection against the other factions and they become indoctrinated into one of the prison gangs with its enormously strict code of loyalty. When they're about to be released, they're told that they will be contacted by someone on the outside. They will be asked to do some favors for the 'family', to show their loyalty and gratitude. You can imagine what the 'favors" are. They're immediately plunged into drug trafficking and other illicit activity. They have very little chance of avoiding it."

"That's a very chilling scenario," said Chris.

"Prisons are not nice places," said Bernstein. "Plus, all the drugs you want are often available in prison. And in many places, the guards are part of the lucrative distribution schemes ."

"I was really naive," said Erin. "I was shocked to find out how many of the people in my group have been in prison, or at least in jail. I think that some of them go into treatment because they're afraid of going back."

"Or because it's a condition of their parole," said Bernstein.

"Why aren't all parolees from drug related crimes put into methadone programs?" asked Chris.

"The criminal justice folks tend not to believe in methadone treatment," said Bernstein. "I think some of that skepticism is related to their almost inherent resistance to giving addicting medicine to addicts. Then, a lot of them don't believe it works."

"Why is that?" asked Chris.

"Because much of their experience in this state is related to seeing addicts going into short term detox programs. You were in one, weren't you, Erin?"

"Yes," she said. "And it didn't work for me. I was O.K. on the higher doses, but when the dose was lowered, I got sick and started craving heroin."

"Of course," said Bernstein. "Three weeks is too short a time. The brain is too delicate an instrument. When its incredibly subtle balances have been profoundly disturbed, literally assaulted, by large amounts of opiates for years, it takes a long time to reestablish its balance. By the way, this salmon is perfection itself."

"Thank you. Why do they have such an ineffective program?" asked Mrs. Childs.

"I think it's another crazy reflection of the anti-methadone bias of the politicians and hard line narcotics administrative officials. Because they're fundamentally opposed to substitution programs like methadone, they have remained determined to ensure that if they're going to be permitted to exist, they're going to be heavily regulated. For example, there are states in which there is a limit-- and a pretty low one--to the amount of methadone that can be given to any patient. California used to limit the amount that could be given. This despite overwhelming evidence that indicates that higher doses, tailored to the needs of the individual patient, are far more effective.

"You can also see why the criminal justice people believe that methadone doesn't work," said Bernstein. "The repetitive failure of ineffective programs discredits the whole concept of methadone treatment."

"There's another regulation that I think is bizarre," said Erin. "My counselor explained to me that you can't receive methadone treatment unless you can prove that you've been addicted for two years and have been through detox twice."

"Isn't that appalling?" said Bernstein. "Can you imagine saying to some scared, young person who comes in seeking treatment, 'I'm sorry. You've only been addicted for nine months. You must continue your addiction for fifteen more months, subjecting yourself to all the health and criminal risks inherent in doing so. Then, we'll permit you to come into the shelter and safety of our program,'"

"It's just infuriating to learn these things," said Mrs. Childs. "I'm ashamed that I never knew any of this. Why do they make it so difficult to get treatment with methadone?"

"The argument they use is that methadone is addictive itself and that no one should become addicted to methadone unless they are seriously addicted to heroin for a substantial period of time," said Bernstein.

"Do you agree with that?" asked Dr. Childs.

"It certainly is true that methadone is addictive," said Bernstein. "But I believe that we should be able to give methadone treatment when it is medically evident that the person has been using heroin. It makes no sense to have arbitrary time limits, either for how long a person must be addicted or how long they can be kept on methadone treatment, which is the case in some places."

"Would anyone like some more salmon?" asked Mrs. Childs. "We're having desert so you may want to leave some room."

There being no takers, the table was cleared for dessert.

Dr. Childs poured glasses of a dessert wine that were distributed around the table. Then the dessert was brought in.

"Look at this," said Chris. "I thought you said you weren't doing any work. This chocolate tort is her specialty. Wonderfully sinful."

"You know that this whole dinner is a labor of love, Chris. I consider this a very special occasion. Now, Dr. Bernstein, why is it so difficult to stop taking methadone?"

"Because it lasts so much longer in your system than heroin does, which is one of its great benefits, it also takes longer for it to be removed. So patients, physicians and counselors must be willing to be very patient in getting someone off methadone."

"If it's that difficult, why is it better than heroin?" asked Mrs. Childs.

"Because heroin is so destructive," said Dr. Bernstein. "Continuing to inject heroin virtually guarantees destruction of the person spiritually, physically, legally, financially and any other way you can name."

"But isn't that largely due to the fact that heroin is illegal?" asked Chris. "Wouldn't it be better to make it legal?"

"There are certainly many responsible, thoughtful people who believe so," said Dr. Bernstein. "They argue that drug abuse, like smoking, is something we should have the freedom to inflict on ourselves if we choose to do so and that making drugs illegal is an infringement of our basic freedoms. Plus, they make the strong economic argument that it is the restrictive legal code that creates the black market and the enormous economic opportunity which drives the import and sales of all illicit drugs."

"How do you feel about that?" asked Dr. Childs.

"I disagree," said Dr. Bernstein. "I don't believe that our society should make a substance as dangerous as heroin available to innocent people. As with other dangerous chemicals, the pharmaceuticals which are used for treating diseases, we've made the appropriate decision to limit the availability of these drugs by requiring that those professionals who are trained, licensed and therefore accountable should be the ones to ensure that they're used safely. On the other hand, I do think marijuana should be decriminalized. Physicians should certainly have the prerogative of prescribing it in certain forms. Oh, this torte is spectacular."

"So what's the prospect of ever having a national drug policy that makes social, medical and legal sense?" asked Chris.

"I believe, as I said earlier, that the current chaotic, ineffective, cruel drug policy is a reflection of the attitudes of the public in general and the politicians in particular. I also believe that we'll never have a drug policy worthy of the greatness of this nation until we reach out our in compassion and concern for the people who've gotten themselves ensnared in this terrible affliction. We should all read what's inscribed on the base of the Statue of Liberty. 'Give me your tired, your poor, your huddled masses yearning to breath free, etc.', and apply those lofty sentiments to our own fellow citizens who have become tragically addicted. When we do that, we'll change from being harsh and vindictive. We'll remove drug treatment from the hands of the regulators and deal with addiction primarily as the medical problem it is. Then our messages of education and prevention will resonate with a power they currently lack. Addicts will be able to obtain effective, appropriate treatment early in their disease, before their lives are destroyed.

"Don't misunderstand," said Bernstein. "Penalties for drug dealers and all those who profit from this cataclysm should be very harsh. But every effort should be made to engage users in effective treatment before sending them to prison. And if it becomes necessary to imprison them, the major thrust of their incarceration should be education and rehabilitation.

"Another change that I support would be to permit the methadone patients, after they have become stabilized and are clearly on the road to recovery, to be able to leave the rigid programs and receive their methadone from community physicians who are knowledgeable and committed to the treatment of addiction.

"Well, enough of my soapbox presentation and its gloomy portent," said Dr. Bernstein. "There's a lot of wonderful science and investigation that's now going on in this field. I can't tell you how happy I am to have you join me, Chris."

"Can I offer brandy to anyone?" asked Dr. Childs. Everyone declined.

"We're also very pleased," said Mrs. Childs. "I was excited when Chris told us, but after learning some of the things you told us this evening, I'm even more thrilled that he'll be working with you. You make it sound like a very exciting crusade."

"That probably means that I had a little too much of your excellent wines," said Bernstein. "But thank you for the compliment. It is a very worthy battle. But look at the time. I must take my leave. I have an early meeting tomorrow. Thank you for a lovely evening. Chris, I'll be in touch. We have some details we need to go over. Good night."

As they drove home, Chris and Erin discussed the evening.

"I can certainly understand why you were so excited about working with Dr. Bernstein," said Erin. "He's so brilliant and so kind."

"He's a very fine man," said Chris. "I just try to picture him in New York dealing with all those addicts. It amazes me."

"Careful, buddy," she said. "All us addicts aren't so bad."

"If they were all like you, everyone would want to be in this business," said Chris. "But how did hearing all that effect you? Did it bother you?"

"I have mixed feelings," said Erin. "On the one hand I feel very comforted to know that there are wonderful people like him involved. That, plus having a great counselor like Margo, and learning more about the whole process makes me feel more secure. On the other hand, all the rigidity and the bureaucratic rules that govern the program make me feel a bit uneasy. It's Kafkaesque. I have this concern that people could get crushed in the cold, impersonal machinery."

"I can certainly understand that," said Chris. "But that's never going to happen to you. We wouldn't permit it."

Chapter Twenty-Six

With a comfortable rhythm to her days, time was passing smoothly for Erin. Getting up early to go to the clinic and get her methadone provided an immediate impetus to her day. Depending on the weather, she would then go for a vigorous walk in the neighborhood or to a small gym she had joined and exercise on the treadmill or Stairmaster, listening to books on tape.

She would then run any errands on her agenda and return to the apartment and do whatever cleaning and laundry was necessary. Then she would take a leisurely shower, eat and drive to the book store. It was a very pleasant pace, punctuated by her group and one-on-one counseling sessions.

She was feeling no side effects from the methadone and had no hint of any cravings for heroin. The dark days of her addiction were slowly receding into the past as she built her present and began to think of their future.

She had become interested in California literature and history, so the bookstore was a perfect environment since the neighborhood and the structures reflected the past so clearly in their architecture and their layout. She began to appreciate and recognize the subtle differences that characterized different times and styles from the late nineteenth and early twentieth centuries.

On weekends, she and Chris planned walks that took them through areas of special interest to her. They wandered through North Beach or Chinatown, the financial district or the South of Market area, carrying maps and books that helped them recreate the past.

They studied books on the great 1906 earthquake and fire and walked through the streets that had borne the burden of the cataclysm that threatened to reduce San Francisco to a residue of ashes and memories.

Sometimes they would return to the wharf in Tiburon or find another outside bar on the water at South Beach or one of the other piers and enjoy the sun and scenery sipping wine or beer, engaged in conversation and laughter.

The days were going into a ledger of recovery. They were like the particles of sand, measuring her accumulated progress and she was cherishing each one with growing confidence.

One morning, Erin and Sandy met in the line waiting for their methadone. Since Sandy had earned take-home privileges, she came to the clinic only twice a week.

Sandy went to the window first, presented her ID card and was given her oral dose for the day. Then she presented a small lock box and was given three small plastic bottles, labeled with her name and ID number each containing one liquid daily dose of methadone. She placed the bottles in the box, locked it and stepped out of line.

When Erin had received her dose, Sandy said, "Let's go get some coffee someplace and have a talk. I've been wantin' to have a chance to chat with you."

"Sure." said Erin. "I'd love to. Do you have some place in mind?"

"Yes," said Sandy. "There's a place I like a lot. It's only a few minutes from here. Where are you parked?"

"Right over there," said Erin. "The little red one."

"O.K. I'll pull around. Just follow me," said Sandy, placing the box in her trunk and making sure that both were locked.

They drove to a small, older neighborhood and parked separately near a small coffee shop that featured home made pastries. A few tables were distributed around the interior, about half of them being occupied. At some were couples or small groups engaged in spirited conversations. At others people sat alone, reading newspapers or books.

"I like these little places better than the chains," said Sandy. "I'm worried about this one, though. It used to be full all the time."

They purchased their coffee and pastries and selected a table near the window which looked out onto the quiet street.

"So, how's it goin'?" Sandy asked. "You was real quiet when you first got here but you been talkin' a lot more. I like what you say. You make real sense. You been to college?"

"Yeah," said Erin. "I've been."

"I thought so," said Sandy. "I can usually tell. Some like to talk like they been but I can usually tell. You, you're real natural. So, How's it goin'?"

"It's going good," said Erin. "I'm really doing well. I think it's really working for me."

"I thought it would," said Sandy. "You look real serious. Lots of people come onto the program and they just aren't serious. You know what I mean? They're just bull-shittin' themselves. They stick around for a while, takin' methadone, but they're still usin'. Then they leave or get kicked off the program 'cause their urines are dirty and they say that methadone don't work. I say it's 'cause they don't work.

"Me? It took me a couple of times before I really got serious. I was with this guy---a real asshole. He was usin' and dealin'. He was doin' speedballs and crack and he'd get violent and abusive. I mean he was really an asshole. So I left him. I couldn't take that shit. Now I got a real good man, Vernon. He used to use but now he's clean. He got clean on methadone and now he's even off that. He's real supportive. Got a good job. In sales. He's a real charmer, you know what I mean? So, how about you?"

"What do you mean?" asked Erin.

"I mean, how'd you get hooked?"

"Somebody I trusted gave me the stuff to smoke," said Erin.

"You got hooked from one hit?"

"Well, I kept going back," said Erin.

"Yea. I've heard about people that get hooked real fast," said Sandy. "It took me a while, but then I really did it. I was using two grams a day plus a bunch of other shit. Man, I really got strung out.

"I was in the joint a lot and they took my kids away. But I'm gonna get them back now 'cause I'm clean and I got a job. 'A stable living environment' they call it."

"That's great," said Erin. "You've really turned your life around, haven't you?"

"Yeah," said Sandy with a big grin. "I really have. And I know I couldn't have done it without methadone and without Margo.

She's the best. She's tough, but she cares. I owe her big time."

"She's mentioned you to me as an example of someone that's done extremely well, so I don't think you owe her anymore than that," said Erin. "So, are you going to marry this guy you're with?"

"Yeah," said Sandy. "I think I will. How about you? You ain't married are you?"

"Not now," said Erin. "But I'm pretty sure I'm going to. I want to, but I want to get off methadone first."

"Don't rush it," said Sandy. "I've tried to taper off a couple times and I got sick and had to back off. But I'm not worried about it. I don't mind taking methadone. It makes me feel secure. And now that I have take-outs, I only have to come in a couple of times a week. And I like goin' to group. Margo's great."

"Tell me," said Erin. "What ever happened to that other guy? The asshole?"

"He's still around," said Sandy. "He comes by every once in a while. Not at our place. He'll cruise by the clinic and try to get me to go back to him. He knows now what a good thing he lost. Just kiddin'."

"Not at all," said Erin. "He did lose a good one. But you're much better off without him."

"Don't I know it," said Sandy. "It's one of those things. He's so bad that I can't even believe now that I was with him. But then sometimes when I see him, I get these strange feelings. Well, I gotta go. Glad we could do this."

When Chris met with Dr. Bernstein to discuss some administrative details, he took the opportunity to raise an issue that had been troubling Erin. "She's concerned that she'll have to stay on methadone for a long time, maybe forever," he said. "What's the reality?"

"The reality is that she and you and everyone concerned will have to be very patient," said Dr. Bernstein. "I'm sure you remember your basic physiology and the concept of homeostasis; that state in which all the body's systems such as oxygen supply, temperature, blood pressure, are all in balance. The organism defends that balance protectively. Diseases disrupt the balance and therapy is successful when the homeostasis can be restored. "For example, an infection causes disruptions that result in fever and generalized discomfort. If the infection is in the respiratory system, there will be a cough which represents the system's efforts to remove the organism. If antibiotics are effective, the organism is killed and removed from the body, the fever and cough go away, and homeostasis is restored.

"Our central nervous system develops very gradually and carefully over many years, maintaining an exquisitely precise equilibrium. Every time there is a signal for one system to speed up, there is a countervailing signal to slow down to prevent excessive, disruptive movement in either direction. The circuits can respond very quickly, but there is always another circuit alerted to prevent destruction of the precious equilibrium. It's like an enormously complex neurochemical gyroscope, dynamically maintaining the homeostatic balance.

"When someone takes a psychoactive drug for weeks, months, years or decades, the old equilibrium is destroyed and a new one that includes the presence of the drug is tenuously established. When that person stops using the drug, it's very difficult to reestablish the original balance. That's what recovery from addiction is really all about; reestablishing neurochemical homeostasis, in a way that permits that person to live a normal life and respond normally to the wide variety of situations they will have to face without having to take drugs.

"Each person is unique. So it's impossible to predict how long it will take. The treatment has to be tailored to the needs of each patient. What works for one, won't for the next. That's why patience is so important; patience and a lot of support."

"Do some people have to stay on methadone for the rest of their lives?" asked Chris.

"Yes," said Dr. Bernstein. "Some will. And that can be very frustrating. Particularly to family members who don't understand that the neurochemical derangement caused by addiction can last for a life time. They see only the top of the iceberg, the drug taking. But they don't understand why the drug is being taken or the incredible force of the powers that drive the addict to take the drug. They believe it's only a matter of will-power. 'Just stop taking the drug.'"

"But can't some people kick the habit that way?" asked Chris.

"Yes," said Dr. Bernstein. "Some do. Some unusually strong

236

people can do that, and they deserve enormous credit. They have to endure not only the enormous physical torture of acute withdrawal but also the long term suffering which may go on for many months or even years.

"You mustn't confuse going through withdrawal and being cured. Many addicts are forced to go cold turkey when they're incarcerated. They're just not given any drugs and they go through withdrawal. But their addiction isn't really changed. The balance has not been reestablished so as soon as they're out of prison, they go back on heroin. And the same thing happens to people who come off methadone too quickly. They can be drug free for a while, but they are likely to relapse unless their treatment has slowly prepared them, and their nervous system, to live without any opiates, methadone or heroin."

"So unless their equilibrium has been restored, they have a high probability of relapse?" asked Chris.

"Yes," said Dr. Bernstein. "Understanding the mechanisms of relapse is the most challenging question in addiction medicine. In spite of all the obstacles, we can do a pretty good job of achieving stability for well-motivated people on methadone. Getting them back to that homeostatic equilibrium without methadone in the picture is our challenge."

"What causes relapse?" asked Chris.

"It's very complex," said Bernstein. "Every addict has certain environmental 'triggers' that cause intense craving for the drug. It might be as overt as watching someone else fix, or even just the sight of a needle or a syringe. For some, it's as subtle as even going by or seeing a certain place where they used to fix. When the triggers are intense they may even experience some of the symptoms they associate with taking the drug itself."

"It sounds like a conditioned reflex," said Chris. "Kind of like Pavlov's dogs."

"That's a good example," said Bernstein.

"So memory of the pleasure is one of the problems?" asked Chris.

"Absolutely," said Dr. Bernstein. "You can recall particularly pleasant sensory experiences and experience the same phenomenon. Think about a particularly delicious meal or a special wine and your mouth prepares to accept it and you may experience a real sense of pleasure. I'm certain you can do that with music that's important to you."

"You're right," said Chris. "I can experience a thrill when I think about certain passages that I love."

"There are ways in which repetitive memory functions are tied up with the 'reward pathway' in our brain. For example, dopamine, one our neurotransmitters is involved in the process and it's also involved in the pleasure that drug addicts experience."

"What are some other triggers?" asked Chris.

"One of the most common is stress," said Dr. Bernstein.

"What kind of stress?" asked Chris.

"Virtually any kind," said Dr. Bernstein. "Job stress, marital stress and financial stress, are frequent causes of relapse. Another way in which we see that is that patients who have been stable on a dose of methadone for a long time will begin to feel withdrawal symptoms when they lose their job or their wife leaves them. If their dose isn't raised to compensate, they may relapse and start using heroin to get through the stress."

"No wonder it's so difficult to cure addiction." said Chris. "Who can stay free from stress? But how does stress trigger craving?"

"The response to stress illustrates another dimension of the complexity of our nervous system. Evolution has prepared our species not only for the tranquil parts of our lives, but also for those occurrences in which we have to make a split second decision for "fight or flight". Part of that adaptation involves the adrenal glands, and two other brain centers, the pituitary and the hypothalamus. A series of hormones is released that ultimately results in the secretion of adrenal steroids which play a key role in the chemical preparations."

"Is this in addition to the rush of adrenalin that's also put out by the adrenals?" asked Chris.

"Yes," said Burnstein. "From a different part of the adrenals. The amazing part of the story is that the signal that causes the pituitary to activate the adrenals, also carries with it endogenous opioids, endorphins."

"To help the adrenal steroids?" asked Chris.

"It doesn't appear so," said Bernstein. "It appears that the endorphins are a chemical buffer to help us tolerate some unpleasant

238

effects of the steroids. One of the things we have learned about addicts, and even former addicts who have been drug free for months is that they over-react, hormonally speaking. They produce excess amounts of adrenal steroids when they are provoked. This has also been confirmed in animal studies.

"The problem is that because of their addiction, the amount of endorphins they can produce does not protect them from the effects of the steroids and they become very, very uncomfortable. They feel anxious and irritable, restless. They don't sleep well and they show signs of depression. They also know that injection of heroin will make the symptoms go away.

"So the buffer of endogenous opiods isn't effective?" asked Chris.

"Exactly," said Bernstein. "The adaptations the brain has had to make to long term addiction has rendered the endorphins ineffective as a buffer and the perception that they need one is translated by addicts into a need for heroin. As you said, there isn't anyway to keep anyone free from stress, so addicts are always at risk of relapse. Relapse is the hallmark of addictive disease."

"Does the system ever completely heal?" asked Chris.

"That's a tough question to answer," said Dr. Bernstein. "For some people, like Margo Sutherland, the answer is 'yes'. But then there are some people who have been completely O.K., off methadone for years, and then they relapse. I think the keys are to be very judicious and taper methadone patients very slowly, which gives their system the best opportunity to restore its equilibrium. The stress buffer system will also have a chance to re-establish itself when they are drug free. But, as I have to continue to emphasize, each person is different, and presents a unique challenge."

"Well, I guess that's hopeful," said Chris.

"Cautiously optimistic," said Dr. Bernstein. "But it takes a lot of strength, patience and support. If any part of the triangle fails, the whole system can fail, the patient will relapse and that can be devastating, even tragic. That's why some people who try to leave methadone completely and relapse are unwilling to take the risk a second time. They feel safer just taking the methadone every day, like a diabetic takes insulin."

"I can understand that," said Chris. "If they've gotten their life back together, they wouldn't want to take the chance of relapsing and losing it all again."

"And I completely support that decision," said Dr. Bernstein. "Taking methadone is infinitely preferable to taking heroin."

"Well, I'm just very glad that Erin's at least in a program," said Chris. "I really think she's doing well. She's starting to think and talk about school again. And we're starting to talk about getting married. So there's some good news."

"Wonderful news," said Dr. Bernstein. "I'm very happy for you both. You must be able to imagine how these kinds of human successes validate the beliefs which have been the foundation of the work we do here. And, even better, Now you're going to be a part of that work."

"I can't wait," said Chris.

When Chris got back to the lab, there was a voice mail message from Rick. He returned the call. "What's up?" he asked.

"We've got an opportunity for a great deal," said Rick. "There's a big party at that new hotel at Squaw Valley and they want us to play."

"I don't know," said Chris. "It sounds great but I don't want to leave Erin. Maybe I could bring her."

"Not this time," said Rick. "We thought we'd stay up and do some skiing. A guy thing. Listen, I know you don't want to leave her. Maybe this isn't such great timing. I just thought---"

"No," said Chris. "It sounds good. I'd like to think about it a bit and talk to her. When do you have to know?"

"In the next couple of days," said Rick. "They really want us so I can stall a bit, but if we're not going to do it we should give them an opportunity to get someone else."

"I agree," said Chris. "I'll let you know tomorrow.

Chapter Twenty-Seven

Erin walked into the conference room where her group was meeting. She poured herself a cup of coffee from the urn and took a seat. She looked around for Sandy, but didn't see her.

"O.K.," said Margo. "Let's get started. What do you want to talk about? Does anyone want to comment on the tape we saw last time?"

"Yeah," said Barbara, a quiet intense woman who always wore sweat suits.. "I want to. It really got me thinkin' cause I've been having' a lot of trouble staying clean. I mean, I want to, and I'm not cravin' and all. And I don't even get high when I do use, so I'm askin' myself, 'Why are you using? I'm just wastin' money, and I ain't got money to be pissing away on no junk."

"So what did the tape teach you?" asked Margo.

"I think I gotta move," said Barbara. "You know they was talkin' about 'Triggers to Relapse' and I just looked at my life. Man. Everywhere I go that shit is in my face. I go to the grocery store, you know what I mean? Like I turn down an aisle lookin' for some soup or some shit like that and there's my connection. Man, I don't need that. I go to buy gas and the motherfucker just happens to pop up."

"I had to move three times just to get away," said Elvira. "But you got to do it. As long as you're around people who are dealin' or using', you aint gonna get clean and if you do you sure aint gonna stay clean."

"Then I don't have a chance," said Barbara. "My old man's using. My brother's dealin'. My sister-in-law is always comin' around wanting me to do some shit with her."

"What do the rest of you think?" asked Margo. "What should

she do?"

"You've got to cut it off," said Elvira. "Even if it's family. You've got to tell them you're gonna get clean even if you got to cut them off and never see them any more. You got to tell them not to come around you. If they got junk, they ain't welcome. If they're using, they ain't welcome."

"That's right," said Edna, a woman in her mid thirties. "I had to cut off some friends I'd known since grade school. They were draggin' me down. I had to move, get a different phone and just put up barriers to get away from that world. Otherwise, there's no way I could stay clean. I mean, you feel bad about cutting people off, but if they were real friends they wouldn't be draggin' you down. You gotta take care of yourself and your kids. You don't want them to go through this shit."

"O.K.," said Margo. "So we all agree. You have to erect barriers as Edna said. You have to avoid the triggers. What about you, Jennifer? You're on step five. How did you do it?"

"You know, it's kind of like starting an exercise program," said Jennifer, a trim professional-looking woman. "When you start out you don't have any stamina, but gradually, you get better and stronger, and then one day you realize that you're doing stuff that you could never do when you started. Then you stop and figure out how many muscles you've built up, so that things that seemed impossible when you started, are now routine."

"That's a great way to think about it," said Margo. "You have to build up your muscles of resistance. Does that make sense to you, Barbara?"

"Yeah," said Barbara. "I can see that. I know I'm all flabby and I got to get strong."

"And you do it one day at a time," said Margo. "You keep doing it and you get stronger. That doesn't mean you're not going to have setbacks, but when you do, you're stronger and you can deal with them better. You have more support and confidence than you did, so when you get stressed you can get help and talk it through, rather than going into a panic and using.

"But, to extend the analogy a bit further, you can't start if you don't have a place where you can do your exercises every day. What I'm trying to do here is get us back to Barbara's problem about how to avoid the triggers. You have to have a safe place to

242

get started. You can't exercise in a place that's all choked with bad air and contaminated with filth. You have to have a clean place to start. To me, that means you've received from very good advice from those who have been through it.

"You're going to have to find a place that's clean enough for you to have a chance. I think you're going to have to move or do whatever it takes to get away from the triggers that are going to drag you down."

They continued the discussion for another half hour, until Margo said, "O.K. Time's up. See you next week."

When Erin left the group she went to the public phone in the lobby and called Sandy's number. After several rings, a sullen voice answered, "Hello."

"Hi, Sandy. It's Erin. You weren't at group. Are you O.K?"

There was a silence. Then, "No."

"Can I help?" asked Erin. "Do you want me to come over?"

Another pause. "No. Don't come here. I'll meet you."

"At the coffee shop?" asked Erin.

"No," said Sandy. "At that little park that's in the next block from the coffee shop. I'll be there in about a half hour."

Erin parked her car on the street adjacent to the small park. She walked to a bench and sat down. It was beginning to warm up as the sun was burning through the overhanging gray clouds. Some large, fat gulls strutted imperiously on the damp grass. Children of pre-school age were watched by sitters or playing on the swings or slides. As she watched them, Erin wondered about what it would be like to have children with Chris and bring them to a park and play with them together.

She took out her book and began reading. After a time she looked up to see Sandy approaching along the pathway. Her shoulders were hunched forward, her hands plunged into her jacket pockets. She had dark glasses on and looked uncharacteristically disheveled. She slumped onto the bench beside Erin and sat silently, her head bowed forward.

"Sandy," said Erin, reaching out to put her hand on her shoulder. "What is it? What's happened?"

Tears were slipping under the frames of her glasses. "Man, you just can't catch a break," she said. "Just when you think you've got something going, wham. And you are down. Way down."

243

Erin put her arm around her shoulder to comfort her and Sandy's anger and resistance dissolved into convulsive sobs. She continued to cry for several minutes, then gradually was able to compose herself and dry her eyes and face on the Kleenex that Erin offered. When she took off the glasses, Erin was able to see the swelling and redness they had concealed.

"God," said Sandy. "This can't be true. This cannot have happened."

"Can you tell me?" asked Erin softly.

Sandy took several long deep breaths and steadied herself. "I just got my laboratory tests back. I just had my annual exam." She took another deep breath. Her face was dissolved in an agonized contortion. "I've got AIDS," she blurted out and began to sob again.

Erin stiffened. She was unable to breath. She felt a numbness in her face and limbs and tingling on the back of her neck. She was unable to speak for what seemed like a long time. Then she heard herself say, "Oh, my God."

She sat there, holding the crying woman on her lap, her eyes filling with tears, unable to shake herself free from the numbing force of the terrible revelation. She felt paralyzed, physically and emotionally. She had the sensation of having been suddenly projected into an unreal, dream-like place.

All the terrible fear she had experienced when she was concerned about her own potential for being infected gradually oozed into her consciousness and she began to feel a knot tighten in her abdomen. She felt nauseated and her mouth and throat were dry.

"How," she asked hoarsely, woodenly. "How could this have happened?"

Sandy gradually regained her composure and was able to answer coherently. "You know that dude I told you about? The one I used to be with?"

"The one that was still hanging around?" asked Erin.

"That's him," said Sandy. "Well, I told you he was after me. A few months ago I was feelin' low and I let him get to me."

"Sexually?" asked Erin.

"Yeah," said Sandy. "I always had this thing for him. He could really turn me on. So I let him do it. That had to be how I got it."

"Oh, Sandy," said Erin.

"After I was with him, I heard from some people that he had tested positive," said Sandy. "But I didn't want to believe he'd passed it to me. And you know, that son-of-a-bitch is still hangin' around. He hasn't got no treatment or anything. I think he wanted to do this to me. I'm gonna get a gun and kill that mother fucker before he messes up other people like he's done to me."

"Oh God," said Erin. The numbness was gradually wearing off and she could see the terror pain and anger in her friend's face. The evil of the act was reminiscent of the beginning of her own addiction.

"And that ain't all," said Sandy. "I told Vernon, you know, my new guy and that really hurt him. He was really pissed off. He slapped me a few times and then he left. I know he was really hurtin'. I told him I wasn't goin' to mess around no more.
He left. Took all his clothes. I can't blame him. Man, I hope I didn't infect him. He'd probably kill me. And I'd deserve it."

"What are you going to do?" asked Erin.

"What I done was I used," said Sandy. "After he left I was hurtin' big time. I couldn't take it so I fixed. Who gives a shit anymore. I'm gonna die. I might as well die loaded. Fuck it."

"You can't give up," said Erin. It's different now. They have drugs to treat AIDS and newer ones coming along. It's not like it used to be."

"Yeah," said Sandy, "but those drugs make you sick. I don't want to live like that."

"Right now, the important thing to do is to find out what your options are. Did they refer you to the AIDS clinic?"

"Yeah," said Sandy. "I'm supposed to be there now, but I'm not goin'."

"Oh yes, you are," said Erin. "Come on. I'll drive you. It's not going to hurt to find out what the truth really is. Come on, Sandy. You've worked too hard just to throw it all in. How about your kids? You've got to show them how to deal with real adversity. You just can't let them see you like this. I know this is as tough as it gets. In a lot of ways, I don't know what I'm talking about because I've never had to deal with the kind of agony you're going through. I just know you've go to hang in there. You can't give up without knowing what your options are. Come on."

They drove to the hospital and went to the AIDS clinic and

walked up to the registration. Sandy gave her name to the receptionist.

"You're late," said the woman. "Have a seat. We'll be with you in a bit."

The two of them sat on some benches and waited silently. Erin was holding Sandy's hand firmly. After ten minutes, Sandy's name was called.

"I'll wait here for you, then I'll drive you back to your car," said Erin. "Hang in there, Sandy. You can do this."

Sandy gave her a weak smile and nodded and then followed the nurse who had called her name.

While she waited, Erin's mind whirled back through a multitude of thoughts that were competing for her focus and attention. Her heart was aching for Sandy and the cruel blow she had suffered. There was also a sense of relief that she had dodged a similar bullet as a result of her trials in El Centro. "It could have been me," she said to herself.

She thought about the immediate consequences of the diagnosis. Sandy had lost one of her most important sources of support and comfort at the moment when she needed him most. Again, Erin compared her own situation, knowing how important Chris' strength and commitment to her were and what an integral part they played in her life and her recovery.

She thought of the cruel irony of Sandy's having everything taken from her at the moment when things seemed to be going so well. There was an unpredictability and a fragility about life that she had never fully appreciated. That awareness made her feel her own vulnerability. There was a net supporting her now which seemed strong and resilient. She was grateful, but still disquieted by her sudden awareness of the chasm beneath her.

When Sandy returned, her walk had regained much of the rhythm and strength that was so characteristic. She sat down and grabbed Erin's hand. "Well, you were right," said Sandy. "Things have changed. They're optimistic. They have to do a bunch more tests. They drew some more blood. Talkin' about things I don't know nothin' about. 'T-cells and viral load.' Anyway, it's gonna take a few days. I have another counselor, just for the AIDS stuff.

"She said I should get away for a couple of days, so I think I'll go see my sister. The counselor says I need to let people know who can help me and be there for me. I need to tell my sister. I also got to talk to Margo. She'll be important. I'll talk to her today.

"I want you to know this, Erin. You really mean a lot to me. You were there for me. That was tough. I really love you for what you did."

"We have to take care of each other," said Erin.

In the following weeks, Sandy regained her equilibrium. The blood tests indicated that she had very early disease. The viral load wasn't heavy which indicated a favorable prognosis. Her white blood counts including her "T" lymphocytes were also normal. She was started on aggressive therapy which she tolerated with only minor side effects.

Her man, Vernon, returned when his fury over her infidelity diminished and was eclipsed by his own genuine concern for her. The support she needed was assembled and she was feeling much more confident.

Chris had gone to Portola Valley in the middle of the day to pick up mail and attend to some other details. When he finished he drove back to the campus, past the golf course and to the Faculty Club. He parked in the parking lot and walked past the student union and the small musical auditorium.

He went up to the host and told him that he was a guest of Dr. Current. He was shown to the table where Jack had turned around and was chatting with some friends at a nearby table.

"Hi," said Chris. "Sorry I'm late."

"You're not late," said Current. "I was early. I was just talking to some of my tennis budies. They're trying to get me to go with them to Wimbledon."

"That sounds great," said Chris. "I'd love to do that. Are you going to go?"

"I don't know," said Current. "It's awfully tempting. Marcia couldn't care less about going to the tennis matches, but I think I could talk her into a week in London with only slight restrictions on shopping spending. These guys have some really good tickets. I think it's too good to pass up."

"Then you have decided?" asked Chris.

"I think I just did," said Current. "I'm gonna go for it. What the hell."

"Good for you," said Chris. "Are you going to do some work while you're there?"

"Oh, sure," said Current. "There's a guy at Oxford that I've been corresponding with. I want to see his lab. I think he wants me to take on one of his post-docs so we could do some good collaboration."

"Then it would be a business trip," said Chris, smiling.

"But of course," said Current. "These are the kinds of opportunities we academic types have to take advantage of. If I haven't taught you anything else, I hope I have taught you something about academic style."

"You're a wonderful model," said Chris.

"Thank you," said Current. "Here, have some of this sauvignon blanc. It's a treasure." He filled Chris' glass and then raised his. "Here's to you, Chris. I guess the only thing that would have made it better for me was if I had had a place for you myself. But, no shit, working with Bernstein is going to be a wonderful opportunity for you. The guy's so goddamned smart and such a good human being He's really made some wonderful contributions."

"Sounds like you," said Chris.

"Thanks, but you didn't have to say that," said Current.

"I know," said Chris. "But I meant it. It's one of the reasons that I'm so eager to do this. I want to see if I can do it as well as you and he do it. No compromise. No bullshit. Solid science and a wise appreciation of how it fits into the big picture."

"Well, If you see me that way, I must not be doing too badly," said Current. "I really appreciate that. By the way, how close were you to taking a job in industry?"

"Closer than I was comfortable with," said Chris. "I really felt uneasy about it, but I didn't want to move, particularly after I met Erin."

"Wouldn't she have moved with you?" asked Current.

"Probably," said Chris. "She would have, if I were convinced that I was really committed to the move. She would have supported me."

"And you couldn't do that?" asked Current.

"I really couldn't," said Chris. "Not with the band. I really didn't want to move."

"Well, now you have it all," said Current. "That's as it should be. How's Erin doing?"

"Just great," said Chris. "She's really back to normal. She's absorbing California literature and history like a sponge."

"Are you talking about marriage?" asked Current.

"Yes," said Chris. "That's what I want. She does too. It's just a matter of timing. It's too right not to happen."

"Well, then," said Current. "Here's to both of you." They touched glasses. "And the great thing, from my point of view, is that I'll be able to see it all happen."

Erin and Sandy were in the dosing line at the clinic having an animated conversation. Sandy backed up and unintentionally bumped into another woman, knocking the woman's dose box and coffee mug out of her hands and onto the floor. The woman turned on Sandy with fury.

"Goddamn you," she shouted. "I ought to slap the shit out of you, you clumsy bitch." She delivered a blow to Sandy's chest.

The unexpecting Sandy was shoved up against the wall, lost her balance and fell, dropping her own lock box and coffee. As she was getting to her feet, the woman advanced again, her arm raised to deliver another blow.

Erin was aghast. Her protective instincts took control and she grabbed the woman's arm to prevent her from hitting Sandy. Having heard the noise, one of the male nurses in the dispensary interceded and separated the two women.

"Now knock that off," he said. "I mean it. We're not going to have any more of this."

The woman backed off, cursing, and Erin helped Sandy retrieve her dropped objects. When everything had settled down, the dosing continued. Walking to the car after receiving their methadone, Sandy and Erin laughed about the incident.

"I've never been involved in anything like that before," said Erin. "She was just furious."

"I've had a couple of minor run ins with that dumb bitch before," said Sandy. "Just words, but she don't like me. Sorry you had to get involved.

"Don't worry," said Erin. "It was just such a shock. It happened so fast."

When Erin arrived at the apartment that afternoon, she was carrying some extra books. She and Chris had discussed his leaving to go to Squaw Valley and she had urged him to go. So she was gathering some additional reading material to occupy her time while he was gone.

She noticed the light blinking on the answering machine and pushed the play button. "Erin, this is Margo. Please stop by my office after you dose tomorrow. I need to speak to you."

She made a note to herself and erased the message.

When Chris arrived, Erin eagerly told him about the incident at the clinic.

"My God," he said. "You actually got involved in a brawl. It must be the Irish in you."

"It was such a shock to find myself involved in something like that," said Erin. "I guess it's that old impulsive part of me. I don't think I've ever seen any kind of a 'brawl' as you call it, let alone been in one."

"A likely story," he said. "I'll tell you this, I'm not about to mess around with you. I'm going to be on my best behavior. As a matter of fact, I'm going to take you out to dinner tonight."

"So you can celebrate our impending separation?" she said feigning a pout.

"I just want to spend a romantic evening with the woman I love savoring the romance of our relationship."

"We can do that right here, my dear," she said, putting her arms around his neck and kissing him.

"Yes, but then you'd have to cook, or I'd have to," he said, returning the kiss.

"All right," she said. "You've convinced me. Where shall we go?"

They chose their favorite Italian restaurant which was within walking distance of the apartment. The waiter recognized them and sat them at the table they preferred. "The risotto is particularly excellent this evening. It's never been better," he said.

They ordered the risotto, salads and a bottle of wine.

"We always talk about exploring all the new restaurants in this city, but when it comes right down to it, we end up going back to the places we've already been," said Chris.

"I know," said Erin. "But I love it that we have some favorites that we found together. We'll just slowly add to the list."

"How would you feel about moving down to Portola Valley?" he asked.

"I love that place," she said. "In many ways it's ideal. And I hate it that you have to commute so far. But right now, I'd rather stay here. The book store is really important to me. Can we stay here a while longer? Maybe when I get some take-home privileges and I don't have to dose at the clinic every day I'll feel better about it. Is that O.K.?"

"Sure," he said. "I just feel a little uneasy about leaving that place unattended. I think I'll see if I can get a student to move in there for at least the next quarter. Then we can have some time to decide what we want to do."

"I really appreciate that," she said. "Thanks for understanding."

"Listen," he said, taking her hand in his, "The only understanding we need to have is that we're completely in love. I just adore you. Are you certain that you feel completely O.K. about my leaving for a couple of days?"

"Completely O.K.," she said. "It gives me a chance to express my inherent Irish independence."

"Independence in moderation, if you please," he said.

On the way home, they climbed the steep streets hand in hand. It was an unusually crisp, clear night.

"So tell me what you see in the stars, professor," she said.

"I see a bright future for us," he said in a theatrical German accent. "I see us growing old together with all our children and grandchildren gathered around singing anthems in our praise."

"Do you really see children?" she asked thoughtfully.

"Well, they're a little more distant," he admitted. "But, the near future is clear. Just the two of us, enjoying each other."

She stopped and put her arms around him, burying her face in his chest. "I feel so good about us, about me. I do so want to believe in that future."

"Don't you believe in it yet?" he asked.

"At times like this I do," she said. "There are times when I still feel a bit fragile, but they're becoming less frequent. I really feel that I'm making progress."

He lifted her chin and kissed her gently.

"Huge progress," he said. "I can't tell you how thrilled I am that you're doing so well. I really want to start planning a wedding."

"I've also been thinking about that," she said. "Please, give me just a little more time."

"We have plenty of time," he said. "I don't want to rush you. As long as we're together I can wait."

When they reached the apartment, they turned on his CD and switched on the bedroom speakers. He turned off the lights and turned to her. She was in his arms instantly. They kissed, gently at first and then with increasing fervor as they both became aroused. They undressed each other hastily and fell into bed locked in a mutual embrace. The physical boundaries that defined each of them fell away as they were swept up into a molten amalgam of passionate spiritual unity.

Chapter Twenty-Eight

Chris left early the following morning after kissing Erin tenderly. When she got up, she followed her usual morning routine and went to the clinic. After she received her methadone, she went to Margo's office and knocked on the door.

When she entered, Margo said, "Sit down. Tell me what happened in the dispensary yesterday." She appeared somber and concerned.

"Oh that," said Erin, laughing. "It was just a silly misunderstanding. No big deal."

"I'm afraid it is a big deal," said Margo, whose expression reflected the seriousness she attached to the matter.

Erin was immediately sobered by Margo's demeanor. "Sandy unintentionally backed into that other woman and knocked some things out of her hands. It was just an accident. The woman just went crazy. She started cursing and knocked Sandy into the wall. She was about to hit her when I grabbed her arm. The attendant came out and stopped it. That's all that happened. What's the matter?"

Margo looked at her seriously. "Erin, physical violence among the clients is taken very seriously. It's not tolerated, for reasons that I'm sure are obvious to you. Violence cannot be a part of the clinic. The nurse who reported the incident says he saw you physically grappling with the other woman."

"Well," said Erin. "That's true, I suppose. But I was just trying to stop her from hitting Sandy. After what Sandy's been through, I just couldn't let her take another blow." Erin could feel her mouth becoming dry. Anxiety was increasing the tension in her neck and shoulders.

"I talked to Sandy," said Margo. "She validates your version of the story. I believe it, too. The problem we face is that the nurse didn't see the early part of what happened, only you wrestling with the other woman. The other part of the problem is that the other woman and the one who was with her say that you started the whole thing; that you were the aggressor."

Now she was alarmed. "Margo," said Erin. "That's not true. It didn't happen that way. You know me well enough to know that I wouldn't behave like that. That's not me." She was beginning to become agitated and having difficulty maintaining her composure.

"Take it easy, Erin," said Margo, leaving her chair and putting her hands on her client's shoulders. "We'll just have to sort out those facts before a determination is made."

"What would they do to me if they accept the other version?" asked Erin, her eyes filled with tears.

"As I said," said Margo. "Violence is taken very seriously. They'd terminate you from the program."

"Oh my God," said Erin, in panic. "What will become of me?"

"Now don't jump to any conclusions," said Margo. "I'm going to be your advocate. I think I can persuade them that this was a matter of self-defense rather than an act of aggression. I think Sandy's situation and your defense of her should also help."

"Who decides?" asked Erin.

"The counseling supervisor and the physicians," said Margo.

"Is there any avenue of appeal?" asked Erin.

"Usually there is," said Margo. "But not for violence. In this case the decision will be final."

Erin sat speechless, unable to believe that this could have happened. She was staring out the window in numb terror.

"I'll do everything I can," said Margo. "Your record is in your favor and I'm a strong advocate."

"When will they decide?" Erin asked, almost distractedly.

"This afternoon," said Margo. "Why don't you go on home. I'll call you as soon as I have the answer."

On her way to the bookstore, Erin regained her composure. She was still badly shaken by the discussion, but her confidence in Margo gave her reason to hope that truth would prevail. She was able to convince herself that things would turn out favorably.

At the bookstore, she found an assortment of small jobs to occupy her mind and help pass the time. She tried to read during some quiet intervals, but was unable to keep her mind from returning to the clinic and the discussion that was taking place there while she waited.

When she arrived at the apartment the light on the answering machine was blinking. She pushed the "play" button.

"Hi Honey," said Chris' voice. "Just wanted you to know we got here safely, despite Rick's erratic driving. Just kidding. I love you. I'll call back later. I miss you already."

Then the second message: "Erin, this is Margo. Please call."

There was a queasy feeling in her stomach as she dialed the number. "This is Margo."

"Hi. This is Erin."

"Oh, Erin. Let me shut the door." There was a pause. "I'm sorry. I don't have good news."

"Go on," said Erin numbly.

"The decision has been made to terminate both of you from the program. Your dose will be tapered starting tomorrow."

The words struck her with the force of a physical blow. She was unable to speak.

"I thought they were going to be more lenient with you," said Margo. "But Dr. Carter was adamant. I guess I shouldn't be telling you this, but I'm really pissed off about it. The rest of us were willing to believe your story and give you a chance since you've done so well. But Dr. Carter wouldn't budge. 'Violence is violence and it must not be excused. If we do it for her we'll destroy our discipline and lose the respect of the clients,' he kept repeating. Then he brought up that crap that you shouldn't be in the program in the first place. For some reason that really stuck in his craw. I'm really sorry."

Erin's hold on her emotions was deteriorating rapidly. "But what am I going to do?" she blurted out.

"I don't know," said Margo. "I'm going to see if I can get you onto another methadone program in the area. But since you're really not eligible by law and you've been terminated for violence it's going to be tough."

"How long do I have to stay off the program?" asked Erin.

"One year," said Margo.

"Oh my God. Oh my God," said Erin as she hung up the phone though Margo was still trying to assuage her feelings.

She collapsed to her knees on the floor, holding her head in her hands and sobbing, "It's gone. It's gone," she moaned. "My life is gone. Oh my God."

The order which had been restored to her life was dissolving. The confidence, slowly and carefully constructed, melted before the blast of her terrifying circumstances. The foundation on which she had been standing, and looking to the future, was the presumption of her success in the methadone program. Without it, she felt, there could be no future.

The waves of pain, panic, and then terror spread over her. She felt as though her brain and her body were spinning out of control. She began to feel nauseated. Her skin became wet with perspiration but she felt cold. She went to the bathroom and vomited several times.

She was becoming increasingly miserable, physically as well as from the fear and panic that enveloped her. Then she realized that she was having an intense craving for heroin. She didn't even try to resist.

She went to the closet where she had hidden the small box in one of her suitcases. She frantically unwrapped the rig and the powder. Surprised at her own dexterity, she measured out a portion of the powder, added water, heated it to bring it into solution and injected into a vein in her left arm.

Almost instantaneously, all the pain began to recede; both the physical agony and the deeper spiritual torment. They were lost in a soft cloud of pleasant sensations that enfolded and comforted her, removing her from the brutal onslaught of reality, disconnecting her from the overwhelming circumstances that threatened not only her happiness but her mental stability. She became less lucid and more free as she floated, suspended in the chemical haven.

Somewhere in space and time, she heard the ringing of the phone and moved slowly toward the sound. She heard Chris' voice but couldn't understand what he was saying..

She drifted into the bedroom and fell into a pleasant dream that gradually merged with a deep, drugged sleep.

When she awoke, she re-entered the world of pain and torment.

256

Now, in addition, there was shame, guilt and self-loathing.

She felt as though the safety net she had believed in had been shredded into ineffective ribbons and she was left poised on the precipice, terrified as she looked into the vast, vacant void of her own vulnerability.

"God, I'm trash," she said looking at herself in the mirror. I'm a filthy, fucking heroin addict. I don't belong in polite society. I'm a no good junkie. There's no place for me."

She began to vacillate between self-pity and bitter recrimination. "Why me?" she shrieked. "Why would they throw me out of the stupid goddamned program? I'm the best junkie in the whole place and they throw me out like a piece of human garbage."

But the guilt was most painful and powerful.

"How could I do this to Chris? He trusted me to stay clean. God, he even wants to marry me. What a joke. Someone as fine and decent as him and his family connected with some like me, a fuck-up and a junkie."

The thought of Chris produced another convulsion of pain and guilt. "I can't face him. How could I face him and admit that I'm so weak and useless that I need heroin to make it in this world?"

The thoughts of Chris and marriage led inevitably to having children. "I wanted to have his children; wonderful, beautiful, bright, talented children. Maybe geniuses. Our children. Inheriting the wonderful gifts from their father. But how could I subject him and the children to the risk of being drug addicts like their mother and grandmother. Even if they were normal we'd both keep watching for signs of that flaw. How terrible to subject innocent children and Chris to that."

She shook her head, sobbing, and said again and again. "No. This terrible flaw, this disease, mustn't be passed on. I am guilty of my weakness, but I must not be guilty of passing this horror on to our children. I will not do that. I'll put an end to it now."

She was pulled together by her resolve. She went to the desk, took out some stationary, and wrote quickly and with determination. She folded the page and inserted it into an envelope on which she wrote the words, "To my Darling Chris."

Then she went back to the closet, prepared the remaining heroin and injected it into her arm.

Chris returned to the apartment in a panic. Unable to reach Erin by phone he had immediately left the mountains to drive home. There was no sign of her in the apartment. Then he noticed that the light on the answering machine was blinking and pushed the button.

"Chris. This is Carlos. Call me immediately. It's very important." His mind swirled in terrified anticipation as he dialed the number. The woman who answered asked his name and he was barely able to form and deliver the words. He gripped the receiver and closed his eyes as he waited for Carlos to come on the line.

"Chris, thank God you called," said Carlos. "It's Erin. Did you know she was using again?"

He was at once shocked and relieved, the latter at knowing that she was again under Carlos' care and protection.

"No," he said. "She wasn't using. She was doing fine. I just left to go up to Squaw. She was fine." he repeated.

"She got some bad news from the clinic. Margo said she was devastated. When Margo couldn't get through by phone she went over to your place and had your tenants let her in. They found her unconscious and called 911. I guess Margo cleaned up the place."

"How is she?" he asked.

"It's bad," said Carlos. "You'd better get here right away."

"Oh Christ. I'll be right there."

He drove as quickly as he felt safe in doing. Over and over he kept thinking, "I should never have gone. Lord, please let her be all right. I'll never leave her again. Please let her be all right."

He parked his car and ran to the ER entrance. He identified himself to the clerk and asked her to reach Dr. Garza. She did and told him that Carlos would be right there.

Time seemed to stop for him. He felt dazed and numb except for the nausea that was churning through his abdomen. He paced in misery, repeating, "Please, Lord. Let her be all right."

He looked through the glass in the doors that separated the physician's area and saw Carlos coming toward him. Carlos pushed the doors open and walked toward him, carrying an envelope in his hands.

Chris looked into the face of his friend and saw unspeakable pain, anger and frustration. He didn't have to be told.

He knew she was gone.

Carlos embraced him and held him for a long time. "God, Chris." he said in a voice choked with emotion. "I've never wanted to save someone so much in my life. I just feel terrible that I couldn't do it. Maybe if they had gotten to her earlier. We just couldn't bring her back. I feel terrible. I'm so very, very sorry."

They walked slowly to the doctor's lounge and sat down, both silent as they faced the enormous pain of Erin's loss. After a long interval, Carlos walked to Chris.

"This is for you," he said. "Margo found it in the apartment."

He opened the envelope which was addressed, "To my beloved Chris."

As he began to grasp the import of what he was reading, he felt dizzy. He wanted to stop reading, as though by doing so, he could prevent the inevitability of what was being imparted to him. But he read on, his mind whirling through a confusing maelstrom of panic, accompanied by a cacophany of internal sounds, dreadful music that forced itself out of the well of his soul.

My Darling Chris,
Your love brought wonderful music to my life. I
wish I had the strength and courage to continue and live
up to what you have a right to expect, but I know now
that I can't do it. This monster has me in its grip and I
will always be vulnerable to another fall. I cannot, will
not, inflict my weakness on you any longer. Whatever
chance we might have had for a beautiful future together
would have been destroyed by the cloud of this
affliction. I carry an incubus within me. I will not
permit it to destroy other innocent lives.

Forgive me and go on with your life.

Adoringly, Erin

He sat with his eyes closed, the music still throbbing through his body, but now it was no longer disturbing. As he had begun to understand what she was asking him to accept, the panic had receded and the music had become more elegiac. He realized the enormity of her torment and the complexity of her decision. It was a flight, but it was also protective. It acknowledged the profundity of her vulnerability, but it did so with great courage.

"I had them move her to a room," said Carlos. "Do you want to see her?"

Chris nodded and Carlos led him down the hall. He opened the door and then left as Chris walked in a few steps and then stopped. His breath caught as he saw her. She looked so peaceful, so beautiful. There was no agony, no desperation. The horror of her terrible ordeal had not disfigured the intrinsic splendor of the human being she had been.

He went to the bed and wrapped his arms around her still figure. His face was buried in her beautiful hair, which still carried the scent of her that he cherished so much. He touched her lips with his for the final time. As he straightened up he winced as he noticed the tiny mark of the fatal sting on her arm.

In the darkness of his terrible pain, in the empty vacuum of the realization that they would share no more time together, there was a small flicker of light, the realization that her ordeal was over, and that she would suffer no more. He nodded to Carlos and left the room.

As he left the hospital, he looked up into the night sky. His internal music was quiet and serene. It seemed to flow from a place he had never before experienced. It was comforting and regal, profound and yet elegantly simple. He knew he would hear that music for the rest of his life. It was Erin's music.